PRAISE FOR *CHASING MONEY*

"Gritty descriptions, simmering threats, and a wry sense of humor contribute to a countdown to disaster. Exceptionally clever and compelling." - Midwest Book Review

"Grows funnier and more surprising every step of the way. Balter's gift for pacing and dialogue make this a series to watch." - Publisher's Weekly

"A strong voice paired with authentic dialogue … Packed with action" - The BookLife Prize

"A heart-pounding thriller that grabs you from the first page and won't let you get away." - Michael Lindley, author of the Amazon #1 Hanna and Alex Low Country mystery series

PRAISE FOR THE *VATICAN DEAL*

"We can't remember the last time we read a mafia thriller that was this fun" - BestThrillers.com

"An electrifying blend of suspense, intrigue, and razor-sharp wit, where the stakes are as monumental as the Vatican's own secrets." - Gary McAvoy, author of the Vatican Secret Archive Thrillers

"A fast-paced, action-packed crime thriller that will have readers on the edge of their seats until the very end." - The Feathered Quill

"A brilliant mix of danger, deception, and intrigue … with complex characters, unpredictable twists, and high-stakes action" - Al Warren, House of Mystery Radio Show

DEAD
EXIT

Mission Point Press

Published by Mission Point Press
www.MissionPointPress.com

Design by Mark Pate

Printed in the United States of America

ISBN hardcover: 978-1-968761-46-2
ISBN softcover: 978-1-968761-47-9
Library of Congress Control Number: 2026911260

DEAD EXIT

A MARTY AND BO THRILLER

MICHAEL BALTER

M·P·P
www.MissionPointPress.com

To my best friend,

Roy Rose,

a man of great character, relentless optimism, and wonderful humor.

Our adventures now fill my books.

He can make me laugh so hard I cry.

CHAPTER ONE

The Call

IF MY PHONE RINGS AFTER MIDNIGHT, someone's been born or someone's died.

As far as I knew, no one was expecting. So, when my phone rang at 1 a.m., unease settled in before I was fully awake.

The Russian accent on the other end didn't help.

"Marty? Marty Schott?"

I recognized Natalya's stepson's voice immediately. "Yes, Alex."

"I wake you?"

"No." I glanced at Abbie, sprawled on her stomach, one leg over the blanket, the other tucked beneath. Her head turned toward me, eyes shut, though stirring. Boomer stared at me from the foot of the bed, ears perked, eyes wide and alert. "But you woke my dog."

"I have a situation."

"You're making me nervous, Alex."

Alex Danilenko, owner of Shangri-La, the most popular strip club in Portland, wouldn't call me at this hour to complain about a bad tipper.

"I need to talk to Bo, right away."

"Then why'd you call me?"

"I not have Bo's number—but you are on my speed dial."

"That's not comforting news."

Alex kept going. "Bo's sister's husband is dead in my parking lot."

"What did you just say?"

Abbie pulled a pillow over her head as I sat up and swung my legs over the side. Boomer jumped off the bed and sat next to me, panting.

"Tadeo Ramírez. He is Bo's brother-in-law, yes?

"Ye-es."

"He is lying dead in my parking lot."

"Heart attack?"

"Yes—his heart was attacked by a bullet."

"Are you serious?"

"I cannot be sure, but it looks like he was attacked by other bullets as well."

I should've been picturing Tadeo lying in a pool of blood, but instead the thump of club music blasting through the phone had my mind drifting to naked women spinning in neon around brass poles.

Thank God no one can see inside my head.

"Have you called the cops?" It wasn't a stupid question. We all had a thing about not calling the cops.

"Yes. There is no choice. This can shut me down. I called 911 just before I called you."

I glanced at the blue glow of my bedside clock and did the math. Shangri-La would be swarming with uniforms by the time we got there. "Try not to say too much," I said. "We'll be there as fast as possible."

"I cannot say too much, Marty. I don't know anything."

I groped my way into the hall. My phone's thin light skimmed the floor. Boomer padded after me, sensing something was wrong. Thank God Abbie's a heavy sleeper. I speed-dialed Bo, but Katherine answered with a slurred "hello."

"Sorry, Katherine, please pass the phone to Bo."

An exhale, a pause, and then his voice: "Marty. What's up?" Bo answered every call as if it were the start of a new day—fresh, alert, like he'd just sat down to breakfast.

"Step out of the room for a second."

"What?"

"Just step out. I don't want Katherine to see your face when I tell you this."

I heard rustling sheets and muttering, "Go back to sleep; it's nothing." Then, after a beat—"Who died?"

Bo and I tend to think alike.

"Tadeo."

"What!? … Are you sure?" I could almost hear his heart accelerate.

I relayed Alex's call. Bo swore under his breath, then said, "I'll pick you up in twenty."

He did. I was already outside when he pulled up.

"You tell Abbie?" he asked, peeling out of my driveway.

"No. You tell Katherine?" I replied, tightening my seat belt.

He shook his head.

I knew Bo would take back roads to avoid speed traps, and I braced myself to be tossed around. Neither of us spoke as his racing instincts kicked in and the city blurred into a kaleidoscope of sheen and shadow. Bo's brain was doing the same as mine—sorting through threats and possibilities. Was Tadeo's shooting connected to us?

It didn't feel random.

Bo and I kept a mental ledger—bodies never found, acts never reported, debts owed to the living.

Was this a new entry?

"Think it's a message?" Bo asked, adjusting his jaw after grinding his teeth.

"If it is, it's a weak one. Tadeo's …" I hesitated, struggling to find the right word, but as usual, I failed, "… peripheral."

"Wow, Marty. Your sympathy is overwhelming. He's family, and he works for us."

"I don't want to be cruel, Bo, but Tadeo's death hits your sister harder than it hits you—and definitely more than it hits me. It doesn't add up."

He exhaled and nodded.

Bo had hired Tadeo—over my objections—after his sister, Laura, asked him to find her husband a job. Tadeo was always between opportunities, and Bo wasn't especially close to either of them. But when their mother died, everything shifted. He stepped into the role of reluctant patriarch, calling in favors and twisting arms until he found Tadeo an executive position at Corner24—our chain of convenience stores.

I barely knew Tadeo, having met him only a handful of times at Bishop family gatherings, but I'd heard about him. He was a regular topic of family gossip. Bo rarely mentioned him, but others often did—not kindly, but in a 'you won't believe what he did today' way.

"Shangri-La is a strange location," I said. "What was he doing there? It's weirdly coincidental."

Bo glanced over. "I don't believe in coincidence, weird or otherwise."

"Me neither."

"Have you been going there a lot?"

I knew why he asked the question. His discretion was admirable.

"A little. Not often."

Staying loosely connected to Natalya's stepson, however tenuously, kept me in her orbit. Bo understood this, and since we both knew it, there was no need to say more. That's one thing I appreciated about Bo—he knew when to leave things alone.

"Could it be Dmitry?" he asked after a long pause.

"I don't think so. If Dmitry wants to send a message, he'd make sure I woke up next to Boomer's head in my bed."

"That's you, Marty. What if he wants to send a message to me?"

"He doesn't. He'd pick me."

Bo took a hard left, tires squealing, his face set in a grim line. He squinted at me.

"Why?"

I let it hang a minute.

"Because you never fucked his girlfriend."

CHAPTER TWO

The Club

THE SHANGRI-LA ROAD SIGN STILL ADVERTISED, "Drinks 50% off until 8 PM." Alex had recently upgraded it, so the neon glowed bright and new. The parking lot was alive with cop cars, their red and blue lights pulsing rhythmically, dimly reflecting off the dry asphalt and cutting through the darkness in a hostile warning. Uniforms and plain clothes milled about in tight clusters. We tried to pull into the lot, but a uniform stopped us while another stretched a long strip of yellow "Do Not Cross" tape across the entrance.

We parked across the street and tried to walk onto the grounds, but once again, the same angry uniform stopped us. Maybe he was sour because of the late hour. "Get outta here," he yelled. "The place is closed. All the girls have gone home."

Perhaps that was the reason for his mood.

"That white F-150," Bo said, nodding toward the Ford sitting dead center in the lot, caged by an ambulance and a ring of uniforms, "is my brother-in-law's."

The officer nodded, and within minutes, Alex Danilenko, club proprietor and caller, emerged with a husky guy in a light blue shirt, no tie, and a battered brown sports coat that hung loosely on his frame. Alex wore a sharp expression of annoyance, along with the more typical black pants and starched white short-sleeved shirt that showcased his muscular arms and garish tattoos. He was clearly calculating how many days this headache would shut down his business and what its lasting impact would be.

The man accompanying Alex had a dark, sharp-boned face, unreadable. His hollow eyes held a dull fatigue; any trace of sympathy had been snuffed out long ago. The last time I'd seen him, he'd had a thin mustache; now his face was bare, making him seem even more detached.

He introduced himself as Detective Adams and asked for our driver's licenses. As he scribbled our names in his notepad, I turned to Bo and gave a slight nod. It took a full breath, but he'd recognized him too. Alex began to explain how he had found Tadeo, but Adams cut him off.

"Mr. Danilenko, this is an ongoing investigation. It's just getting started, so I'd appreciate it if you kept quiet until I've had a chance to learn more."

Alex dropped his head, the red and blue strobes skating across his bare scalp. He had no hair—anywhere, according to rumor—and under the lights, he looked almost antiseptic, a pale canvas disrupted by tattoos lurid in their meticulous detail: knives, crosses, and a heart on his chest accurate enough for a medical journal.

He knew this was going to be a long night.

"Mr. Bishop, you said you're the brother-in-law of the victim?"

Bo shrugged. "From here, it looks like his car, but the ambulance is blocking my view. Can I go look?"

"No. You'll contaminate the scene. I have the victim's driver's license, which was in his wallet." Adams motioned toward a uniform standing near the car, who jogged over with a plastic bag. "Don't touch the bag—just look at the license."

Adams pulled out a small Maglite and lit up the bag. It held a wallet already flipped open, exposing the driver's license. Bo sighed. It was definitely Tadeo Ramírez. "Yes, that's my brother-in-law," he said softly.

"Okay," Adams replied, lifting the yellow tape between us. "I'd like you two to come inside the club to talk some more. Do me a favor and give the area a wide berth. We're looking at shoeprints, and I don't want yours to become part of the mix."

We nodded and followed him along the lot's perimeter into the building.

Bright overhead lights replaced the strip club's usual low, intimate glow. Under the harsh glare, illusions fell away, and everything looked a little seedier—like a mini-mall arcade in daylight. The velvet ropes were thin and sagging; the faux-leather booths were cracked, with fraying corners.

I remember thinking this was how the cleaning crew must see it: bargain laminate straining for a manufactured luster, grime settled into the creases, and the lingering scent of sweat and perfume.

A small booth, tucked out of view from the dance stages, was cordoned off with yellow tape. Another plainclothes detective was on his hands and knees, flashlight in hand, probing the space under the table and scanning the booth's floor.

"Tadeo sat there for several hours, drinking," Alex said, nodding toward the booth.

Detective Adams shot him a stern look, his lips pinched into a straight line.

"Am I committing a crime?" Alex shot back, his glare just as stark.

Adams directed us to a small table and told us to sit. Then, muttering inaudibly, he excused himself and moved toward a tight cluster of uniforms gathered by the bar. He read our names off his notepad to one of them, who then left through the front door.

"This is going to cost me," Alex lamented, hands in his pockets. "It'll take months before my regulars feel comfortable to come back."

"I want to feel sorry for you, but you know there's a dead guy outside, and Bo's related to him," I said, every word edged with sarcasm.

Alex rolled his eyes. "*Da,*" he snapped. "And why is that? Why do you know so many people who die?" He hesitated, searching for the correct English. "With you two, death doesn't get a breather."

You don't know the half of it.

"This isn't the time, Alex," Bo hissed, voice tight with frustration. "Tell us what happened—before Adams gets back."

"I don't know anything," Alex muttered, shaking his head. The top of the heart tattoo that marked his chest shifted, visible through the strained button of his tight shirt. Alex wore his shirts one size too small to spotlight his muscles.

Not for the women.

For the men.

"Tadeo came in," he continued. "I don't remember exact time. I was covering for my bar-girl—she took extra time in the bathroom. You know …" He pointed at his crotch and frowned. "She is in her week. But I recognized his drink when I poured it. Tadeo always gets a Mexican mule—like Moscow mule but with tequila, not vodka. Not common. So I recognize him by his drink. When my bar-girl came back, I went over to say hello."

"So he's quite the regular," I said, not trying to be subtle.

Alex shot me a glare. He wanted his words to sting. "Just like you."

"Bite me," I shot back.

Bo stared at us both, face set in disbelief. "Is this really happening? I've got a dead brother-in-law out there. I've got to deal with my sister soon, and you two are pissing on each other?"

He was right. I offered an apology, and Alex followed suit with less sincerity.

"Tadeo was nervous about something," Alex said.

We watched Detective Adams talk to the uniforms.

"He wouldn't tell me why," Alex continued.

"Do you think it was personal, or something else?" Bo asked.

"How do I know?" He paused, his expression shifting. "Maybe 'nervous' isn't the right word. Maybe it is 'scared.' He kept looking over my shoulder at our door like he was expecting someone—watching the door bouncer check IDs. He drank five mules, which is a lot."

"Did you water them down?" I asked, knowing the club's protocol.

"*Konechno*—of course," he answered, meeting my eyes. "But still … it is much tequila."

The cop who Detective Adams had read our names to came back into the club and whispered something to him. He glanced over at us. My stomach sent an immediate warning. I tapped Bo on the knee. Adams jotted something in his notebook as he walked toward our table.

"Gentlemen, do you remember me?" he asked. "A few years back?"

He remained standing, so we had to look up at him.

Bo and I shook our heads.

"I remember you," he said. "Not your faces—your names. Martin Schott and Bo Bishop. They stick in the mind."

Here it comes.

Adams pulled a chair from a neighboring table and sprawled wide-legged, his eyes steady, never leaving us. He exhaled slowly.

"I spoke to both of you about the …" He glanced at his notepad. "… Baron Von Baltruschat murder case." His gaze shifted from Bo to me, measuring our reactions with the patience of a man holding four aces.

A long silence followed.

"It's still an open case," he said. "A double homicide someone tried to cover up with arson. Never been solved. Like a stone in my shoe."

He let the words hang; his fingers tapped the notepad in slow rhythm.

"You remember me now?"

CHAPTER THREE

The Detective

KARMA DOESN'T KNOCK. It just lets itself in, makes itself comfortable, and waits for the fallout. Tonight, it wore a badge and answered to Detective Adams. I forced my lips to twitch into what I hoped would pass for a smile—nonchalant, a little casual, but the warmth didn't reach my eyes.

Bo adjusted the cuffs of his shirt, his eyes flicking to me for an instant before returning to Adams, his face impassive. I let my gaze drift around the room, taking in the tattered corners of the club as if I were searching for lurking memories.

Bo and I have the same talent: maintaining a serene exterior while our insides coil tight—like walking down a dark alley with footsteps close behind and never breaking stride. When I finally looked back at Adams, I knew he saw right through me. He was too sharp to be played.

"I *do* remember you," I said, snapping my finger emphatically and annoyingly. "You split us up and questioned us in separate rooms."

"SOP," he replied.

Standard Operating Procedure—cop-speak for "it wasn't personal."

"You had a mustache." My lips tightened.

"And a few more pounds." His lips did the same.

The strained silence swallowed the room. Bo cut through it,

dropping his palm heavily onto the table. "My brother-in-law's been shot, detective."

"And I want to get your statement, but I'm trying to reconcile the fact that both of you were involved in another murder just three years ago. What are the odds?"

"Involved is a serious charge, detective," Bo said. "You questioned us. We'd spent a few hours visiting Baron Von Baltruschat earlier that day. His house was invaded that night after we'd left. We certainly weren't *involved*."

"Wrong place, wrong time," I added.

"Yeah, that's very unfortunate," Adams mumbled, looking down at his notebook. "Didn't you go there because you were looking for someone? I can't remember."

"We were looking for Nico Scava, our business partner at the time," I said.

"Yeah, that's right. Ever find him?" He sounded sincere, unaware that Nico was still missing, which made sense because Nico's case was in Washington State, across the river, not part of Adams's jurisdiction or caseload. But I knew he'd check.

"No," I said, keeping my eyes locked on his.

"That was fall of '02—and here you are again, summer of '05, with a murdered brother-in-law."

"We were alerted by Alex," I asserted.

"He's my fucking brother-in-law detective," Bo said angrily. "He's family. Why *wouldn't* I be here?"

"Yeah, yeah, but still, here you are—both of you—just like the Baron's house. You two live together?" A flash of amusement in his eyes.

Bo tilted his head, a smirk, or a scowl—I couldn't tell.

"It's not a crime," Alex interjected. "They came because I called Marty first. I don't know Bo's number."

"So this time—you're not just visiting," Adams said, his lips curling. "Seems like your luck hasn't improved."

A shallow shudder slithered up my spine. Adams wasn't just being a smart-ass—he was a new nemesis. When he got back to his desk, he'd pull old files—Homicide—Arson—Baltruschat—and make our lives hell.

"I have to go," said Bo, glancing at his watch. "I have to tell Laura, my sister."

"No, you don't," Adams said, standing up. "I'm heading out there now to tell her myself."

"More SOP?" I asked.

He shot me a smug smile and nodded.

Bo got up. "Then I'll go with you."

I could practically see Adams's brain working. He'd be able to sweat Bo the entire way there. "Yeah, you do that," he agreed. Then he turned to me and handed me his business card.

"Stay here. One of the unit guys will get your info."

His card, with the PPB logo, read: Detective Chuck Adams Homicide Division

Seeing his name in print brought back memories of how Bo and I used to call him "Chuckles" because, well, he wasn't. Even back then, he had the warmth of a brick wall.

I nodded, agreeing to drive Bo's car back to my house and meet him at the office the next day. As Adams walked off, I grabbed Bo's sleeve, pulled him close, and waited for the detective to get out of earshot. I whispered, "Be careful."

Alex leaned in as well and hissed, "You're doing a very stupid thing."

"Tell me something I don't know," Bo whispered back, then turned to catch up with Adams.

///

Three years ago, our business partner, Nico Scava, took a bullet to the head—courtesy of a deranged Russian sociopath named Vasili

Bobrov. That was our introduction to Natalya Danilenko and her oligarch boyfriend, Dmitry Chernyshevsky.

Natalya believed Bo and I had stolen a painting and a large sum of money from her and Dmitry. To retrieve them, she sent her nephew Vasili, a *Bratva* mob enforcer. In his eagerness to please her, Vasili went rogue, killing anyone in his path—including Baron Albert von Baltruschat and his wife, Crystal. As the chaos escalated, Natalya tried to keep Dmitry, the oligarch, in the dark—because if he learned the truth, he would have had us all killed.

During this horrible time, Bo and I straddled the line between criminal behavior and desperate necessity until I finally crossed it by putting Vasili down with a Browning .223 bolt-action varmint rifle. *Varmint* being the operative word.

We managed to escape the consequences. Nico Scava's *disappearance*—a polite euphemism for *"we don't know what happened to the body"*—hardened into a fact of life. The money was returned, and the painting was recovered because we hadn't stolen anything. Without that twisted and oddly fortuitous misunderstanding, we would never have crossed paths with Natalya and Dmitry. They would never have invested in our startup company.

Bo and I would've lived simpler lives—poorer, but simpler.

Instead, Natalya joined our board of directors as chairman—more a figurehead than a driving force—and, with Dmitry's bottomless pit of money, we built our small conglomerate, Paladin Holdings.

Along the way, I had an affair with Natalya, and Dmitry ignited the largest mafia war in modern Italian history. I learned two hard lessons: one, don't sleep with your chairman; and two, oligarch money spends as easily as any other—but it carries a barbarity that corrodes decency and leaves a void.

Now, Bo and I were carefully dismantling that company and severing ties with both Dmitry and Natalya.

It's a complicated story—and not one I was eager to explain to Detective Chuck Adams.

CHAPTER FOUR

The Bedbug

I ONCE READ—maybe on a coffee mug—that intuition is your soul whispering. At that point, mine wasn't whispering. It was staging a full-blown panic attack.

Sitting in Shangri-La—a fluorescent cave of iniquity—in the middle of the night, I exchanged awkward glances with Alex while waiting for a cop, any cop, to take our statement. Dread pressed inside me like an air bubble expanding under my ribs. It became harder to breathe. I jammed my hands deep in my pockets, clenching them to stop their shaking. I had too many secrets to be drowning in this much blue. I was a cat in a dog kennel, desperate to get out.

Alex and I watched the uniforms move with quiet efficiency. New faces drifted in, and I knew at once the body van had arrived. Tadeo was headed for the morgue.

"How's your stepmother?" I asked Alex, breaking the uncomfortable silence.

"She's good," he said. "I don't see her as much as before."

His gaze lingered just long enough to make me wonder if he knew about us. When Natalya and I were together, she'd visit Portland frequently. Now, not so much.

I'd never known exactly how close Alex and Natalya were. He was only a few years younger than her—his father had married Natalya late in his life, after Alex had already grown. He called her "mother," but it always felt more formal than affectionate. In reality, she seemed more like an older sister. I never asked if she'd told him about us. I didn't want to know. He already knew too much—it was his gun that Vasili used to kill Nico, for starters—and that was more than enough to keep me tethered to him. We were reluctant allies, bound by mutual interests and ghosts, hiding behind the illusion of friendship.

"Is Tadeo friends with Bo?" Alex asked, still talking about him in the present tense.

"Not really," I said.

He gave a little nod. "Makes sense."

"Why?"

"Because Bo does not make friends with fools."

"You think Tadeo was a fool?"

"I don't want to insult the dead," he said, then shrugged. "But yes. He isn't smart."

"Wasn't—wasn't smart."

He nodded his head solemnly. "*Da,* yes—wasn't."

"How so?"

"Because I talk to him when he comes here. I don't talk to many customers, but I talk to him because you introduced us."

I shook my head. "That's not possible—I hardly knew him."

"It was a bachelor party, yes? For a work comrade."

A memory sputtered awake. A year ago, after Bo and I returned from Italy—after Natalya had ended our affair and I was trying to repair the cracks in my marriage with Abbie—Bo pushed to hire Tadeo as "Director of Store Standards" at Corner24 despite Jeff Noble, the company's president, hating the idea.

Nate Radford, Jeff's operations V.P. and second-in-command, was getting married—for the umpteenth time—and I attended the bachelor party at Shangri-La. Apparently, I made introductions.

Alex went on about Tadeo's drinking—which, like mine, tended to be excessive—and his interest in naked women, which, unlike mine, bordered on obsessive.

"He came too often, drank too much, and was a big bedbug," he flicked his wrist with a calypso flourish.

I remembered that *bedbugs* were what the dancers called aggressive and handsy customers who were always bugging them to go to bed. Hence, the name.

I shifted the conversation. "How's your life? Any new friends?"

Alex had always worked hard to keep his sexual preferences quiet—he owned a strip club, after all. The women he employed liked him because he wasn't interested in them—his bouncers felt otherwise.

"I have a new friend, but you know, Marty, they never last."

"Is that their fault or yours?"

He grinned broadly for the first time that night. "It is mine."

A Black woman detective walked over to us, flipping through her notepad. I wondered if every cop in Oregon was issued one along with their badge. She made almost no impression on me—plain clothes, plain face, plain eyes, neatly braided hair, a boxy frame, and white Converse sneakers. The Chucks stood out, though.

She introduced herself as Tasha Hayes and picked up where Detective Adams had barely begun. I took the fact that she didn't separate me from Alex as a good sign—neither of us was a suspect. Her questions were routine, except for one. She turned to Alex and asked, "Did Mr. Ramírez ever record his conversations with the ladies in the club?"

Alex looked confused, shaking his head. I just shrugged and furrowed my brows.

What an odd question.

Then she told me I was free to go, adding that either she or Detective Adams would be in touch. I left Alex marinating in a pool of cops; the poor guy was equal parts dejected and combative.

CHAPTER FIVE

The Walk

I DROVE BO'S MERCEDES BACK TO MY HOUSE and pulled in at exactly 3:30 a.m.

Boomer, our golden retriever, greeted me at the door, tail wagging like it was the best part of his day. Unlike some, he was always happy to see me. Abbie followed in his wake, not as happy. She tightened the sash on her bathrobe, her eyes bleary with sleep.

"Where did you go?" she asked. "Boomer woke me, bounding out of the bedroom."

"It's too early for coffee. Let me make you a tea before I tell you." I turned toward the kitchen, hoping a little normalcy might soften the landing.

"That sounds ominous," she replied, following me, her bare feet silent on the cool floor.

Even with sleep-crusted eyes, no makeup, and pillow hair, she had a grace and an emotional gravity that steadied any room when the walls began to tilt. I told her everything that had happened, and once she'd absorbed the shock, she sank into a quiet slump, staring into her mug as if it held answers.

"I need to call Katherine."

"Let her sleep, Abbie. This news needs to come from Bo."

"Isn't Shangri-La Natalya's stepson's place?"

I nodded, a bit surprised she remembered.

"Tadeo getting shot is strange enough, but to be shot there seems peculiar," she said slowly, her voice edged with skepticism. "Did he hang out there? Was it random—wrong place, wrong time?"

I huffed at the comment. "I said those exact words to the detective. He didn't like it."

Her eyebrows lifted. "Why?"

"Remember a few years ago, when we had that blowup with the cops looking for us, while Bo and I were in Vegas?"

She nodded. It wasn't a favorite memory, and I could tell she wanted to move away from it.

"Remember, they were looking for us because Nico had gone missing, and we'd shown up at the Baron's place that same night it was torched—and the charred remains of Albert and his wife were found in the rubble?"

She narrowed her eyes and shivered slightly. "Where is this going, Marty?"

"The detective who was looking for us back then was at Shangri-La tonight. He remembered us."

She let the silence hang between us. Everything about that time was an ugly memory. Nico's disappearance, our startup on the brink of collapse, and our crumbling marriage.

"It's a weird coincidence," I finally said.

We talked a little longer before she decided to go back to bed.

"I won't sleep," she said. "Come, keep me warm. Bad news like this makes me want to be near you."

I checked my watch—4 a.m. "Let me take Boomer for a quick walk. I'll be up in fifteen." She smiled meekly, her fingers trailing over my shoulder.

I'd spent the past year carefully rebuilding our marriage. The quiet indifference that had crept in—the distance that dulled what we once were—was finally gone. It had taken months to restore what I'd let slip away: relearning the shape of her laugh, how she curled into me at night, how affection is given when it isn't asked for.

Without ever saying it, she had let me try—let me earn my way back.

Boomer had heard the word *walk* and was waiting for me at the front door. He understood English—at least the important words: *walk*, *sit*, *don't*, *food*, and, of course, *bacon*. He barked at the TV when a bacon commercial came on. I would fast-forward to spare him the disappointment.

Boomer and I had an understanding about leashes. He hated them, and so did I. I promised him I'd use them rarely, and he promised not to run away. To borrow a term from Detective Adams, Boomer's SOP was to saunter about twenty feet ahead of me, then sit or sniff things until I caught up. We kept each other in sight, as kindred spirits do.

We took the trail in the wooded park across the street, and I walked carefully, trying not to trip over exposed tree roots and the usual tangle of growth. I talked to Boomer because he always listened—or pretended to. Lately, though, the urge to talk to him had grown stronger, like with an aging friend, when you're unsure how much time you have left together.

Boomer was getting on, and I saw it in the white creeping into his golden coat, especially around his nose, as if he'd stuck it into snow. His eyes, still warm and dark amber, always happy and curious, now included a quiet melancholy—a gentle pity for me, as though he understood something I didn't. As if he knew that, by being merely human, I could never fully grasp the depth of his wordless wisdom.

"Boom-boom, I'm gonna call Natalya. It's just after seven in Florida. She should be awake." I could see his silhouette against the black forest, sitting, panting, staring back at me in what looked like a silent scold. "Yeah, I know. I should wait, but I'd rather talk to her privately without others listening in." His silent skepticism didn't waver as I pressed the autodial button.

"Did I wake you?"

"Almost," she yawned. "You missed my alarm by five minutes."

I pictured her lying in bed and shook my head—*stop it.*

I explained what had happened, uninterrupted but for her breathing.

"Who is Tadeo Ramírez??" she finally asked.

I told her.

"I am sorry. How is Bo?"

"I don't know."

"Does this man have a family?"

"Yeah. He and Laura have two daughters. Both younger than Bo's."

A long silence.

"Where are you right now?"

"Walking Boomer."

"I will call Alex."

"Wait an hour," I said. "He's probably still with the cops. They'll go through their standard protocol, and after that, he'll be alone—tired, but alone."

"Yes. I will text him. Let him know I am thinking of him. I'll invite him to visit me for a few days. He enjoys the South Beach scene."

"Good idea." I hesitated. "If I ask you something, will you give me an honest answer?"

"Why do you insult me, Martin?"

"Does Dmitry have anything to do with this?"

A beat of silence. Then, sharp but heavy with history—"Why would you ask such a thing?"

"I have plenty of reasons. Dmitry doesn't do subtle—he bank-rolls bloodshed like it's a line item in his budget. Is it unreasonable to think he might be throwing violence around just to jam things up—maybe drag out the negotiations?"

"You think he would hurt someone in Bo's family?" She took a long breath. "You always see devils where there are none." The exasperation in her voice was obvious, but under it was something colder. She wasn't just offended on Dmitry's behalf—my question also cut at her choices, her instincts, her judgment in men.

"Take Boomer home. I know you took him out at 4 a.m. just so you could call me, away from Abbie, to ask such a question. Don't forget, Martin, I know how you think."

"It's a fair question, Natalya."

She sighed, the sound distant but heavy. "Oh, *milyy* …"

She hadn't called me sweetheart in a year. The weight of the word hung between us. I let out a slow breath. "I'm sorry, Natalya. It's been a long night. But it's just so … calculated."

She paused. "How do you mean calculated?"

"Deliberate. Intentional," I said. "Another dead body in my life—in Bo's life. Before I met you, my world was as dull as a grocery receipt. My only run-in with cops was doing forty through a school zone. The only dead person I'd ever seen was my father before they carted him off to be cremated. Not even in Vietnam. And if you're gonna see dead bodies, a war zone's a good bet.

"But now? My life is littered with bodies—and none of them from natural causes. Bullets through eye sockets. Ice picks in ears. Heads blown off. A guy shot in the chest just so he'd stay alive long enough to know he was dying. And tonight, Bo's brother-in-law, shot in your stepson's parking lot."

I exhaled. "I don't know what it is. I can't put my finger on it. Maybe it's fate, maybe a twisted inevitability, maybe just bad luck baked into my DNA, but something dark is stalking me, closing in."

She was quiet for a long moment. Then, softly, "Oh, Martin … fate stalks everyone. It caught you the moment you found me."

CHAPTER SIX

Dead Exit

JUNE WEATHER IN PORTLAND IS FICKLE, trapped between breaking up with winter and seducing summer. It teases you with a day or two of perfection, then follows up with a few days of misery. That morning, misery had returned—low, thick clouds spilling an uneven drizzle, temperatures dropping sharply from the day before.

I drove the Z8 to the office, my new toy, a private reward for winning back Abbie, making peace with my teenage kids, and staying away from Natalya. That last part—staying away from Natalya—had been excruciating for a long time, but it had grown easier with every passing month.

Bo hated the car. Too tight. Too flashy. Too much work to fold himself into. Decades ago, he'd squeezed into Formula GTP cockpits that offered more room than this. Getting him into the Z8 was like stuffing a bear into a phone booth—awkward, a little painful, and downright comical. It also meant I'd be the one driving that day.

Paladin Holdings's offices are on the ground floor of Lake Oswego's only commercial building, offering an unbroken view of the water. Floor-to-ceiling windows, just five feet from the lake, create the illusion that you could leave your desk and dive straight in. We call it the glass cage. With its plush furnishings, living-room layout, and sweeping panorama, it's always the preferred setting for business meetings.

When I arrived, I greeted Christine, our office manager. Her cubicle, located just outside the glass cage, was affectionately called the C-suite, and her nameplate read "Chief" because she ran the place. Bo was already there, pacing, his weary eyes fixed on his coffee.

"I haven't told anyone yet," he said as the glass door closed behind me. "I'm still trying to get my head around it."

"Everyone will know soon enough. It'll be in *The Oregonian* today," I said, filling my own mug. "What happened with Laura?"

"It was a mess," he said, rubbing his face. "I called Kath, and she came over. We stayed with Laura all night. Watching her deal with it tore me apart. She let the kids sleep, then told them this morning. I couldn't take it, so I left. Katherine's still there. A female cop came to stay with them for a while. I went home, took a shower, and came here."

"Your car's at my place," I said.

"I'll get it later. I drove Katherine's car."

"Tell me what happened with Adams."

"That guy is going to be a problem, Marty. He stepped into something he can't scrape off. He wanted me to repeat every detail of our visit with the Baron, as if Tadeo's murder didn't matter at all. He's obsessed with our connection to both homicides. Christ! That was three years ago. Feels like thirty. I had to dig deep to remember our story. I'm sure he's already pulling everything he has on that old case, ready to start digging."

"There's nothing there," I said. "The Baron's case is as dead as Tadeo, and his goddamn murder isn't connected to us for a change."

Bo nearly dropped his cup. "Jesus, Marty! Tadeo's my brother-in-law. How about a little consideration?"

I held up both palms. "Sorry. You know what I meant. I already called Natalya—asked her if Dmitry was behind it. She said no, and I believe her. He's not moving pieces around the board. You're connected, but by marriage, not by motive." I dropped onto the couch. "So, who the hell wants Tadeo dead?"

"Who doesn't?" Bo exhaled and lowered himself into the opposite end. We spent the next hour running through possibilities—gambling debt, get-rich scheme gone bad—all plausible.

Over the years, Bo and I had learned how to talk about sensitive things in our aquarium. The office couch faced the lake, its back to the interior glass wall, where people walked by—but Christine's watchful eye was always on us, ready if we signaled. We'd developed the habit of keeping our voices low and our eyes on the water whenever we discussed things that justified our paranoia.

"The suddenness and randomness are what bother me the most," Bo said, his gaze fixed on the gray expanse where fog rising off the lake blended seamlessly with the drizzle.

Christine knocked lightly on the wall. I turned, and she formed her hand into a mock phone, thumb and little finger extended, holding it to her ear to signal an incoming call. She'd long ago learned our code for privacy and knew better than to interrupt when the lake held our attention. I nodded, signaling her to put the call through.

I hit speakerphone, and a low, congested growl rolled out.

"Gentlemen! You're not having a good morning," said Marek Sokol.

"How the hell do you know?" Bo asked, surprised.

"I'm omniscient."

"You talked to Natalya," I said cynically.

"That too," he replied.

Marek worked for Dmitry Chernyshevsky and Natalya. Bo and I didn't like him as much as we respected him. He was the attorney handling the dissolution of our partnership with the oligarch. Managing the various legal and financial teams. We'd been dealing with him for months. Slick, sharp, smart, loyal to Dmitry, and—most importantly—morally flexible, Marek earned our respect not for those qualities, but for being upfront about them. He never pretended to care about our best interests, and we appreciated that blunt honesty. In a world of blurred lines, shifting allegiances, and sudden violence, his lack of pretense made him a valuable collaborator, even if we never fully trusted him.

"I'm sorry for your loss, Bo," he said, his voice low and measured.

"Thanks," Bo replied.

"Do you want to push things out a few weeks?" He referred to the upcoming meeting to finalize the documents and arrange the money transfers related to the final agreement. The legal teams had been working on the papers for months.

"No," Bo answered.

///////////////////////////////////////

When Bo and I returned from Italy over a year ago, we had made it our mission to separate from Dmitry. We discussed it incessantly, calling the plan a "dead exit"—"exit" being the goal, "dead" being the risk. What we had braced for as a life-threatening move, however, turned out to be nothing more than a matter of careful concession and compromise.

Still raw from what we'd endured in Rome, we spent months figuring out how to approach Dmitry without getting ourselves killed. We already knew enough to be afraid. During the Chiurazzi foundry acquisition, Dmitry had turned Naples into an abattoir, sending the Moscow Vory to wipe out the Di Lupo clan of the Camorra. The papers called it the Scampia Feud—223 people shot down in stairwells, alleys, and market squares. A cold, methodical slaughter. All because a single Di Lupo had dared to cross him. By then, we understood exactly what Dmitry was capable of.

We'd stalled all new acquisitions, bringing Paladin's growth to a standstill. Even Natalya began to question our sudden inertia. Then, one afternoon, we sent everyone home, opened a bottle of Glenlivet, and put Natalya on speaker. We told her we would be willing to let her and Dmitry buy Paladin Holdings from us. Everything was on the table—we were prepared to walk away from it all in exchange for a fair return.

Her voice was calm, almost detached. "I had a suspicion about this," she said. "But I have a better plan."

Bo and I exchanged glances, fortifying ourselves for whatever was to come.

"I think you should buy Dmitry and me out instead."

The words hit like dropped glass—sharp, splintering. We flinched, instinctively checking for unseen cuts. Unfazed by our silence, she continued. She and Dmitry would approve the dissolution—on one condition: Dmitry would recoup his investment and retain the Italian foundry that held the Vatican license, attached to the Vatican Bank account—the keys to the kingdom.

Bo found his voice first. "You sound like you've already had this conversation with Dmitry."

Natalya let a beat pass. Then her voice dropped. "Tell me, Bo, do you think Dmitry or I cannot read the minds of our partners?" She let the question linger. "I told Dmitry months ago that you and Martin have lost your passion for Paladin. You haven't worked on a single acquisition since Chiurazzi."

"Italy was … a lot," I admitted.

She exhaled softly—not a laugh, but something like recognition. "For me, too, yes?"

We all understood what she meant. Her kidnapping. The torture. Dmitry's retribution. The gap between those past horrors and the present calm felt too vast to bridge.

"But understand," she continued, her tone rising again, "Dmitry invested in Paladin because of me. He has more companies than he can count. His only interest is the Chiurazzi."

We talked a while longer, but in the end, Bo and I were suspended between disbelief and reluctant relief. Leaving Paladin had seemed momentous—an act sure to trigger Dmitry's wrath. And yet here was Natalya, laying it all out like a simple business transaction. (Maybe that's all it ever was.) No threats. No bloodshed. No reprisal. We had braced ourselves for savagery—and instead, got mercy.

Negotiations for the conglomerate's breakup were surprisingly smooth. Each company inside Paladin Holdings operated independently, so the division was straightforward. Beaumont Enterprises, the company Natalya and Dmitry had initially set up to move Dmitry's capital through to Paladin, would take the three luxury hotels and the Italian foundry … and the Vatican Bank account—an asset not listed on any balance sheet, but whose strategic value overshadowed every other part of the portfolio. After all, he laundered more than a billion a year through it.

The transaction, therefore, wasn't a one-for-one swap. It was a carve-out where the usual metrics didn't apply. The Vatican account was a black box with a value no analyst's formula could quantify. So, we adjusted the distribution: all the other companies—the boat builder, the plastics company, the sawmill, the microbrewery, and Corner24—ended up with us.

I had my own theory about why breaking free of Dmitry was easier than expected, but I never shared it with Bo. Maybe Natalya still felt something for me—enough to strike a private deal with Dmitry. I knew how persuasive she could be when she wanted something. He got to keep her, and I was the forfeit. A kind of asymmetrical exchange—a lover's bargain. Or maybe it was just my ego, clinging to the idea that I still mattered to her. Either way, it's the story I tell myself to sleep at night.

<hr>

"I understand you might have a police problem," Marek Sokol said.

Bo turned to me, his expression practically shouting, *Why do you tell Natalya everything?* But his voice stayed even when he spoke. "I think we've got it under control. The cop who questioned us last night recognized us as being part of another murder investigation from a few years ago—he didn't like the coincidence."

"I don't either," Marek rumbled, his voice low and deliberate. "You think last night involved you?"

Bo's eyebrows shot up. "Do you know something we don't?"

"No—but a dead man can be a message without the envelope," Marek said, his words landing like a cryptic eulogy.

"We already went over this," I cut in, sharply. "The only messenger would be your client—and we're hoping it's not him."

"It isn't." Marek shifted his tone just enough to make me cautious again. "But I think you should look into Corner24. He worked there, didn't he? Your brother-in-law?"

"Tadeo Ramírez," I clarified, my mouth feeling chalky, as I reached for the coffee.

"The dead guy."

"To repeat myself, Marek," Bo said, frustration edging his voice. "Do you know something we don't?"

"To repeat *myself*—no. But Corner24 isn't as clean as you think."

"Meaning?"

"During due diligence, I reviewed their numbers. Things didn't add up. Don't misunderstand—I don't care. Dmitry doesn't want the business. You can have it with our blessing. The damn thing's too unwieldy. Too many parts, too little oversight. One hundred and twenty cramped stores across three states. It's like navigating a dark room covered in spilled Legos."

"It's profitable," Bo said.

"Is it?"

Bo bristled. "What the hell? I see the numbers every week. It's my job—they look fine." He took a breath and steadied himself. "And I'm good with numbers."

"I'm sure you are, Bo," Marek said. "But you look at them with trust—I see them with suspicion. That's my job. To me, they looked cooked. Not messy like lasagna—more refined, like a soufflé."

Bo shot me a look—I shrugged in response.

"Okay, Marek, we'll check into it," said Bo. "But it doesn't make sense that you'd catch something I missed."

"I'm not sure I did. But I'm more distrusting than most. I study the fine print."

With droll flippancy, I said, "The fine print is where the bodies are buried."

"No, Marty. It's not where you find the bodies—it's where you find the shovel."

CHAPTER SEVEN

The Funeral

TADEO RAMIREZ WAS BURIED FIVE DAYS LATER.

Inside the funeral home, the cool air carried a faint scent of lilies, dust, and something else—something indeterminate, timeless. A brooding bleakness. Abbie and I awkwardly shook hands with strangers, avoiding eye contact and exchanging the usual condolences. In the main room, a photo collage of Tadeo stood on an easel beside a dull-gray metal urn. Faces frozen in moments I hadn't shared.

Bo said Laura planned to place the urn on the mantel. I shivered at the thought, stirred by her vulnerability. The urn wasn't just metal and ash—it was absence, sealed in a container. A mournful presence that should be allowed to recede into the quiet corners of memory. But everyone carries grief differently, and who was I to judge?

The widow sat with Bo and Katherine, surrounded by their children—Tadeo's two daughters and Bo's three. The adults wore black; the kids wore muted colors. Everyone looked somber and distant. Katherine held Laura's hand while Bo gently stroked the back of his youngest daughter, Natalie. There was almost as much pain in Katherine's eyes as in Laura's. I didn't know Laura well, but I knew Katherine. She had a kindness that felt effortless, a quiet charity so deeply rooted it seemed part of her bones. When Abbie and I first met her many years ago, we were almost incredulous—unable to believe someone could possess such consistent, natural goodness.

Over the years, we learned it wasn't just real—it was the architecture of who she was.

When Bo saw us, he excused himself from the group and joined me. Abbie quietly took his place beside Katherine.

I hadn't seen Bo in a few days. He'd been home, helping comfort the girls after losing their uncle. Bo was never close to Tadeo. Tadeo's overbearing bluster repelled him, but Bo's daughters received it as warmth and humor. He had been their favorite relative.

At funerals, people tend to murmur politely and avoid discussing the host. Bo was no different. When he walked over to me, Tadeo wasn't top of mind.

"Marek's flying in next week," he murmured. "And Paladin's about to get sliced up like a birthday cake."

"Let's not talk about it," I said. "The folks here from Corner24 can't know about this until it's done."

The entrance door opened, and a soft ripple flowed through the room as Natalya and Alex Danilenko stepped in. Natalya's gaze locked onto mine before anyone else's, a silent reminder that old habits die hard. Her lips curved into a faint, weary smile. I gave a subtle nod in return, already feeling that old sting—loss and longing, like shrapnel buried in a wound that had healed but still throbbed with every change in the weather.

She wore a tailored black dress that flattered her figure without revealing it. A dark gray stole was draped over her shoulders, and her modestly heeled shoes were buffed to military precision. Her nails were polished and immaculate, showing no sign that one had ever been ripped from her finger. Her only jewelry—a small, pearl bracelet and a simple watch—felt understated and deliberate. Alex, by contrast, looked like he'd just tossed a black sport coat over his usual black pants and white shirt. His jewelry was gone—except for the diamond earrings, which were more a trademark than an ornament.

"I didn't know they were coming," Bo said, turning slightly so only I could hear.

"Me neither," I replied, walking toward them and extending my hand to shake Natalya's.

We brushed cheeks as she whispered, "Good to see you, Martin."

I led them to the guest book, and as they signed in, Bo, Katherine, and Abbie walked up to say hello. They exchanged brief, amicable hugs, but my attention stayed on Abbie and Natalya. In the three years since Natalya had joined the company, we'd all been in the same room only a handful of times.

I'd avoided talking about Natalya with Abbie for obvious reasons. Whenever Abbie asked about her, I would give one-word answers. Bo, on the other hand, was more transparent with Katherine about Natalya, so any impressions Abbie had likely came from Katherine, filtered through her unerring kindness.

I studied their faces, noting how effortlessly attractive the three women were, as if their features had been shaped by the lives they led. Katherine carried a refined composure—her hair perfectly arranged, her posture soft yet assured, a steady brightness that made people settle when she entered a room.

Abbie had a more gentle allure—less managed but no less striking—genuine and unguarded, with an easy confidence that didn't need to announce itself.

And Natalya—born with arresting features—held a poise honed through her climb from poverty to privilege. She carried a deliberate reserve, admirable from a distance, held behind a pane of hard-won certainty.

Curiosity brought a cluster of mourners over to greet Natalya and Alex. No one had ever seen them before, and I'm sure they'd all heard the Russian accent and immediately wondered how they had fit into Tadeo's life.

"Who's the Russki babe?" Ed Cruz, the company's logistics manager, whispered in my ear.

"Always the gentleman, Ed," I replied, my voice detached and cold.

"Okay, then—the *chick* with the accent."

"Natalya Danilenko, the chairman of Paladin Holdings."

"That's where I seen her before," he said. "Her photo's in our annual report."

"I didn't know you read," I said.

"I wouldn't kick her outta bed for eatin' crackers, if ye know what I mean," he leered sideways.

"I do know what you mean, Cruz, and you're walking a fine line. She's a friend of mine."

Ed Cruz ran the supply chain for Corner24, which included three large warehouses, a few stocking outposts, and a fleet of trucks that always smelled like cigarettes and stale coffee. Plump and suety, he looked like the type who'd outmaneuver you long before he'd out-work you. His face was round and fleshy, and his black hair slicked back as though he'd dipped it in a tub of pomade on a dare. But what stuck with me most were his fingers. Long. Restless. Always moving, like worms on a hook.

"Just admirin' your taste in bosses."

"She's not my boss, Ed." I locked eyes with him. "But she *is* yours."

His lids drooped, disguising his sentiments, and he took another sip from the flask in his pocket. The suit was expensive, well cut, and entirely wasted on him. Taste and subtlety were absent; crude passed for couth. I didn't like him. Bo liked him even less.

"I recognize the bald muscle with her," he said. "Ain't he a bouncer at Shangri-La?"

"It's her stepson. He owns the place," I answered.

"Jesus. Our chairman's kid owns a strip club. Think you can get me a discount?"

"I'll get right on that."

"Call it a company perk."

"Let's not," I answered. "Speaking of perks, you have an idea why Tadeo was at Shangri-La that night?"

His lids opened just enough to let me know he was lying. "Nope."

"Didn't think so," I muttered, turning back toward Bo, who stood across the room with our VP of Operations, Nate Radford, watching us.

Nate reported to Jeff Noble, the company president and the man we'd bought Corner24 from. Noble still ran the show—that was part of the deal. He hadn't been to the funeral, and Bo and I knew why. Officially, he was "under the weather," though in a way we couldn't explain to anyone.

As soon as I joined them, Bo leaned toward Nate without breaking his gaze from Ed and whispered, "Did Ed marry well?"

"What? I don't—" Nate paused, following Bo's eyes. "Oh. You mean, did he marry rich?"

"Exactly. Did he marry into money?"

"Ed?" Nate snorted. "Hell no. The guy doesn't even act married—he chases anything with a pulse. His wife used to wait tables at Hooters out at Jantzen Beach. She's a number herself. It's not a marriage; it's a cage match with cleavage."

Bo glanced at me. Without a word, we exchanged a quick conversation:

Bo: *Follow me, outside.*

Me: *Right behind you.*

Bo: *Leave this asshole here.*

Me: *Still right behind you.*

We stepped out onto the well-worn gray steps of the funeral home, its bleached white walls reflecting our shadows. A small sign, *Willamette Memorial Chapel*, hung crooked in its metal frame, as if it had grown tired of standing straight—or didn't care anymore.

"Ed Cruz is stealing from us," Bo said, his voice low even though no one could hear.

"I'm not surprised, but how do you know?"

"I'm assuming the eighty-grand Porsche Carrera with the CRUZIN vanity plate over there is his," he pointed to the parking lot. "The suit he's wearing costs more than a month's mortgage. His boots are croc leather—easily three figures. And when I asked him the time, he checked his platinum Lange chronograph."

"That's a thirty-thousand-dollar watch," I said, not hiding my shock.

"As I said, the son-of-a-bitch is stealing from us."

"Maybe Sokol was right, and he saw something we didn't."

Bo raised an eyebrow. "After this, let's go see Noble. Something stinks."

"It's Ed's cologne," I said.

Bo grinned. "I'm not sure what bothers me more—that Nate doesn't notice Ed dresses like a rich pimp, or he notices and doesn't care."

We lingered for another half hour, making polite conversation while keeping our distance from Nate and Ed. Bo hovered near Katherine and the girls. Abbie stayed close to me, her fingers slipping gently into mine. I caught Natalya watching us. Our eyes met; I broke away first. Moments later, she and Alex murmured their solemn goodbyes and left.

I was about to ask Abbie if she was ready to do the same when I noticed Laura standing with Nate and Ed, her back rigid, her chin angled as she spoke in low, clipped tones. Her voice—strained and taut—rose with each sentence.

Bo heard it too. His brow tightened as he moved toward her, puzzled. I followed. Laura's composure was splintering into sharp fragments. Her red, brimming eyes darted between Nate and Ed, searching for something they weren't giving her. Her breathing quickened. Something was building.

"Laura," Bo said softly, touching her shoulder.

She jerked away, spinning toward him, her face flushed and trembling.

"I just want to know what's been going on," she hissed.

"Going on where?" Bo kept his tone level, though his jaw had set.

"At the company, damn it. At Corner24." Her voice shook, but the words cracked across the room.

"Laura," Bo said, his voice low and steady, though I could hear the strain beneath it. "I don't know what you're talking about." He glanced at Nate and Ed, who both shrugged—but I caught the faint flicker of a smirk on Ed's lips. I decided right then that I'd fire his fat ass on Monday.

"Bullshit!" Laura's voice sliced through the murmured conversations. Heads turned. "It's all bullshit."

"Laura," Bo said again, softer this time, trying to draw her back from the edge. "Let's take the girls and go home. This isn't good for them … or anyone here."

"You're lying to me, and it won't work anymore."

Abbie and I knew better than to intervene. Her fingers tightened around mine. This wasn't ours to fix. This was Bo and Katherine's storm to walk through.

"Lying about what, Laura?" Katherine asked. Her voice stayed calm, but her eyes flipped to Bo, searching for something he wasn't saying.

"That's what I want to find out." Laura's voice cracked. But as her gaze slid from Bo to me, something changed. The pleading drained out, replaced with something sharper—probing, calculating. The hair on the back of my neck rose.

"Just tell me one thing," she said.

"What?" Bo's voice had gone tight.

Laura fixed him with an unblinking stare.

"Why the hell was my husband wearing a wire?"

CHAPTER EIGHT

Jeff Noble

JEFF NOBLE WAS ALIVE.

Barely.

I didn't know if the cancer would take him or AIDS. He didn't either. There was a time he thought he did—back when his AIDS was under control, and the cancer was just a diagnosis. But then the chemo treatments tightened the race. Now they were nose to nose, the finish line in sight.

He lived on the far side of the lake. Not visible from our office without binoculars and a reason to look. Even then, his place was only a rooftop behind the pines. The house was huge—an inheritance from his father, who founded Corner24 and left it to him. Jeff didn't do much with either. He lived well, spent fast, and became a favorite with the lake crowd—old money, wine clubs, always the preferred auctioneer at every charity event in the Portland metro area.

But Jeff gambled.

A lot.

The tribal casinos knew his name. Vegas knew his whiskey. He lost enough to keep the comps rolling—suites, steaks, markers on file. After the AIDS diagnosis, his gambling slid from careless to reckless. When the money finally ran out, he sold the company to us.

Jeff owed everyone—banks, backers, and probably the valet at the Bellagio. To mitigate our risk, we structured the acquisition as seventy-five percent cash and twenty-five percent earnout. It paid off his debts, gave his investors a decent return, and left him in charge for the next five years to earn his remaining twenty-five percent. If he failed to run the company well, it would cost him more than it would cost us.

It was a solid plan—until lung cancer came knocking. Jeff smoked Marlboros like he was on Philip Morris's payroll. The chemo, meant to slow the cancer, kicked his AIDS back into motion. That's when the race tightened. He kept it private until the doctors said it didn't matter which disease crossed the line first. They were running neck and neck.

The unraveling had begun months earlier. He'd become just a voice on the phone, deflecting every attempt at face-to-face contact. We didn't push. With Jeff, detachment was part of the package. So when he reluctantly disclosed his condition, we didn't ask questions—we just listened. He told us he'd had AIDS for years but had kept it quiet, not even disclosing it when we bought the company—he didn't want us to cancel his earnout. Then came the cancer—like tossing lighter fluid on a low flame. He no longer had a choice. He asked us to keep it private. He had a daughter he wanted to protect. We honored that.

A handsome Latino man in his mid-thirties, with close-cropped hair and a neatly trimmed beard, led us into the living room—if you could still call it that. The furniture had been pushed back to the walls as if in preparation for a wake. A hospital bed now occupied the space where the giant sofa once stood, an IV pole beside it like a misplaced flagstaff.

Jeff stood next to the bed, gripping its white frame to keep himself upright, an oxygen tank at his side replacing Queen—his copper-colored pointer—who had once shadowed him from room to room until the doctors insisted she go. Too many germs. Tubing snaked from the tank into his nostrils. The room smelled faintly of antiseptic and microwaved soup, with an undertone disturbingly close to the funeral home we'd just left.

"How was the funeral?" asked Jeff, his voice still carrying the fight his body had already lost.

I didn't know how to answer since he was so close to attending his own.

"Sad," said Bo.

"You just come from there?"

"Yes, we dropped everyone at Bo's house. They're having a small reception there, and we came directly here," I said.

"I'm flattered."

"Don't be," said Bo flatly.

Jeff glanced at the silent Latino man. "Alisandro, can you give us a minute?"

Alisandro smiled and stepped out of the room. We'd not seen him before, but the car in Noble's driveway had let us know he had company. I figured he would listen from the vast hallway—there was a baby monitor on the nightstand, and he carried the receiver in his hand.

"Then it's not a courtesy call," said Jeff, moving slowly to the front of the bed and leaning against its mattress.

"My brother-in-law was found wearing a wire," Bo said. We both watched Jeff closely for a reaction.

"When he was shot?" Gaunt, gray, dull-eyed, his bones stuck out like tent stakes. He hacked, dredged up phlegm, and swallowed like it hurt.

"Yes," I said.

"What kind of wire?"

Bo and I shrugged, not sure what he meant.

Jeff's annoyance flared in a mild flush beneath his translucent skin. "Was it official? You know—cops in a van out front with antennas … like on TV?"

"No," Bo said. "My sister said it was jerry-rigged; a mic taped to his chest, wired to a small recorder in his pocket. The cops have it, but they won't tell her what was on it."

"So, your brother-in-law gets off recording strippers talking dirty while giving him a lap dance?" It wasn't a question.

Jeff had always been a cynical asshole—flippant and arrogant. The past few months had added a sting, curdling his usual irascibility into bitter enmity. If he hadn't already had one foot in the grave, Bo might've decked him. I stepped between them, just in case.

"We think he was trying to get someone from the company on tape."

"My company?" Jeff looked startled. "Shangri-La is quite the detour from Corner24."

"We think he was going to meet someone there," I said. "But they didn't show."

"Maybe Tadeo was trying to get some dirt," Bo added.

"Dirt on what?"

"You tell us. You're running the place."

"What are you implying?"

"What are you hiding?"

That did it. Jeff started coughing—hard, wet. His flush went crimson, spittle oozing from his lip, which he wiped with the sleeve of his terry robe.

"Get out!" he rasped, yanking the oxygen tube from his nose. "You come into my house—while I'm rotting in real time—with your bullshit accusations? You think I'm running a crooked house? Some kind of racket? That my company is dirty?"

"It's not your company anymore, Jeff," Bo said coldly.

"Piss off!" he wheezed.

The Latino reappeared, but Jeff flicked his wrist for him to leave again. "Ignore him. He's just here to keep an eye on me."

"Your day nurse?"

"Yeah. That's what he is. My goddamn day nurse."

Alisandro glanced carefully at each of us, then backed out with a slight bow, still silent. There was a strange weightlessness to him.

An unctuous geniality that felt practiced, as if he were playing a role. He hovered just outside the doorframe, listening.

"You made me hire Tadeo. I never wanted him. Sharp as a marble. But you insisted. Now he gets himself clipped at a titty bar with a recorder in his pocket like some comic book detective—and your first thought is me? *My* company? You can kiss my withering, bony ass. Both of you—just get out."

"I plan to rip Corner24 apart," Bo said, in his standard stolid way. "Shelf by shelf, box by box, and I better not find anything."

"Or what?" rasped Jeff. "What will you do? Kill me? That position's been filled."

Bo didn't answer. He just stared.

"Tell you what," Jeff muttered, waving the day nurse back in. He grimaced as Alisandro—still smiling smarmily—eased him back into the bed and reattached his oxygen tube.

"I'll be meeting up with Tadeo soon. When I do, I'll ask him what vulgar little ditties the strippers whispered in his ear to make it worth strapping a damn mic to his chest."

Alisandro lifted his legs onto the mattress, straightened them, and drew the sheet and blanket over himself.

Jeff rasped after us as we left. "If you have any other stupid accusations to make, send me a memo next time."

//

We rode in silence for a few miles. I hadn't expected Bo to drive the Z8, but not driving would have been even more uncomfortable for him. He looked like he'd been shoved into it with both hands, as if it were a cage built for something smaller.

"Where are we going?" I finally asked.

"Corner24 main office."

"I know this is personal, Bo, but Jeff made a point. We're making leaps in logic, connecting tenuous dots."

I was probably the only one who could say that to him without getting punched.

"I don't think Tadeo was a perv—recording strippers," Bo said.

"Neither do I. But Jeff's right. If the cops are to be believed, it wasn't an official wire. After you left the club that night with Adams, a woman officer—his partner, I think—questioned me. It was all basic stuff, but she caught me off guard by asking Alex if Tadeo had ever recorded the dancers. I thought that was strange."

"Yeah. The cops haven't given Laura any details. She only knows about it at all because they tried to search the house for tape recordings. When she demanded an explanation or a warrant, Adams finally told her about the makeshift contraption."

"Have they searched his office?"

"No, just the house. They're pushing the perv angle—it's the simplest explanation. Find the pissed-off boyfriend of a stripper, and they've got a suspect. Everything else is messier, harder to prove. You and I are the only ones thinking differently."

"Noble sure turned fast," I said, reflecting on Jeff's gratuitous tirade. "He went from his usual surly to batshit crazy in a sentence."

"I caught that, too."

"Makes me think he's hiding something. Deploying anger to deflect."

"That wasn't anger, Marty—that was fear."

//

We arrived at Corner24's corporate headquarters and parked at the entrance. It was Saturday afternoon, so the lot was empty. Bo and I didn't come here often—we preferred our lakefront office, intimate but expansive, over this glass-and-concrete box that looked more like a regional IRS bureau. The late afternoon sun turned the tinted windows into mirrors.

Bo pried himself out of the Z8 like a stubborn cork, and we let ourselves into the dark lobby with my security badge, which I kept in the glove box. The main corridor curved gently, a long arc of glass-walled offices along the outer wall and a grid of beige cubicles inside—each identical, each a cell in the hive, distinguished only by the personal photo mosaics pinned to the walls.

Tadeo's office was near the end of the curve. We hadn't reached the halfway point when we heard it—faint thumps, a drawer sliding open and slamming shut, the rustle of hurried movement. Bo slowed and tilted his head. I nodded, raising a finger to my lips—not that I needed to.

We slipped off the main corridor into the cubicle maze, ducking low, moving as if we were about to breach a mafia compound. The noises grew louder as we crept closer: paper shuffling, the universal clatter of metal cabinet doors sliding open, and something falling with a dull thud. Then the voices became recognizable.

Nate Radford and Ed Cruz.

I peeked from my crouch. Nate stood behind Tadeo's desk, rifling through drawers as if he'd lost a winning lottery ticket. At the credenza, Ed's fingers twisted and twitched, flipping binders open and tossing them aside. They hadn't yet changed out of their funeral attire.

Bo nodded at me, and we both stood up.

"Lose a stapler, gentlemen?" he said, deadpan.

Nate and Ed froze, like junkies caught digging through a dumpster. I saw Ed's lips form the word *shit* before stretching it into a grin.

"Hey, guys," Nate said, aiming for casual—and missing. "What are you doing here?"

"Back at you," said Bo.

"You know that whole thing at the funeral? Wearing a wire. Very bizarre."

I knew where he was going and gave him kudos for thinking fast—thinking at all.

"It freaked us out," he continued, and Ed gave a lumpish nod.

"Made us wonder what Tadeo was into. Recording people? Recording dancers? Maybe stashing the tapes here in the office. Company liability—you know?"

Bo tapped a finger to his chin. That was our signal—he'd take the lead.

We'd created nonverbal signals for us years ago: a chin tap for "follow my lead," an ear pull for "I'm lost, take over," and a head scratch for "you're on your own." This was the first time we'd used them in a while. I put on my thinking face.

"Funny you say that," Bo said, stepping into the office like it was his. I followed. "Marty and I were thinking the same thing."

"Great minds …" Ed said.

"You find anything?" Bo asked.

"Clean as a nun's conscience," Nate answered.

"You think Tadeo was recording something other than strippers?" Bo asked, flipping open a manila file on the desk. Empty.

"I don't know."

Ed quietly straightened the binders he'd been shuffling through.

"I mean, employees. Did he ever ask you guys weird questions?"

"Jesus!" said Ed. "You think he was trying to get personal shit to blackmail us?"

"Did he?" I asked.

"Nah. He knew better. I'd have killed the moth—" He caught himself, but the sentence had already landed.

Bo raised an eyebrow. I didn't say anything. I didn't need to.

"When was the last time you talked to Jeff?" Bo asked.

"Noble? Yesterday. He told us he wouldn't come to the funeral."

"We just came from there. We told him about the wire."

Nate gave a fake sigh. "I don't bother Jeff with shit like that. You know what he's dealing with. I'm not about to give him more to worry about."

We exchanged a few more pleasantries before they left. No handshakes. We didn't like each other, and no one felt obligated to pretend otherwise. Afterward, Bo and I walked to their offices; both were locked.

"They were lying," I said.

"Yup."

"They got here fast. Didn't even go home to change. Whatever they're looking for, it's important."

"We have a serious problem, Marty," said Bo, as we walked back down the hallway to the lobby. "Marek Sokol was wrong."

"About what?"

"Sokol asked if killing Tadeo was a message—it wasn't a message."

He stopped walking.

"It was cleanup."

CHAPTER NINE

Ransacked

"MARTY!" ABBIE'S VOICE CAME THROUGH THE PHONE, tight and strained. "Where are you? You need to get here. Now."

"I'm just leaving the Corner24 building—what's happening?"

"You're with Bo?"

"Of course."

"Tadeo's house has been ransacked. Laura's on the phone with the cops. You both need to get here fast."

I hung up and told Bo. He stepped on the gas, shifting gears. The car lunged as if we were coming out of a pit lane at Daytona.

"They waited until the funeral," Bo said, checking the mirrors. "They knew the house would be empty."

"They who?"

"Don't know, but they're connected to Nate and Ed."

"Looking for what?"

"Whatever Nate and Ed were after in Tadeo's office."

"Whatever it is, it's not recordings of 'dirty ditties'."

"You got that right."

Bo nearly collided with the cops as he and I arrived at Tadeo's house. Two black-and-whites with their lights flashing—no sirens—rushed from the other direction, and right behind them, an unmarked Ford with Chuck Adams and Tasha Hayes. We all braked hard at once, like a spontaneous drug bust.

Laura sat on the porch bench in her funeral dress, arms tightly folded across her midsection as if warding off a stomach cramp. Abbie had one arm around her shoulders. The girls were stretched out on the lawn, quiet, picking at the grass. The front door of the two-story colonial stood wide open.

Bo barely put it in park before jumping out. Detective Adams passed us without a word, jabbing a finger at us to keep clear of the house. Detective Hayes followed him inside. I noted she was wearing her Chucks again.

"The 911 operator told us to get out," said Abbie as Bo and I walked up. "She said, 'Don't touch anything. Just leave and wait outside.'"

Laura looked up at us, blinking rapidly, her eyes glassy and wide. "It's all trashed, Bo. Like they wanted to punish us. Not steal anything—just tear it apart."

I glanced toward the house. "Was anything taken?"

"We don't have much worth stealing, but what little we do have is still here. Just tossed around."

"How'd they get in?"

"The backyard door in the kitchen. We rarely lock it. I leave it open in case the girls forget their key."

I was reminded that we did the same thing at our place.

Abbie stood, and Bo slid in beside his sister. I fell in step behind her onto the lawn, giving him and Laura space to carry the weight of what was happening.

"Marty, what the hell is going on?" Abbie snapped, her voice low but angry, as if I'd had a hand in it. "We were all at the Bishops' for the reception, but you and Bo left the funeral home and never showed. Then I drove Laura home—and thank God I did. She's at her edge. She's about to lose it."

"Bo and I went to Tadeo's office," I said quietly, watching the two uniforms idling near the curb. I didn't mention the stop at Noble's house—no reason to pile on. "We were trying to find anything that seemed ... *off.*"

"Off how?"

"If Tadeo was wearing a wire, that's more than a little unnerving."

I left the rest unsaid. For Abbie, Katherine, and Laura, *unnerving* was enough. For Bo and me, it was a different kind of danger. If Tadeo had been spying on us, our history with Dmitry and Natalya could put us in a cell. Abbie knew none of that, and I intended to keep it that way.

"Did you find anything?"

"No." I lied again—a reflex by now as natural as ducking a punch.

Over the next half hour, Bo and I handled our families the way we handled everything else—another piece of business. We booked Laura and her daughters into the Governor Hotel, which we still owned until Dmitry's deal closed, ensuring they got two of the largest suites. Katherine and Abbie helped Laura pack under the watchful eyes of Adams and Hayes, then all three headed out in Abbie's car. Katherine drove home to take care of Bo's daughters. Abbie called our kids, Andrew and Ali, and told them to get over to Bo's house for dinner. It was time to circle the wagons.

Detective Adams asked Bo and me to stick around after everyone left, which we did. He permitted us to wander through the house to see if we might notice anything specific.

We didn't.

I'd never been there before, so I couldn't be much help. It looked like a crime-movie set—cushions gutted, drawers yanked and dumped, picture frames cracked and left face-down. Upstairs, closet doors hung open like broken jaws, clothes flung out in frantic handfuls. It felt deliberately violent. Not just a search but also a warning.

Adams had us sit at a four-sided table by the front bay window. The white tablecloth lay in a rumpled heap on the floor, the vase broken, the sympathy bouquet of gladioluses strewn across the room.

"What's happening here, Mr. Bishop?" Adams asked.

"How should I know?"

"Because weird shit happens around you—the two of you."

Detective Hayes sat quietly, her tired, brown eyes opaque, as if she were thinking about something else. She flipped her notepad to a half-blank page. I could see that at the top she'd scribbled: *Scava, Nico—02-HOP1047 – U/I.*

"I'll bet weird shit happens around you, too," said Bo, most of his steam gone.

"I'm a cop," said Adams. "What's your excuse?"

I cut in. "Why are you leaning on us, detective? Bo's brother-in-law was killed. We're trying to help, and you treat us like we pulled the trigger."

"Did you?" Hayes asked, tapping her pen.

"You think I looted my dead brother-in-law's house?" hissed Bo.

"Did you?" Hayes kept tapping.

Our gazes circled each other like predators.

"Are we suspects?" Bo asked.

"Not yet," said Adams. "But bad things stick to you. You're Murphy's Law walking. I've never had the same two people be material witnesses in three separate crimes. Not in twenty years."

"Material witnesses?" I said. "We never witnessed anything. Our partner, Nico Scava, disappeared—never to be found. Baron Albert Von Baltruschat and his wife were killed in their home; we weren't there. Tadeo was shot while we were asleep at home." I flipped my fingers in the air, counting each point. "How are we witnesses?"

Adams gave a tight smile. "You're always in the blast zone, Mr. Schott."

Detective Hayes gave a low laugh. "Yeah—like a husband with three wives who all disappear mysteriously."

Bo glared at her. "I have one wife, met her in high school."

"We know," said Adams. "We're looking into it."

I knew what he was doing—scaring the bejesus out of us and letting us know we were in for a full proctology exam. I avoided glancing at Bo. I wanted to show no fear.

"What do you think they were looking for?" Hayes asked, steering us back to the house.

"Maybe more recordings," Bo said. "Tadeo didn't wire himself up for stripper gossip. He was after something else—maybe he kept notes."

Adams leaned in. "Or maybe he was digging for *leverage* on you two."

Bo shook his head. "Detective, he wore the recorder in a strip club, not our living rooms or office. Marty and I were in bed at the time."

Adams didn't miss a beat. "Maybe one of the girls overheard something you let slip." He looked directly at me. "Guys say all kinds of things when there's a naked woman on their lap."

"Jesus Christ." I slapped the table. "You've got a fixation, detective. At this point, I should call a lawyer."

I pushed back from the table. "Let's go, Bo. This is a waste of time."

Adams's posture softened. "Sit down. No one's pulling out cuffs."

I sat, glaring, knowing Adams wasn't done.

"We're busting your balls," Hayes said. "We don't think Ramírez was recording strippers."

"There was nothing on the tape," Adams added. "Just static and music. The club owner—Danilenko—talked to him a bit, but no one else. Told him he looked like he was on a blind date."

"Tadeo?" Bo asked.

"Yeah. Like he was waiting for someone," Hayes said.

"Someone showed," Adams continued, "just not in the club."

I raised my eyebrows for more. Adams was sharing, and I didn't want my voice to break his mood or make him stop.

"At the end of the tape, you can hear Tadeo breathing heavy as he walked. Then, he says, 'Finally,' and you can hear a vehicle pull up. Sounds like another truck. A second later—three shots. Then lots of rustling. Someone's searching him. Then nothing."

"Searching him? He was robbed?"

"No, his wallet had been taken from his back pocket; we found it next to him. It was opened, but money and credit cards were still inside. Nothing was taken as far as we could tell, not money, not jewelry, not the recorder—and if anything screamed 'please steal me,' that was it."

"So, someone watched him leave the club, walked up, and shot him," I said.

"Close," Adams said. "Shangri-La has no security cams—Danilenko says customers wouldn't come if they thought they were being recorded. There's a Taco Bell across the street, though. We pulled their footage. Garbage—low-res VHS. All we got was a shape, some movement. No one approached Ramírez on foot. They drove up. Looks like a truck—slightly taller than his 150, so maybe lifted, off-road tires. They pulled up on the passenger side and shot him. Glock nineteen, nine mil. After that, the driver got out, ran around the vehicle, then jumped back in and peeled out. The video's so grainy, we're guessing at parts—the truck blocks most of the view."

"That makes no sense," said Bo. "Who gets shot three times in a parking lot of a busy dance club, and no one hears or sees anything?"

"Where's the bouncer?" I added.

Detective Hayes leafed through her notebook. "It happened shortly before 1 a.m. The street wasn't that busy anymore. The club doorman, Mr. Tyrone Harris, was inside, behind a door built to keep the noise in, which also keeps it out. The music was playing loudly. It's not clear from the video, but it appears the shooter kept the gun inside his own vehicle."

"Ballistics showed he might have used a silencer," injected Adams.

"So, Tyrone didn't hear anything?"

"He probably heard *something*," Adams said. "But nothing that registered as a gun. No screams, no chaos, no reason to abandon the door and lose his job. People don't go running every time they hear a weird noise."

We sat in silence. I glanced at Hayes's notebook. She'd gone back to the last page and written one word: *leverage?*

I pointed to her earlier scrawl. "What's that code after Nico Scava?"

"File number for your missing partner," she said.

"I figured. What do the letters mean?"

"HOP means homicide—open—presumed dead. UI is under investigation."

"You're still looking for Nico?" Bo asked. "He's been gone three years."

"Technically? Yeah. Practically? Not so much. More of a desk job than a manhunt."

"But you're going to look into it now," I said.

"It's a lead."

"Tadeo never knew Nico Scava. Trust me, his murder has nothing to do with our missing partner."

"So you say," Adams said. "We have other leads. I'm gonna look at everything."

"SOP," Bo said, and Adams's lips twitched.

I stood. "Well then, we'll let you get some work done." I paused, and then added, "While you're shining that light up our ass, let us know if you find any polyps."

Bo shook his head like a weary parent.

Back in the car, Bo drove down the street and parked in an empty driveway.

"What's the plan?" I asked.

"Wait till they leave, then we hoof it back. I want to check the garage."

"You don't think it was searched?"

"It probably was, but Tadeo had a secret location. He showed it to me once. It's where he kept his stash of weed and cigars. If he was hiding something, that's where it'd be."

"I didn't know he smoked."

"That was the point. He told Laura years ago that when his daughters were born, he'd quit smoking cigarettes, weed, and cigars. But he liked the occasional puff. So, he'd pull from his reserve whenever he left for a few days, like to go hunting or fishing."

To kill time, we talked through plans for the company's remaining assets after the divestiture. The sun dipped below the horizon. Adams's Ford drifted past, and we let the moment pass, sitting in quiet for another half hour.

"Why would Tadeo keep the recorder running the whole time he was in Shangri-La?" Bo asked. "If he was sitting alone, what was there to record?"

"Maybe he didn't know it was on. It was in his pocket. Could've turned it on without realizing."

"Or maybe he was nervous. Didn't want to fumble around in his pocket if someone showed."

"True," I said. "Or maybe he was just a perv."

CHAPTER TEN

The Stash

THE WINDOWLESS GARAGE WAS AS DARK AS A MINESHAFT and smelled like motor oil and broken plaster. Bo's flashlight beam punched through the blackness.

We'd jogged over from where we'd parked, staying clear of lit windows. Bo had gotten Laura's house key before she left for the hotel, and we'd come in through the same door the vandals had used and locked it behind us. We reached the garage through the kitchen. It had been a long day, and we were still in our funeral suits, looking like dollar-store *Reservoir Dogs*—Mr. Black and Mr. Midnight Blue—slouching through middle age.

"This feels like breaking and entering," I muttered.

"SOP," Bo said.

"You got a new buzzword, don'tcha?"

"I'm gonna get a T-shirt with it."

Bo swept the beam along the wall, past bikes, old lawn tools, and folding chairs stacked in a crooked pile. I stayed close behind, careful not to trip over the clutter. He stopped before a red fire extinguisher mounted low on the wall, between a shelf of faded paint cans and a whitewall tire that shouldn't still exist. He ran the light over it, checking for wires or alarms. Two metal brackets held the extinguisher to the wall. With a quick motion, Bo popped the brackets, and the tank dropped into his hands.

"This is it," he said. "Tadeo showed me once. Said it was his version of a humidor."

"For weed and Cubans," I said. "Classy."

"He couldn't afford Cubans," Bo muttered, dragging the fire extinguisher across the workbench. The scraping noise rumbled through the darkness. Bo didn't seem to care.

In the faint light, I noticed a seam near the tank's base, half-hidden under the bracket grip. Bo twisted it open and stuck his arm in. He pulled out a beat-up carton of Camel cigarettes, a plastic sandwich bag stuffed with weed, a dozen Romeo y Julieta tubes, and a yellow prescription bottle labeled *Tiger King*. He frowned and wiped his hand on his pants.

"What?" I asked.

"Boner pills,"

I took a step back. "There are things you can never unknow."

He waved the flashlight over the carton of cigarettes. "Tadeo didn't smoke Camels. He was a Marlboro man."

I picked up the carton and turned it over. Packs of Marlboro, Camel, and Newport spilled out. A folded paper from a legal pad drifted onto the dusty workbench. Bo picked up the paper and handed me the flashlight. While unfolding it, two crisp one-hundred-dollar bills fell out, and I caught them mid-air.

"Hello," I said. "What's this?"

Bo shrugged. "Cigarette money?"

I gave them to Bo, and he stuffed them into his pocket. "Remind me to give it to Laura."

The paper was a list of numbers. Nothing else.

4-30 – 1 – 1407	6-11 – 2 – 750	<u>8-5 – 2 – 1407</u>
5-7 – 2 – 750	6-25 – 1 – 1407	8-20 – 1 – 750
5-14 – 2 – 750	7-9 – 1 – 1407	9-3 – 1 – 1407
5-28 – 2 – 1407	7-23 – 2 – 750	9-17 – 1 – 750

"What the hell is it?" I asked.

"Don't know." Bo squinted and leaned into it. "Maybe combinations: those are addresses to our warehouses."

"What's the underlying?" I asked.

"Let's figure it out later," he said, folding it back up and tucking it into the pocket where he'd put the money.

He nudged the rest of the pile with his finger, as if it were contagious.

"What's with all the different brands of cigs?" I asked.

"Maybe he liked them?"

"You've never smoked, have you?"

"No," he answered. "My coaches would have kicked my ass."

"When I was in the military, I smoked like it was a direct order. Two packs a day. Smokers don't change their brand—only if they've run out and have to bum one off somebody. It's part of the addiction—like an infidelity."

I picked up a pack of Marlboros. It was my brand twenty-five years ago. Something about it felt wrong—off-balance. I couldn't say why, and I slipped it in my pocket.

"For later?" Bo quipped.

I rolled my eyes.

From deep inside the main house, I heard a door shut, and my eyes locked with Bo's—no words, just a flash of panic.

"Shit!"

"Hide!"

"Where?"

"I don't know!"

I waved the flashlight around. The garage offered nowhere to hide. Footsteps approached—quick, deliberate. The only exits were the door to the house, from where the sounds grew louder, and the garage door, which rumbled loud enough to wake the neighbors. Bo pointed to another option: a janky plywood structure tacked to the back wall, a ten-by-ten shed shoved into the corner, cramped and crude.

We stumbled over, and Bo pressed on the door—a slab of cheap fiberboard bolted to warped hinges. It budged an inch and stopped. My eyes bulged. Bo gripped the edge, levering it with a grunt, and swung it open. We slipped inside just as the door to the house creaked open. I shoved a small rusty bolt into place.

The air smelled of mildew, earth, and freshly cut grass.

Two sets of shoes tapped across the garage floor.

"*Blyad*," muttered one voice—Russian for *fuck*. Bo and I knew the word well.

Then, in the same rough tone: "*Dǎ kāi dēng.*" Chinese.

Inside the shed, a thin line of brightness flared through the seams—the garage lights had been switched on. The cubby was barely big enough for the two of us: a lawnmower in one corner, hoses dangling overhead, every surface filmed in dirt. I figured Tadeo had gutted an old darkroom and turned it into a garden shed.

We heard the fire extinguisher tank roll across the workbench, then tools clatter.

The men weren't locals. One voice was low and rumbly, stiff around the edges, like someone who'd memorized English but never relaxed into it. The other was higher and faster, clipped, nasal. Chinese, no question.

"What's in there?" the growl asked.

"I look," said China.

The fiberboard rattled with the first hit but held. I felt Bo shift beside me, his shape blocking most of the faint light leaking through the seams. He pressed his back to the door, bracing. A second slam followed—harder. The board groaned.

"It not open. Stuck from inside," China panted.

I slid over and leaned into the hinges, ready for the next hit.

It didn't come.

"Quiet," hissed Growl. "Listen."

Outside, a car rolled up, engine idling. A door opened.

"Cops," whispered China.

"*Yebat'*," hissed the growl. "*Shā sǐ dēng.*"

The seams vanished as the lights snapped off—the garage plunged into darkness. The two men moved quickly, quietly; it sounded like they ducked under the workbench, but I couldn't be sure.

A sudden burst of static crackled through the black.

"Unit four, status check."

"Four's on scene. House looks quiet. Want me to check the neighbor?"

"Negative. I've got a possible domestic at 3214 NE Eagleton, same area. Respond code two."

"Copy. Show me en route."

The car door slammed. A moment later, the cruiser backed out of the driveway.

China and Growl shifted in the dark, murmuring to each other in Chinese. I heard them leave the garage, then the house door open and close. Bo and I stayed frozen, listening for another ten minutes. I could smell our sweat.

Nothing.

At last, we pulled open the shed door and slipped into the garage—prisoners climbing out of an escape tunnel. Bo didn't speak. Neither did I. We exited the house quickly and headed back toward the car, several blocks away, retracing our steps and avoiding lit windows again.

As our car rolled out onto the street, my muscles turned to mush. I'd been holding my breath too long; now I filled my lungs slowly, steadily, trying to clear my head.

"One of those guys spoke Russian *and* Chinese," I said.

"Tadeo was into something bad," Bo said. "We've got to figure this out on our own."

"Déjà vu," I said wryly.

Bo didn't answer.

Three years ago, we would have been screaming at each other—Bo insisting we go to the cops, me insisting we handle it ourselves. My hands would've shaken. My guts would've clenched. My pants would've smelled of urine.

But not now.

Not anymore.

Over time, fear grows quiet, like a dog that's learned no one's coming and stops barking. We were still pulling shrapnel out of our conscience after Rome, dragging the wreckage of choices we couldn't undo. We weren't the same men anymore.

It's not that we were tougher. We were practiced.

We didn't know who killed Tadeo.

But we'd find out.

CHAPTER ELEVEN

The Delivery

AFTER I DROPPED BO OFF, I DROVE HOME. Abbie was alone and anxious, every light in the house blazing. A funeral followed by a house invasion will do that to anyone.

I told her about searching Tadeo's garage. I left out the part about "Growl" and "China" having the same idea. I described the cigarettes, the cigars, the boner pills. I said nothing about the sheet of numbers. I justified the omission as a kindness. Lies always go down easier when you dress them up as chivalry.

I rummaged through the kitchen drawers and found an old, red Bic lighter, the faded outline of a tiny beer ad still clinging to its side. I told Abbie I'd be back in a minute and took Boomer into the woods for his nightly excursion.

I walked deep into the trees and pulled out the Marlboro pack I'd plundered from Tadeo's supply. Boomer sniffed it once, decided not to pick up the habit, and went back to nosing through every bush and fern in his path. I crouched under the beam of my flashlight and took a closer look. The tax stamp looked fresh—glossy, almost wet, as if it had been slapped on minutes earlier. I picked at one corner with my thumbnail. It peeled clean off. That wasn't supposed to happen.

I told Boomer I was about to do something stupid, preempting his judgment. I smelled and then lit one. I didn't inhale—I wasn't about to put my lungs through that again—but even dry-puffing, it tasted like something scraped off a radiator. Bitter. Metallic. The tip sparked faintly when I touched it with the flame, then flared. It burned fast and unevenly, like it had been packed wrong. The Marlboro wore the right clothes but didn't carry itself well. I hadn't smoked in twenty years, but I knew crappy tobacco when I met it.

///////////////////////////////////////

It didn't take long to solve the number puzzle.

The paper wasn't a cipher so much as a reminder—something someone had scribbled down so they wouldn't forget. The first numbers were dates; that part was easy. The last numbers were obvious. We had two large warehouses serving our chain: one at 1407 Emerson, the other at 507 East Palm.

That left the middle digit, always a one or a two. We let it taunt us for a while, turning it over until the only thing that made sense was time—1 or 2 a.m. or p.m. Business hours didn't fit. It had to be a.m.

One detail gave Bo pause. He was sure Tadeo hadn't written the schedule.

"This looks like Cruz's writing," he said.

"It's just numbers," I said. "How can you tell?"

"I've read enough of Cruz's reports," Bo said. "His fives look like that."

I looked at the paper again. "Could this be what everyone's looking for?"

"Seems thin," Bo said. "It's just a schedule. Why ransack a house and an office over it? Just change the schedule."

"Good point."

///////////////////////////////////////

Bo parked two blocks from the warehouse. It was a week after the funeral. The night lay still, flat as a windless lake. A half-moon sagged low, its pale light frosting the hood. The dashboard clock glowed: 12:52.

I held the sheet of numbers, its crease worn soft from being folded and unfolded too many times.

"Delivery or pickup?" Bo asked.

"We'll know in a minute," I said.

But I already knew. If I were a betting man, I'd have put my last shred of cynicism on delivery. I looked at the paper again: *6-25-1-1407*. June twenty-fifth. One in the morning, at 1407 Emerson. Our engine ticked as it cooled. A semi downshifted a block away. We slouched lower in our seats.

A plain red truck—no markings, diesel grumbling—rolled past and swung wide into the warehouse lot. Bo turned the ignition. We crept forward with the lights off until we had a clean view.

The truck maneuvered up to the loading dock, brakes thudding, red lights glowing. The overhead door cranked open, and a weak yellow spill of light pushed out into the lot. Three figures followed, moving with the kind of efficiency that only comes from repetition.

Bo pulled a small pair of Nikon Travelite binoculars from the glovebox, and we got out of the car and stayed in the shadows. The warehouse lot was surrounded by a ten-foot chain-link fence topped with razor wire and was overgrown with weeds and brush. We found the side entry gate just past a stack of splintered pallets and a reeking dumpster that hadn't been emptied in a month.

Bo twisted the combination lock without hesitation. With one hundred and twenty stores, all the padlocks used the same combo— cheap thinking dressed up as efficiency. The lock's bolt snapped open. We slipped through and crouched low, hugging the fence line.

Bo scanned the building with the binoculars and leaned closer. "Indicator lights are off," he whispered, nodding at the security cameras above the dock doors.

We crept toward a familiar side entrance we'd used before when accompanying Nate Radford on inspection tours. The push-button lock had an override—1960, the year the company was founded. It allowed executives access to any warehouse, eliminating the need to memorize local codes.

The metal door grudgingly resisted, heavy and stubborn, before we stepped inside. The air was thick and silent, carrying faint smells of cardboard, degreasing cleaner, and something sharp I couldn't name. My brain jumped to blood—but the floor was cement, smooth, and empty. I warned myself to relax.

Only the lights above the dock were on—dim and yellow, the color of tallow candles burning. The rest of the warehouse stayed in shadow as we moved through a maze of racks and pallets. Eight-foot towers loomed: shrink-wrapped stacks of bottled water, canned soda, snack cakes, chips, beer, candy, and coffee. A new scent hit me as we neared the light—not exactly tobacco, but close. The industrial breath of ten thousand cellophane-sealed packs.

Bo and I crouched behind a pallet of paper goods, with a clear view of the loading bay. We traded the binoculars between us. Nate Radford managed the operation with quick hand signals and a tight expression. Ed Cruz drove the forklift, hauling out pallets of cigarette cartons from the truck. Another man—built like he spent his days lifting boxes and his nights on a bar stool—shifted cargo around the trailer bed.

A fourth man drove the second forklift—Chinese, same build as me, not someone you'd peg for warehouse work. His face was smooth but not soft, stern and fierce, like he could bend metal with a stare.

The man inside the trailer grunted and called out something in Chinese. Then he stepped out into the light, and I saw his face— high cheekbones, flat nose, thick brows, wrinkled skin the color of wind-burned earth, and a thin, wide mouth like a fissure in dry terrain—all arranged in a blunt geometry. His hair sprang from his scalp in thick, black whorls, like animal fur. He was definitely not Chinese or American.

He wiped his brow with his sleeve and then swore in Russian, "*Yebat'*"—I'd heard the word too often not to understand.

"That's the bastard from the garage," I whispered to Bo.

Bo nodded. "And I'll bet the Chinese guy is too."

Nate walked over to the pallets, clipboard in hand, eyes scanning the load. About twenty were arranged on the warehouse floor, double-high—forty in all. He marked his clipboard and nodded. "Whole load's here."

Bo passed me the glasses and shifted closer. His elbow snagged a pallet tag sealed in a clear plastic sleeve, hanging loose against the stretch wrap. The sleeve rasped once across the taut plastic—dry and sharp—then snapped back against the cartons with a flat slap that pinged off steel and concrete. The sound cut through the loading bay, climbing into the rafters, alone in the empty space.

We stopped breathing.

The big guy, who wasn't Chinese or American, snapped his head toward us. He took two steps forward, head cocked like a soldier listening for the enemy. Then he raised his hand, motioning for silence.

"Shit!" I mouthed, stuffing the glasses into my coat pocket.

Bo pointed toward the rear of the warehouse and took off. I followed, sprinting deeper into the darkness. Behind us, the clatter at the loading dock went silent—no doubt they'd stopped unloading and were searching. I scanned the dark racks for anything solid and swingable: pipe, hammer, shovel. Bo tapped my shoulder and pointed to a metal door glowing red under an EXIT sign.

"Fire exit," he whispered.

"It'll trip the alarm," I hissed.

"They already know we're here."

"It'll give away our location."

"And your point is …?"

I shrugged.

Bo hit the push bar. Nothing.

He hit it again. Harder. Louder. The fire exit was locked. Our position now known.

"We're trapped," he said.

I exhaled. "Story of my life."

And then—we ran.

We stayed close to the wall, where the floor was clear. The warehouse was huge, the size of a football field, but every yard was a gauntlet of stray boxes, bins, and rolls of shrink-wrap. I was out of shape. My lungs burned, and I gasped at the hot air; sweat ran into my eyes. Bo didn't look much better.

When we reached the far corner, he panted, "Head back to the loading bay."

I scrunched my face. "Why? You wanna say hi?"

"They've scattered. No one's there. If we're lucky, they're searching all the wrong aisles. The bay's our only open door."

It made sense. I nodded.

We kept running. Bo was the athlete, but at least twenty pounds heavier. I started to pull ahead. Then a shout tore through the dark. The Chinese guy had spotted me charging from a side aisle.

"Here! Over here!" I heard him yell.

I didn't stop.

He turned onto my path.

Bo came in from behind, shoulder low, legs pumping, and hit him like a linebacker in a goal-line drill. The crack of impact echoed off the concrete. The guy spun sideways, slammed against the metal shelving, and crumpled like a sack of gravel.

He didn't get up.

I bolted for the light.

The loading dock loomed ahead, raised several feet above the asphalt, wide open, bright, and empty. I hit the edge, leapt, and landed hard—knees buckling, palms scraping the rough pavement.

Behind me, Bo landed smoothly and yanked me upright. The warehouse lights burned like stage lamps. No one came out. All

I heard was the hum of the truck and the slap of our feet on the pavement as we sprinted across the lot, through the side door we'd come in, and straight for the car.

I didn't look back.

Bo drove like he'd just seen the checkered flag.

"Our company's smuggling cigarettes," I huffed.

Bo nodded heavily. "Yup. And I don't smoke."

"The irony has not escaped me."

We drove in silence for a while.

"It's not Dmitry," Bo said.

"It's not Natalya," I answered.

More silence.

"That big guy," I continued. Face like a warped knuckle—talks in Chinese but swears in Russian. Reminds me of a *Gopnik* without the tattoos."

"You think he's in charge?"

"Nate Radford's supposed to be in charge. But it looked like he was taking his cues from Knuckles."

Bo glanced over. "What do you want to do, Marty?"

I looked out the window. Portland was asleep, but my brain wasn't.

"Don't go to the cops."

Bo laughed—low and dry. I laughed with him. It wasn't funny, but the tension had nowhere else to go. A red light caught us, and we sat still, the car idling. I didn't need to look at Bo. I knew what he was thinking.

"That locked fire exit in the warehouse is a safety violation," I quipped.

"I'll email Radford and Cruz tomorrow," said Bo. "Maybe copy Adams."

"While you're at it, include the FBI and ATF," I added.

CHAPTER TWELVE

I Hope You Know What You're Doing

ABBIE MET ME AT THE DOOR. Every light in the house was again on—living room, family room, game room, kitchen, halls, even the entry and mudroom—lit the way we did for the annual Christmas party. Andrew and Ali were off with friends; school was out, and sleepovers would rule the next two months. Boomer made his rounds along the edges, tail sweeping, a warning to any intruder that they would meet slobbery resistance.

"It's past two, Marty," she said, her voice tight with anxiety.

"I know. I'm sorry," I said.

Bo and I faced the question we always did—how much of the truth to bring home. In the past, we had edited our lives for them, trimming away threats, kidnappings, and my extracurricular missteps, presenting only what could be lived with. We had kept the damage contained. This was different. The rot had taken hold inside the company itself, spreading beyond our practiced discretion. We would have to tell them, though neither of us knew how to explain the danger without inviting it fully into the room.

I chose my words carefully. "Corner24 is being used to smuggle cigarettes," I said. "Bo and I saw them unloading at the Washington warehouse."

Her eyes went wide. "Oh my God. Did you call the police?"

"Not yet. We need more first."

"Are you serious? More what? Call the cops, Marty. You have criminals in your company."

Her blissful naivety was comforting. She had no clue about Nico, Albert, Crystal, Leo, Vasili, Sergei, or even Dmitry. To her, these were names, not epitaphs. From her perspective, this was the first crime to touch our lives. Paradoxically, it was the least dangerous thing I'd faced in a long time.

On the drive back from the warehouse, I asked Bo what he planned to tell Katherine. Coordination mattered. Like Abbie, Katherine had always been kept in the dark. Bo said he'd give her enough to stay informed, but not enough to expose our full history. Our past needed to remain a sealed crime scene, balanced delicately against the present.

"We're running a huge risk," I said.

"I'm tired of lying," he answered.

"Like I'm not?" I rasped.

"You have more to hide."

"That's unfair."

"Yes, it is—but still true."

We drove in silence the rest of the way.

"We'll go to the police, Abbie. I promise," I said later, pouring a Glenlivet from the kitchen liquor cabinet. "But right now, we don't know how deep this goes. For example, is Jeff Noble involved?"

In my mind, I'd already judged him to be. But that wasn't what mattered. What did—what scared me—was the chance that Dmitry or Natalya had a hand in it. Or—if they didn't—what would happen when cops started digging in our sandbox, where so many landmines were buried.

"Is it the reason Tadeo was shot?" she asked.

"I don't know," I said. I guessed it was, but didn't want to say it aloud.

"Is this putting all of us in danger?"

The phone rang before I could answer—Katherine. Abbie took it and disappeared down the hall.

I dropped onto the couch. Boomer followed, climbed up, and rested his head on my lap. He always knew when Abbie and I were tense. He could hear it in our voices, smell it in the air. Usually, he'd slip away. Not this time.

I stroked behind his ears. "How do I handle this, Boom-boom?"

He didn't answer—he was crafty that way.

Fifteen minutes later, Abbie returned and took a deep breath.

"Okay. Katherine and Bo just had it out. She's not calling the police, so I won't either. But we're all moving to the Governor Hotel and staying with Laura—kids, dogs, everyone. We're taking the entire top floor. You own the hotel, so make it happen. We're not moving back until the police are involved and all danger has passed, including finding Tadeo's killer." Her voice wasn't angry. She was tired, surrendering to a kind of reluctant pragmatism.

Abbie is a woman of simple truths. She once said, "Bad things don't happen to me." And mostly, they didn't. Her moral compass runs inside a very narrow range. She's the kind of person who'd drive an hour to return a dollar of incorrect change. She never had to teach our kids right from wrong—they just watched her.

We stayed up another hour talking. Abbie kept saying, "I hope you know what you're doing." And I kept answering that I did.

A year ago, when our marriage was on the rocks, and I was consumed with Natalya, she would've fought—demanded more. But I'd won her back. The affair ended without her ever suspecting. Now she trusted me, trusted us again. Repairing the distance between us had also given her a flawed confidence in me.

I thought about that as I lay awake—the irony.

I got to the office early. Bo was already there, guzzling coffee like it held the formula for eternal youth.

"I didn't get to bed until four and slept 'til six," I grumbled.

"That's two hours more than me," he shot back. "Radford and Cruz will know it was us last night."

"How do you know?" I asked, filling my mug with the youth elixir. "They never actually saw us."

"There are fewer than a dozen people who know the override code on all the warehouse locks. You and I are two of them. Jeff's practically tethered to an oxygen tank. Nate and Ed are another two. It's simple math."

"Speaking of Jeff … you think he knows?"

"Six months ago, I'd have said yes. But he's not paying attention anymore."

"Yeah—impending death'll do that to you," I said.

"Marek's flying in later," Bo reminded me.

Dmitry's attorney was coming to finalize the company separation and distribution agreements. Our attorneys had already reviewed everything; now it was just a matter of signing and issuing checks.

Our strategy for the company going forward was simple. We'd built a significant conglomerate, albeit with someone else's money, and even after losing the hotels to Dmitry and Natalya, we still had six profitable companies, including Corner24. To maintain our growth trajectory without Dmitry's backing, we secured financing through Refco, a large national financial services firm willing to lend us millions using our subsidiary companies as collateral. Bo had handled most of the legwork. We were about to cut a $100 million check to Dmitry—repaying him the capital he had fronted to buy all the companies in Paladin Holding—plus a healthy profit. In return, he'd trade his equity in Paladin for the three hotels. Then we'd be clear.

"We can't let this cigarette thing get out of hand," Bo said. "We just borrowed millions from Refco. If any of this leaks, they could call the loan—and we're screwed."

"Another reason to shut this down fast," I agreed.

"Listen, Marty …" Bo gave me that look—the kind only a close friend is allowed to use. "Don't talk to Natalya about this. She'll tell Dmitry. We can't risk it getting out. We handle this ourselves."

I made a face, asking, "Why are you even saying this to me?"

"Because you tell Abbie *nothing* and Natalya *everything*." He paused. "To you, she's like a confessional in heels."

"Wow! You're an asshole when you don't sleep," I said.

CHAPTER THIRTEEN

The Revelation

THE SUN SAT HIGH AND CLEAN, not a cloud in the sky, but it might as well have been midnight inside Jeff Noble's house. Curtains were pulled tight.

The air was inert, heavy with the faint rot of used bedding and disinfectant. Heat pressed in from the walls, damp against my skin. But it was the smell that hit hardest—a rank sickroom blend of alcohol wipes, Vicks, and something sour and bodily that clung to the nostrils. I breathed through my mouth to blunt it.

The main room was a mess. The hospital bed still sat in the middle. Pill bottles crowded a coffee mug. A fleece blanket lay balled on the floor. A plate with some crusted-over something and a fork sat abandoned at the foot of the bed. The muted flat screen was on some animal show—lions chasing gazelles.

Bo shot me a glance that said *Jesus* without saying it. We both knew better.

Jeff, in hospital scrubs and down to skin on bone, had let us in and told us to make ourselves at home. His voice was reedy and acerbic—like a crypt keeper telling us where to dig. Then he disappeared down a dark corridor to God knows where.

Ten minutes later, he returned. "Pit stop. You don't want to be near me these days when I do that."

"Didn't want to be near you, even in better times," Bo said.

"What do you want, wise-ass?" he asked, putting the oxygen plugs back into his nose.

"You know Radford and Cruz are using the company to smuggle cigarettes?"

Jeff took a deep breath, sat down on his unmade bed, and for a moment looked like Bo had asked him what he'd be willing to die for. Then he exhaled hard—one long, confessional breath.

"You don't mince words, do you, Bo?" he chuckled. "No foreplay."

"I don't dance either," said Bo.

"Okay, then, let's have at it. Yeah, I know. Radford called me a couple of days ago to tell me that you guys were snooping around like the Hardy Boys."

"You think it's funny?" I asked.

His gaze hovered between contempt and indifference.

"No, Joe Hardy, I don't think it's funny. I think it's—" He shook his head. "Fucking biblical!"

"You made a big deal about Tadeo being some kind of deviant recording strippers," barked Bo.

"Maybe he is," Jeff barked back. "I don't know what that half-wit was doing at Shangri-La that night. He wasn't there on my account."

"I think he was there to talk to someone," I added. "Maybe Radford. Maybe Cruz. To get information on your operation."

Jeff's face reddened, his jaw hard as a clenched fist.

Bo and I took a step back.

He grabbed the coffee mug and slammed it onto the bedside table, spilling its contents. Not coffee, maybe soup. It was red, with little stars floating in it. Then, energy spent, he sagged onto the bed, legs swinging out of rhythm, head down, staring at our shoes. The anger had run its course. Perhaps the fear had also subsided.

Bo and I let the low hum of the intercom fill the silence. Bo tapped his chin again, and I nodded—grateful to follow his lead.

"Where's the nurse?" Bo asked quietly.

"He's not a nurse. He's my handler. He makes sure I don't talk to you or anyone else. Trust me, he'll be here soon. Maybe he's caught in traffic. He's not an early riser, if you catch my meaning."

"How much shit are you in?" Bo asked.

"Are *we* in?" I added.

Bo shot me his stink-eye. "I gave you the signal."

"Sorry."

Jeff snorted, half-grinning. "You're in deep. I'm dying. I swam to shallow water. Now I just sit and wait till I slide under."

"Did they kill my brother-in-law?"

"Who? Radford? Cruz? I doubt it. Radford's too chickenshit. Cruz is too stupid. They're tools—both figuratively and literally."

"So, you didn't tell them to do it?" asked Bo.

"Fuck you."

Under different circumstances, Bo might've stepped forward and shoved his nose up against his—but how far do you push a dead man walking?

"You need to worry about the Mongol—Zor."

"Stop sounding like a comic book," Bo said.

Jeff sighed and motioned us toward the two fat leather chairs facing his bed.

He talked for the next half hour. We let him.

Most of it came out like an autopsy report—dry, familiar, unapologetic.

He'd sold us the company because his gambling debts had finally gutted both his pride and his inheritance. He kept the AIDS diagnosis private—for obvious reasons. He was the scion of a wealthy father who'd built a respected business and earned his place as a community pillar. A bisexual son with AIDS and gambling debts didn't fit the legacy.

Lung cancer was God's final joke—his take-home prize for screwing up his life. He aimed to go quietly and spare his daughter the worst of it. She lived in California. Her mother had kept them apart for years, but they'd reconnected. Now, finally, they were friends.

He stopped paying attention to the business.

Then one day Tadeo Ramírez showed up.

Jeff had never liked him—thought he was a nepotism hire (he was), and more filler than function (also true). But Tadeo brought him something: several packs of cigarettes, poorly made and missing tax stamps.

"I'm an expert on cigarettes," Jeff wheezed. "I got the cancer to prove it."

Tadeo cracked open a pack of Camels and said the whole thing tasted like it had been marinated in dung. Every time he lit one, it reminded him of shoveling horse shit on Bo's home ranch in eastern Oregon. He'd caught him by surprise. Jeff had been derelict in managing the business, but it was only then that he understood how much. The company had always run like a Swiss clock; his father had made sure of that. Jeff's role had been passive, not active.

What he couldn't tell was what Tadeo wanted. To rat or to ride. Was he reporting a crime—or angling to be part of it? Tadeo stayed vague, but Jeff was clear about one thing: he didn't want Tadeo running to Bo. So, Jeff asked him to dig deeper, to help figure out what was happening behind his back. If nothing else, it would keep Tadeo occupied while Jeff went to the people who actually knew what was going on. They always did.

He called Radford and Cruz and chewed them out for an hour. He'd assumed they'd let a few bad packs slip into inventory. The chain moved thousands of packs a day—over twenty brands, across a hundred and twenty stores. Shit happens. He never suspected an entire smuggling operation had taken root.

Nate and Ed lied and stonewalled him. When he threatened a deeper investigation, they held the line and never confessed. A couple of days later, however, they returned—uninvited, and not alone.

They brought guests: a big Mongolian with a face like a catcher's mitt—Altan Ganzorig—and a wiry Asian named Zhao Ming.

"The Mongol calls himself Zor," Jeff said. "And the Chinese guy Ming. They don't talk much. But trust me—those two are nasty mofos."

"We saw that the other night," Bo said.

"Yeah, I heard," Jeff replied. "But they didn't catch you. When they do—you won't like the experience."

"Why didn't you call the cops?" I asked. "Or us?"

"Because they said they'd burn down my house and my business. And go after my daughter." He looked at his feet and sighed. "I might have fought them years ago. But look at me. I couldn't fight a toddler, let alone these guys."

Bo and I stared at him—not because we doubted him, but because we were measuring something else entirely. Not his words, but the cost to him for saying them.

"And to be even more honest, it wouldn't be my problem in the future. It'd be yours, and if I could get my final payout, my daughter would be set for life."

He gave us a slight grin. "Some sins amortize."

A quiet click of clarity registered.

Until then, the risk had felt abstract—bad news from a neighboring town. After the slow-rolling horrors Bo and I had already endured—first Vasili, then the blunt bloodbath in Italy—I'd started grading danger on a curve. If there wasn't a gun to my head, or kidnapping, or torture, peril reached me through a curtain of dulled senses.

But now, finally, I felt it thread its way through the haze.

CHAPTER FOURTEEN

The Numbers

AS NOBLE SPOKE, I ODDLY CRAVED A CIGARETTE.

"What do you know about tobacco smuggling? Not much, I bet. I didn't either—but I did the research, so you don't have to. It's not like drugs. No one gives a shit about bootlegged loosies. It's a victimless crime. Only the taxman gets stung, and who cares about him? Feds chase grass, coke, and meth. Cigarettes? They don't even make the list. That's what makes it perfect—low priority for the cops, lighter sentences if you're caught. Barely a ripple in the system. But the money? Jesus. The money's insane."

"Insane is a relative word," Bo said.

Jeff gave a wet cough, jammed the oxygen plugs into his nose, inhaled, then yanked them out. "You can fill a forty-foot container with fake smokes from China—fifty thousand cartons, which is five hundred thousand packs, which is ten million sticks—for a hundred grand. That same load sells here for close to two million. Do the math—actually, don't. It'll just piss you off."

I did anyway. Ten million cigarettes for a hundred grand—one penny per stick. Twenty sticks in a pack, so twenty cents a pack. Wholesale, before taxes, the pack goes for $3.50. That's a sixteen-hundred percent return.

"With weed, you get about eight or nine times your money. Cigarettes ..."

"Sixteen times," I said, proud of my math.

Bo whistled.

"Coke'll get you fifty times your money, but you've got blood on your shoes and a cartel breathing down your neck. Cigarettes? Twice the profit of weed. No labs, no growing ops. Just a warehouse, a forklift, and some greased customs officials."

"And a shitload of counterfeit tax stamps," Bo added.

"The North Koreans print 'em—millions at a time. They come in rolls, packed in a suitcase. There's a guy—I heard about but never met—who's got a warehouse where they do the prep. He's got a machine that slaps the stamps onto the packs."

"You don't sound all that stressed over it," I said. "Did you invite them, or did they muscle their way in?"

Jeff showed us his palms, as if he'd been caught laughing at a funeral. "Sorry. I'll dial it back. I've been looking up all this shit while decomposing in bed. What else can I do? Want to know how much the ATF cares?"

We nodded.

"Their budget for tobacco enforcement is two percent of operations. I pulled it from the Inspector General's report. It's the only racket worth busting that nobody's chasing. It's a gold mine without a fence."

"Why isn't every gangster from here to Poughkeepsie doing it?" I asked.

"Scale," Jeff said. "It's tricky. You're not dealing in grams—you need warehouses. Forklifts. Shipping manifests. Most gangs hate that. They deal with burner phones and gym bags, not logistics. You need an outfit that can build and run a network. Warehouses, containers. Crooked dockworkers. Trucks. It's a whole Costco operation."

"And Corner24 is its distributor," said Bo.

"Not even close. We get a quarter of each container and mix it with the legit stock. Depending on location, our stores sell about a hundred packs a day—some more, some less, but a hundred's a good average. Across one hundred and twenty stores, we move nearly twelve thousand packs a day. A quarter-container accounts for thirty percent of our sales. It pays the bills."

"Who gets the rest?"

"Anybody willing. Reservation tribal shops. Casinos. Mom-and-pops. Bodegas, Minimarts. Trucks spread it all over the country."

"We've got over five hundred counter employees ringing up sales. How the hell does this happen without anyone catching on?" Bo asked.

"They don't know. They get their delivery once, maybe twice a week, and sell whatever's in the boxes."

"No one ever complains about getting a bad pack?"

"Almost never. They taste it, but when they do, they've already driven off. Most tolerate it. Worst case, they bring it back, and we swap it. But it's so rare we don't even track it. It's cigarettes—five bucks—not a thirty-five-dollar steak dinner or a fifty-dollar bottle of wine."

"How long's this been going on?" I asked.

"I don't know. Radford and Cruz told me the Mongol approached them around the time I started my chemo treatments. They figured I'd be dead before I found out."

Bo and I stayed silent. The casual mention of mortality can shift a room.

"Did those two yahoos think Marty and I would never catch on?" Bo asked.

"Radford and Cruz? Why would they? You barely know their names. You two are famous for hands-off management."

"What if we stop taking delivery?" I asked.

Jeff's feet started swinging in sync. "It's not that easy to *quit*."

He chuckled dryly at his pun. "The profits are too sweet. The guys in charge will do whatever it takes to keep it going."

"And Zor—the Mongolian—is in charge?"

"Hell no," Jeff spat. "He's just muscle. A hammer. Not the brains.

This operation's worth a million a month, easy. Zor's job is to gouge your eyes out with a spoon to protect it."

"Or shoot my brother-in-law outside a strip club," Bo muttered.

///

We spent another hour soaking in cold truths. Jeff didn't hold back. He admitted he'd stopped scrutinizing the company's P&L and had leaned entirely on Radford and the controller, Kennedy Johnson—yes, that was her real name; her parents were deeply political. Radford had recruited her early. She didn't just cook the books—she plated them, like a Michelin-star chef.

Corner24 was a private company with no CFO, no audit committee. Jeff had delegated all financial responsibility to Johnson. That made it easy for Radford and Cruz to keep the circle tight, insulated, and efficient.

On paper, the numbers looked perfect. Profits showed a tidy ten percent bump. Shrinkage down. Everything clean. Bo and I stayed ignorant and happy, thinking the machine was humming. Half the profits stayed in the company to bolster cash flow. The rest? Into the pockets of Radford, Cruz, and Johnson. Warehouse grunts and low-level staff got bonuses and just enough hush money to keep them quiet. Information was fragmented, compartmentalized. Nobody knew enough to blow a whistle.

When Radford and Cruz first brought Zor and Ming to visit Jeff, Zor did most of the talking. Ming's English was too mangled to follow, and Jeff said that suited him fine. Zor spoke slowly and deliberately, the way someone does when they think they're explaining things to children. Jeff mimicked his cadence for us, flattening his voice, stretching the pauses.

Zor knew everything. Jeff's diagnosis. His family. His ownership stake. Radford and Cruz had briefed him down to the blood type.

"I gave 'em my usual *piss off*," Jeff said. "I've got a few months left—why would I crawl into bed with those pricks?"

He leaned forward, the energy draining out of him.

"But then Zor recited my daughter Beth's address. Her phone number. Even her email." Jeff's face tightened as he slipped back into Zor's snake-smooth tone, his lips curling at the memory. "And then that son of a bitch leaned in so close I could smell his hair. He said—word for word—'If you even think about interfering, or opening your mouth, especially to your corporate owners, your lovely Beth will be the first to greet you on the other side.'"

CHAPTER FIFTEEN

Marek Sokol

CHRISTINE HAD LEFT MAREK SOKOL SITTING IN OUR OFFICE, sipping a Red Bull while staring out at the lake. He looked older than us but was probably our age. It was the shock of white hair, piled as if he'd never owned a comb. His face was kind, but his eyes were cynical, scanning for any weakness. He looked like a tall Einstein, just before the hair took over.

We apologized for being late. Told him we'd been at Noble's place, informing him of the divestiture.

"What did he say?"

"Poor bastard's got maybe three months. He just wants to make sure we've got the contingency capital if investors bail."

None of our acquired companies ever saw the real investor behind us; Dmitry's name never appeared on any document or closing. His capital was scrubbed clean, funneled through a layer of domino companies. Russian money isn't illegal—just unpopular, a rotting tooth in a perfect smile, best kept hidden.

"Why'd you think there's something wrong with Corner24?" asked Bo, reminding him of our earlier conversation.

"Starting last year, Corner24's earnings jumped significantly without explanation," Marek said, sipping his Red Bull. "No changes in management, no new policies, nothing. Cash flow spiked. Odd, but I didn't dig—Chernyshevsky doesn't care about the numbers.

You were keeping it, Noble wasn't watching, and I figured you two were busy elsewhere."

Neither of us answered. We just stared, equal parts disbelief and wonder, amazed he'd managed to connect the dots on his own.

He recognized the look and smiled, pleased with himself. "I look for weak spots—things tend to tear where it's thin."

"You have a lot of homilies," I said.

"I have this desk calendar," he replied.

I smiled.

"We're looking into it," Bo said.

He didn't want Marek, or anyone else, knowing about the smuggling. Not because they'd panic, but because they might whisper it to the wrong person. Dmitry's power wasn't just greater than the smugglers'—it was gravitational. He could hoover up the entire operation without leaving a speck of dust or reduce it to slag in a blast furnace. Our immediate priority was keeping Dmitry in the dark—and everyone else, too.

With the new financing we were arranging, caution was essential. If we needed to involve the authorities, we could always do that later. For now, the company divestment was the priority.

"Speaking of contingency capital—how's your Refco line of credit?" Marek asked.

"All approved," Bo said. "Dmitry's money is in escrow, waiting for final signatures."

"Still can't believe you got Refco to fund you. They're a commodities house."

"They've been doing alternative lending for years," Bo said. "Bridge loans, structured debt, high-risk stuff. We didn't want a traditional bank. We looked around. They all had reams of rules to follow to get funding approvals. Dmitry spoiled us. When we found a company to buy, he wired money fast with no red tape. Refco moves big money fast as well, with minimal friction."

Marek gave us a faint parental grin. "Still sounds dicey. They've got a big IPO coming—Wall Street darling and all that. But they're cowboys. Sometimes innovation is just hubris."

"You know," I said, sarcasm loaded, "for a guy who works for Dmitry, you sure spook easily. You don't like much of anything. Have you even met your boss?"

"I have," Marek replied calmly. "And he pays me to be nervous. I do *nervous* exceptionally well."

We penciled in dates for Natalya's arrival and tied off loose ends. After Marek left, Bo and I slumped on the couch, watching fat bass ripple the lake.

At the time, it felt like a breather. I would learn later—it wasn't.

CHAPTER SIXTEEN

Uncomfortable Questions

THE WAITERS AT THE GOVERNOR HOTEL were clearing the wreckage of a twelve-person dinner. There's a predictability to the tableau teenagers leave behind—crumpled napkins, stray french fries, straws in every glass, silverware scattered across the linen like loose change.

Laura's two daughters, Bo's three, my daughter, and the lone male—my son—had all vanished to their rooms for gossip and games. None of them had any interest in enduring the torment of lingering with their parents.

That left the five of us in the quiet vacuum that followed, chairs turned inward, half-slouched under the fatigue of the past few days. The room seemed to expand in the hush, its walls wrapped in moody murals of the Lewis and Clark expedition—ochre sunsets, wind-lashed rivers, brooding skies.

Bo and I had fallen in love with the hotel long before we bought it. A melding of two buildings—the old Seward Hotel and the former Portland Elks Lodge—it still carried the vestiges of midnight rituals and backroom whispers behind its Italian Renaissance façade. The words ELK TEMPLE were still carved into the terra-cotta above the entrance, a dated declaration of its past.

We sat in the back room of Jake's Grill, the hotel's restaurant, long a favored haunt of Portland's politicians, dealmakers, and visiting celebrities. Its stories were already legendary. Tonight, in our wary calm, we were adding another—three families hiding in plain sight from a murderous crew of tobacco runners.

Katherine and Abbie had convinced Laura not to go to the police—not yet. Reporting the smuggling herself wouldn't matter; she'd learned it from us, and so it was third-hand information. She needed Bo and me to make it real. But her patience was wearing thin. She'd agreed to give us another day.

Abbie twisted her napkin into a tourniquet. "Tell us what you're going to tell the detective."

"Chuck Adams?" I said. "Chuckles?"

"Stop being flippant, Marty," she snapped. "Nobody's laughing. We're holed up in a hotel in fear for our lives—our kids' lives. It's not funny, and I don't appreciate your casualness."

Katherine and Laura nodded. They thought I was being cavalier. I wasn't. It was reflex. A kind of defense forged from three years of living in a world of abrupt mayhem.

"We're all under stress," Bo said. "Marty deals with it differently."

I was about to apologize when my phone rang. It was Alex Danilenko. My stomach tightened. This whole nightmare had started with his call. I showed the screen to Bo.

"I need to take this," I said, hurrying out to the lobby, leaving behind three determined women and one puzzled business partner.

"What?" I barked into the phone.

"You always answer the phone angry," Alex said.

"You've always been good at reading the room, Alex."

"I don't understand what you are saying, Marty. But I don't care. I am calling to ask you something important."

"What?"

"I am visiting here in Miami with Natalya. Why is that Detective Adams calling me from Oregon, asking questions about Nico Scava?"

"Nico Scava!" I hissed, bending forward as if the name of my former—and very dead—business partner had just slugged me in the gut.

"*Da!* He called to yell at me for going to Florida without telling him. Just because a man is shot in my parking lot does not mean I am on house arrest! I asked if I was under investigation. He said no. So I said, then, I can go where I want." He paused, as if trying to remember why he called.

"Alex—focus. Nico Scava."

"*Da,* yes. He asked me many things. How long I knew him? What girls he liked? When did he marry Charley? Did he have enemies? What do I know about his business with you?"

Out of the corner of my eye, I saw Bo step into the lobby, phone pressed to his ear. His face unreadable, but his free hand knotted into a fist. Who was *he* talking to? It wasn't Alex.

My stomach twisted tighter.

"I don't want to answer questions about Nico, Marty," Alex said, voice sliding into panic. "I will say something stupid without meaning to. I have too much to lose—my club, my life. You understand this, yes?"

"Adams is a dog with a new bone. He's digging, looking for dirt on Bo and me."

"That is not hard to find, Marty. You and Bo—you swim in shit and call it soup."

"Stay in Florida. Stay with Natalya. Don't come back for a while. Don't answer numbers you don't recognize. Unless he shows you a warrant, you don't need to talk to him."

"I know. Natalya wants to talk to you now."

"Tell her to call me tomorrow. I'm with my family." I hung up before he could spiral further. I'd never refused to talk to Natalya. One more thing to deal with later.

I wandered across the lobby to Bo, who was repeating, "Yes, Charley," like a prayer.

He hung up, shoulders sagging.

"Don't tell me," I said. "Charley's freaking out because Adams is sniffing around about her missing husband."

He nodded, and I relayed what Alex had told me.

"Did you know Dante asked Charley to marry him?"

My eyebrows took flight, and I shook my head.

"They're trying to get Nico declared legally dead so she can move on. The last thing they need is some detective suddenly digging into his disappearance after ignoring it for three years. Charley said Dante's freaking out."

Dante Scava—the world's most prolific art forger, Natalya's business partner, and my personal gadfly—was Nico's younger brother. His forgery scheme had set off the chain of events that permanently altered our lives and ended with Nico's death. Afterward, like any dutiful brother, he stepped in to console Nico's widow, Charley. One thing led to another, and now, apparently, she'd traded one Scava for another.

"Odd that Alex called me and Charley called you at the same time," I said.

"Not really," Bo said, checking his watch. "Adams was at Tadeo's murder scene after midnight. He probably works swing shift. He schedules his call list around dinner to catch people a little off balance."

I eyed him. "That's bizarrely specific."

Bo snorted. "Too much TV."

"We've got to divert him," I said. "He's fixated on Nico and the Baron. They're not loose ends—they're live wires, and if he ties them together, everything comes apart. We need to give him something bigger to chase than a cold case about our missing partner."

"Let's call him," said Bo. "Set a meeting for tomorrow. We give him Radford and Cruz."

I pulled Chuck Adams's card from my wallet and handed it to Bo. He dialed. We sat on one of the lobby's worn leather couches, set the phone on speaker, and held it between us.

"Adams."

"Bo Bishop and Marty Schott," Bo said.

"Speak of the devil."

"Have your ears been ringing?" I asked.

"You've been a busy detective," Bo added.

"Getting annoying calls, are you?"

"Yes, actually," I answered.

"It's going to get worse," he said.

"Let's meet," Bo interjected. "We've found something you'll want to hear—something that could help your investigation."

"Which one? Scava? Von Baltruschat? Or—Schott and Bishop?"

"Ramírez."

"Tadeo Ramírez is off my plate—put on ice for now," he said, pausing just long enough for his words to explode in our ears.

"I'm more interested in Schott and Bishop."

CHAPTER SEVENTEEN

Murder Groupies

JEFF NOBLE'S FRONT DOOR STOOD OPEN.

After a cold, brittle night at the hotel—frustrated wives, restless kids, everyone eager to blame something, anything, anyone—Bo and I drove out. Our plan was to warn him that we were going to the cops that morning, and things might escalate quickly.

Jeff had told us the day before that he'd already taken the first step by sending his daughter, Beth, off to a summer art program in Florence—a fancy holding pen for rich art majors, supervised just enough to keep the sex constrained and consensual. I mentioned that if things turned ugly, Bo and I knew people in Italy who could protect her. Bo narrowed his eyes at me for even suggesting it.

Bo knocked on the ajar door and called out, "Hello?"

Silence.

I stepped into the dark, claustrophobic foyer. A wave of stale, overheated air washed over me, as if the house were exhaling its foul breath.

"Jeff?" I shouted. Then turned to Bo. "What's the watcher's name?"

"Who?"

"The guy Jeff calls his nurse—the one who makes sure he doesn't blab."

"Alisandro, I think."

"Alisandro!"

We entered the living room. The hospital bed was rumpled in heaps. I touched the sheets. "Cold," I said.

A sharp, acidic smell crept into my nose—the ammonia bite of urine.

"Smell that?" Bo asked.

I nodded.

We followed the stench past the bed, past the central fireplace, to the library door—half open, a pale blade of light cutting across the hardwood floor. Bo hesitated, then pushed it wide.

Jeff hung from the banister of the second-floor landing. His body swayed just inches above the floor—so close it looked like he might have still found footing if he'd only tried. A hard wooden chair stood next to him. His hospital gown gaped open, exposing veined skin like discolored rice paper, a sunken chest, and a soft, sagging belly. Below, a dark puddle spread in an uneven bloom, shimmering faintly. The smell hit us fully now—sharp and sour. He'd emptied whatever was left inside him.

I cupped a hand over my mouth and nose.

An orange extension cord, the kind used outdoors, was cinched tightly around his gaunt neck. It was tied to the top rail of the balustrade, disappearing behind his ears, which were pulled upward almost to his hairline. His head twisted at an odd angle, mouth frozen in a half-gasp, eyes wide and glassy, as if searching the dark for us.

"Jesus Christ," Bo murmured.

I threw my arm out in front of him like a traffic guard. "Don't go anywhere near him. Don't even step in the room. Adams will try to blame us for this."

"Suicide?" Bo asked.

"Seems excessive," I answered. "He's got more pills than a pharmacy. Why go out ugly and painful like that when you can just fade out?"

"The stink is too much," Bo said, stepping back into the main room. "You're right. Noble wouldn't go this way. He wouldn't step off the chair. His neck wouldn't break; he'd suffocate. It's too painful. Knowing him, he'd step back on the chair."

"I agree. I think he was pulled up—the chair was put there later."

The scene felt staged—almost elegant in its cruelty. No overturned chair, no struggle, no sign of Alisandro. Just Jeff, strung up and exposed, as if they wanted us to see every last humiliating detail. They hadn't just killed him. They'd reduced him—stripped him of every scrap of dignity.

"More cleanup?" I asked, referencing Bo's earlier comment about Tadeo. I followed him, keeping my hand over my face.

"Could be cleanup. Could also be trimming the herd."

I shook my head in disgust. "One call to Dmitry or Natalya, and the whole Miami Bratva would be here in twenty-four hours to wipe out these cockroaches." Even as the words left my mouth, they tasted empty. I sounded like a movie gangster.

"I think you're overestimating our influence with those two," Bo said. "We're in the middle of a divorce, Marty. The band is breaking up. I'm not so sure they'd race to our rescue."

After a short debate, we decided to call Detective Adams. It was still well before noon, and we assumed he'd be off the clock, so we used the number on his business card, hoping it was his personal line. It was.

"Adams."

"You up?" Bo asked.

"No," he said.

"You need to come to Jeff Noble's house," I said, leaning toward Bo's phone. "Bring a squad car and the coroner."

"What did you do now?" I could hear the sound of running water in a sink.

"We walked into another murder, made to look like a suicide," Bo said.

"Christ almighty! You two are like murder groupies."

"Fair point," Bo said, gave him the address, and hung up.

We sat in the car and waited.

Jeff was the second dead man in as many weeks, yet my hands stayed steady. My stomach was tight but controlled. My system had learned to adapt. Decades earlier, when I arrived in Vietnam, fear perched on my shoulder like a crow waiting for scraps. But then, as the months passed, I had to remind myself I was still in a war zone. You don't grow braver. You just stop feeling the tremor.

My phone buzzed, and I put it on speaker.

"Morning," said Nate Radford. "Are you and Bo around today? I got someone who wants to meet with you."

"Who?"

"Guy's name is Bob Heller. Says he wants to show you something."

"You know him?" I asked.

"Kinda."

"What's he want to show us?"

"I'll let him tell you."

Bo started shaking his head and mouthing, "Not a chance."

"Does he work for the Mongolian?" I asked, tossing a grenade into the conversation—just to see how he'd handle the blast.

Radford hesitated, maybe recalculating. "No—the other way around."

"You want us to meet Zor's boss?" said Bo.

Radford was surprised to hear Bo's voice. "He's not his boss—but he's higher up in the organization. And yeah, it's time, I think."

"Why do you *think* that, Nate?" Bo kept up the deliberate wordplay.

"Well, Jeff's not really in charge anymore. You guys are moving in, and you need to keep up with what's happening."

"We bought the company a year ago, Nate," I said. "We kinda 'moved in' a while ago."

"Could've had me fooled," he said. "I only took orders from Noble. So maybe you didn't *move in* the way you thought."

"Why do you think Jeff's not in charge anymore?" asked Bo.

"I heard the poor bastard's not doing well."

"Not well?" I asked, mockingly.

Dead was about as "not well" as you can get.

"Yeah—I heard he's getting worse," he said.

"Sadly."

"Well—don't take this the wrong way or anything, but I hope the end comes quickly. I don't want him to suffer."

"I would never take that the wrong way, Nate," I said. "Thanks for your concern. I'll let him know when I see him."

I wondered if Nate had been the one to haul him up. Watch him flail.

"Yeah. Give him my best." He hung up, probably thinking he'd handled that well.

CHAPTER EIGHTEEN

Police Report

CHUCK ADAMS LOOKED TIRED, like he hadn't slept well. He smelled of deodorant, and his hair was still slick from the shower. He must've raced here.

When he pulled into the driveway, a black-and-white, lights off, trailed behind. Bo and I stepped out of our car, and Adams joined us. No handshake. Just a stiff nod. His way of keeping distance. The detective wasn't looking to make friends.

He studied the house, one hand raised like a visor.

"You leave the door open?" he asked.

"No," I said. "It was open when we got here. That's why we went in."

"We don't break into people's homes," Bo added.

"Let's let the jury decide that," Adams said, deadpan.

"If you're gonna be an asshole, detective, we'll leave right now," I snapped. "It's too early on a bad day for that shit."

Adams blinked, then gave a slight nod—conceding the point—and pulled out his notepad.

"Touch anything inside?"

"The bedsheets," I said. "They were cold."

He jotted it down. Two uniforms from the black-and-white wandered up. Adams instructed them to tape off the driveway, walk the large front yard, and flag anything unusual. Then he told us to stay put, and headed for the house.

"Shouldn't he draw his gun or something?" I muttered as he disappeared inside.

Bo shrugged. "Figures if we didn't get killed, he won't either."

"Mmm. Optimist."

Adams wasn't inside ten minutes. When he came out, he was already writing, nose wrinkled as he tried to blow the smell out of his nostrils. He grabbed the mic in his cruiser.

"Morning, Marcy," he said in a low, somber rumble. "Can you send CSU and the ME out to …" he glanced at his notes and recited the address. "Confirmed DOA. Apparent hanging."

"Copy," Marcy's voice crackled.

"Send another unit too," he added. "The neighborhood's gonna get curious. I need a perimeter."

He walked back over.

"Saw Noble at a few fundraisers," he said. "Charity auctions. He was the entertainment—ran the bidding like a pro. Funny guy."

"Not so funny the last few months," Bo said.

"That hospital bed is his?"

We nodded.

"Didn't know he was sick."

"Terminal," I said.

"Suicidal?" he asked, scribbling *terminal* and my initials next to it.

"Maybe," I said. "But not like this."

"It's"—he searched for the word—"flagrant. I'll give you that."

We went through the rest—how we knew him, why we were there, whether he drank heavily (yes), if he had enemies (yes), whether he had money problems (yes), anything suspicious in the past few days (yes, if you consider picking up a shadow named Alisandro "suspicious"), and if he'd ever talked about taking a header over the second-floor banister (yes and no).

The usual.

"What's Alisandro's last name?" Adams wrote it down.

"Don't know," I answered. "Jeff never said. Just called him his 'watcher.'"

"Watcher?" he asked. "From committing suicide?"

"No," said Bo. "If anything, to make sure he *did* commit suicide."

Adams's eyes squinted.

I jumped in. "Which brings us to Corner24 and Tadeo."

Another cruiser pulled up. Adams closed his notebook.

"Not my case anymore," he said. A brief flicker of resentment in his voice.

He'd said it to us the night before, but in person it hit harder—the way a breakup stings more face-to-face than over a text.

"Why?" Bo asked. No flicker this time—full anger.

"Can't say. But Tadeo's not my problem anymore."

"Whose problem is he?"

"Don't know. Someone with more pull than me."

"What do I tell my sister?"

"Don't tell her anything. The case isn't closed—it's just not mine."

Bo and I traded a look.

"Detective," I started, "we found something that might change this whole investigation. A crime is happening at Corner24. We think it might be tied to why Tadeo got shot."

He studied us for a second. Then: "Let's sit in my car."

Bo and I piled into the back seat while he took notes up front. We told him everything—names, timelines, warehouses, Noble's admission, all of it. It took a while. Bo and I took turns, and whenever we went too fast, he'd cut in with a question, and we'd circle back to fill in the gaps. He looked genuinely interested, as if we were filling in the blanks of a deactivated case file.

"Noble told us they threatened to kill his daughter if he breathed a word to the authorities," I said. "They assigned this Alisandro guy to watch him and prevent him from going to the cops. He was so close to death that it was a temporary duty. It's probably why he's hanging off the banister right now."

Adams looked skeptical. "But he didn't tell the authorities."

"No, but he told us," I said, emphasizing that telling *us* was the same thing.

"I'll take this to my chief," Adams said, snapping his notebook shut. "Can't promise anything."

Bo slapped the back of Adams's seat. "What the f-ing hell is happening here, Adams?! We tell you there's a cigarette-smuggling ring in our stores. A Mongolian the size of a refrigerator and his Chinese toady are bootlegging millions through Corner24. I can't come up with better reasons to kill Ramírez and Noble." He was breathing hard now, staring daggers at Adams. "And your reaction? 'You can't promise anything'—like we're bitching about a neighbor's stray cat."

He took a beat.

"I know you think Marty and I are some kind of ninja assassins," he continued more quietly. "You want to hang Nico or Von Baltruschat around our necks? Good luck. You're chasing smoke, not fire. But we're handing you a five-alarm blaze right now."

Adams didn't flinch. I had to hand it to him—he was granite.

"Listen, tough guy. Stop telling me how to do my job. Back off. You go near Corner24 on this, you'll get stampeded. You want to be a hero? Solve mysteries and shit? Join the fucking academy. But if you keep sticking your nose in this, you won't see another Christmas. And don't think I'll lose sleep over it. You two yahoos have danced on the edge long enough—one gust and you're over. Stay out of it."

Bo shouted, "It's our goddamn company, detective! What the hell do you expect us to do? There's a smuggling ring operating out of our stores!"

Adams yelled back. "Report it!"

"We just did!"

"Good job!" He turned to look at us with the eyes of a bouncer itching for an excuse.

"Now get the hell out of my car."

CHAPTER NINETEEN

Bob Heller

NATALYA SAID TO ME ONCE: *Kogda volki sporyat, ovtsy stradayut*—when wolves quarrel, the sheep suffer.

Bo and I were back to being sheep. Only this time, it was worse—we didn't even know who the wolves were. It wasn't Dmitry or anyone connected to him. So how did we end up here? Two men dead. Smugglers moving product through our company as if they owned the place. And the cops treating us like kids pounding on a locked door.

Bo didn't say much on the drive back. He held the wheel tight enough to steer a straight line through a windstorm. When we pulled into our office lot, he didn't get out. Just let the engine idle and stared at the building as if he wasn't sure he'd ever seen it before.

"What's happening, Marty?" he asked—his voice holding back fear and frustration. "Who has the power to bury a murder investigation?"

"The D.A.?" I offered. "The feds?"

"Why the hell would they?"

"What if it's us they're watching?" I said. "Paladin. Our cash. Where it comes from. The deals. Dmitry's laundering. What if the feds have had their eyes on us this whole time, and they're pulling Adams back for fear he'll screw things up?"

"You're always paranoid, Marty."

"Paranoid's just another word for cautious."

"On that note, what do you want to do with this Bob Heller guy who Radford wants us to meet? Is it a setup?"

"I doubt it. These assholes need to bring us on board. Once they onboarded Jeff, he was their buffer—primarily from us. They just hung him out to dry—pun intended. Now they need a new frontman."

"Okay, call Radford and get directions," instructed Bo. "I'll get my gun out of the trunk."

"You have it in the trunk?"

"After Vasili, I don't go anywhere without a gun. It's always within reach."

"Vasili was three years ago," I said.

"Your point is?"

"And you call *me* paranoid."

///

Bob Heller stood with his back to the building, working a toothpick like it was lunch. He looked—to borrow a line from Raymond Chandler—like a man who slept well and didn't owe too much money.

The gravel road had announced our arrival a good minute earlier, but he made no move to greet us. The building behind him was a tall brute of warped planks and rusted metal, squatting on a patch of scrubland a few miles from the river port. I could smell fir needles and wet bark pressing in from the stunted timberline around the property.

Heller's face looked older than his frame suggested, especially around the eyes. He wore a clean denim shirt, sleeves rolled to the elbows. His jeans were crusted and worn, cinched with what had once been a belt, now just a faded strip of leather. And logger boots. I half expected him to be carrying a chainsaw.

Bo and I got out of the car and approached him like he was a dog known to bite. Heller stayed pressed against the wall, keeping himself upright. When we reached him, he flicked the toothpick away and offered a handshake, firm and dry—a workingman's hand.

Up close, the age showed more clearly. His face was all edges and erosion—creases around the eyes like hash marks of years lived or sacrifices made. A tight goatee traced his jaw like permanent bristle. His blond-brown hair was cut short enough to stand at attention, as if he'd told his barber, "Make me look like a Marine." He was lean, not skinny—built to last, not to lift. More M&A fighter than boxer. In his right hand, he held a thick wooden cane, nearly an inch around, its rounded grip worn smooth from use.

"Thanks for coming," he said in a light baritone.

"Sure," said Bo.

"Why not," I added.

"Any problem finding the place?" he asked.

"A little," said Bo. "Radford wasn't clear with his directions. I passed it twice before I saw the entry—the gravel driveway threw me off."

"Yeah, the gravel's intentional," he said, pushing off the wall and, with a pained look, flexing his shoulder like it needed to be put back in place. He walked slowly along the building, leaning into the cane to favor his left leg. "The dust it kicks up is kind of an early warning system."

"You need that?" I asked, trailing behind him. "A warning system?"

"Not really," he said. "It's more of a selling point."

That was putting it mildly. The warehouse appeared to have been built during the Nixon years and had since been left to deteriorate. Its sagging shell of barn wood, corrugated steel, and sun-bleached siding was streaked with rust from decades of rain—a forgotten coffin from Oregon's timber-belt years. A broken pallet jack sat in the weeds, half-sunk in a patch of tall grass.

"Want to see the setup?" he asked, but the question was rhetorical. He looked at us for a long second—measuring, in case he'd have to carry us later. It was clear he didn't talk unless it served a purpose. Everything about him felt tactical.

"Which one of you has the gun?"

I pointed to Bo.

"I figured."

"I know karate," I grinned.

"Funny," he grinned back.

He stopped at a dented side door patched with a steel plate bolted unevenly across the middle. Faded spray paint marked a number, unreadable through the grime. He yanked it open, as if it were stuck, though it wasn't—it was just heavy.

I expected the inside to match the ruin outside—dust, rot, maybe a few raccoons claiming squatter's rights. Instead, we stepped into something else entirely. The floor was smooth concrete, worn in places but swept clean, with yellow safety lines marking wide lanes and numbered bays. Rows of industrial shelving stretched up to the rafters, stacked with labeled crates and shrink-wrapped pallets. Everything looked sorted, scanned, and ready for transit.

Bright, fluorescent tubes buzzed overhead, casting a cold light common in morgues and machine shops. A couple of forklifts sat along the far wall, their charging cords coiled like sleeping snakes. Past them, a glass-walled office looked out over the floor, raised a few feet like a control booth.

The outside may have looked like a corpse, but the inside was very much alive—quiet, ready, and waiting for the next shift.

"Nate tell you about me?" he asked, not looking at us but sweeping his eyes across the concrete floor, maybe looking for scattered debris.

"No," Bo answered. "We don't like talking to him. He knows any conversation past two sentences will include the words 'you're fired.'"

"You don't want to do that."

"Why?"

"Because I need him," he said, drawing in a long breath. "Between him and Cruz, he's the smart one."

"It's a low bar," I said.

His eyebrows agreed with me.

Bo gestured at the space around us, palm open. "So, how's it work?"

"I'll tell you—but you understand the rules, right?"

"Not all of them," I said.

"There's a lot of money in play. Muck with it, and the consequences are severe."

"Like shooting my brother-in-law," said Bo.

"Like whittling your entire bloodline down to a rumor." He tapped his cane for emphasis. "Like leaving you the last one alive—so you get to wonder every day what order they all died in."

The comment was so menacing and explicit my heart actually palpitated. "Do you have any idea what we're capable of?" I shot back. "The reach we have? The wreckage we can bring to this circus?"

I looked at Bo, who gave the barest shake of his head. He knew, as well as I did, that my words sounded impotent and juvenile. No different from a celebrity telling a cop, "Do you know who I am?" I could feel the red creep into my cheeks. In the end, I still had a lot to learn about being a tough guy.

"I don't think I'm being clear," Heller said. "They know you. They know everything. And they were counting on your ignorance. A couple of wannabe business titans—too fat and happy to dig into the guts of their own company. You like buying businesses, not running them."

"And yet here we are," said Bo, in his standard, stolid voice. I could tell his anger was climbing.

"Yeah, they know you've got a Russian backer—some big-shot oligarch … Dmitry something. They don't give a shit. This is bigger than you can wrap your heads around. You need to know you're not screwing with some local yokel with a grand ambition and a locker full of AKs. You're dealing with China. With North Korea. Not gangs—actual countries. Think your Russian friend will save you? He steps within a mile of this, he'll fly out a high-rise window without a parachute. You can tell him I said so."

Bo didn't flinch, but something in me cracked—sharp and sudden, like boiling water hitting cold glass. We'd spent years pretending Dmitry Chernyshevsky didn't cast a shadow, burying him under enough denial and deception to pave a freeway. And now this guy— some freaking nobody I'd never seen before—drops Dmitry's name like it's cocktail chatter. I almost laughed. Not because it was funny, but because it felt safer than letting him see how hard it hit.

If he knew about Dmitry, he knew where the fault lines lay. And if he knew that, he could walk the cracks, which meant we were exposed.

We were marked.

CHAPTER TWENTY

The Board Game

"YOU KEEP SAYING THEY," I snapped. "Who is '*they*?'"

"People you don't know," Heller answered, shifting slightly off his cane. "People you don't want to know."

"What do you mean? China? North Korea?" Bo asked as he scanned for chairs. "You sound like we're playing a board game."

Heller picked up the hint. "You want to sit? Follow me."

His cane tapped against the concrete as he led us to the control room. Bo and I followed … kids, being marched to the principal's office. I watched his stiff gait and wondered if it was an old injury or a disability. Hard to tell.

"Why the cane?" I asked, immediately regretting the breach of etiquette. Even with a guy who might shoot me in the face, I still felt the need to be polite.

"Osteomyelitis," he said, tapping the cane against his foot. "Bone infection. Like termites chewing through the marrow."

Both Bo and I winced.

"It's a curse," he added.

Inside the office, a metal desk anchored the center, flanked by two dented file cabinets, the color of chewed gum. A Mr. Coffee sat on a plywood counter beneath a Playboy calendar from over a year ago. Miss July winked at anyone desperate enough to sample whatever Mr. Coffee was brewing. Heller poured himself a quarter mug and topped it with Jim Beam from a nearby bottle.

"Want some Beam and beans?" he asked.

Over the past few years, I'd broken bread with Vasili, a psychotic killer; Sergei, also a psychotic killer; a dozen Moscow Bratva hit-men; Camorra assassins; and a Mafia princess who wanted to both kill me and fuck me—so knocking back a drink with what looked like a semi-retired lumberjack with a bum leg, even if I couldn't trust him with an axe, didn't rattle me.

"Sure," I said.

Bo raised his hand for one, too.

We settled into the metal chairs.

"You work for 'China' and 'North Korea'?" Bo asked, using air quotes.

Heller took a sip and gave a loud, "Ahhh."

"It's an expression. The guys running this operation get their product from China and North Korea—with cover. High-level, government-sanctioned. China's Ministry of State Security—*Guoanbu*—you know, the guys who don't officially 'exist,' but they know what you had for breakfast." He mimicked Bo's air quotes. "And the Norks? They'll counterfeit anything. Money, smokes—whatever keeps the 'dear leader' in whiskey and women. They're not amateurs. It's a state-sponsored syndicate. They fund their black ops from the money they make on contraband. And you two gentlemen are now in the middle of it."

I drank most of my Beam and beans, wondering how it might taste with Scotch.

"Why are you telling us this?" I asked.

"Maybe I got a bleeding heart. Maybe I don't want to see your family wiped off the planet. Maybe I don't want you screwing up my gravy train. Pick one."

"Where is everybody?" Bo asked, looking over the warehouse. "Anyone work here?"

"It's empty till it's needed," said Heller. "It's just a valve in the pipe. One piece in the machine."

"But it's yours," I said.

"Yup. That's how I got in. I showed 'em my setup and got introduced to the top dog one evening in a fancy restaurant, eating campanelle puttanesca. His operation needed a clean way to move containers off the port—half his shipments weren't getting through. I've got friends on the docks who … you know … set 'em free."

"No," I said, purposely obtuse. "What's that mean?"

He squinted. I could tell he wasn't buying it. "We ride the manifest. Make the forms look right, sign off where it's needed, let the scanners do their thing, check appropriate boxes, and go blind when it's called for. Timing's everything—everyone has to work the same shift. Once it clears, it comes here."

He gestured behind him. "We crack the cans, offload, rebox if needed, and dress it up. Then it's onto clean trucks, fake manifests, sealed doors. Most drivers think it's snack food or floor tile. The ones who *do* know generally work for the outfit that ordered the load. By the time the cigs hit a bodega in Queens or a gas station in Trenton, they look like they came straight from Philip Morris."

"Where'd you have the campanelle puttanesca?" asked Bo.

"Jake's Grill. Why?"

Bo shrugged. "I'm a fan."

The whole thing bordered on comedy—the Portland smuggling ring operating out of our chain of convenience stores started over Bo's favorite pasta, in our own restaurant in the Governor Hotel. Apparently, the Gods have a sense of humor.

"Where do they get the stamps?" I asked. "This doesn't work without tax stamps."

Heller nodded. "Same source as the cigs. China or Norks. I don't handle that. I supply the roof and open the dock. Others handle makeup and distribution."

He pointed out the window at two tax-stamp machines—industrial rigs the size of freezers. In front of each sat a bin—one labeled Oregon, the other Washington—each filled with tight rolls of fake stamps, commercial-grade, ready to feed through the machine and press onto cartons.

"The stamps arrive in suitcases," he said. "Judging from the quality, they're probably printed in North Korea but shipped from China."

Heller sipped his doctored java. "You've met our distribution management, Ganzorig and Ming?"

"Not directly," I said.

"They control the territory from Seattle to San Fran and all points between. Corner24 is one of their drops."

"It's a big drop," I said. "We have one hundred and twenty stores across that same geography."

"Yeah, it's a solid outlet, but Indian reservations are even bigger. They move a shitload of product through their casinos. Apparently, drunks and gamblers have more on their mind than the taste of a cigarette." He paused for a moment. "But you get kudos for being clean and corporate."

"You've built quite the operation," I said, using my most sincere tone.

Bo nearly choked. "Ditto," he coughed.

"Shit, I don't do much. My old man left me the land and ware-house. I didn't know what to do with it until the Chinese showed up. I get paid for the space and dock work. Others handle the rest."

"Others?" I asked. "Like Radford and Cruz?"

Heller laughed. "I know they work for you, but Jesus Christ, Cruz couldn't graduate clown college if he had a crib sheet."

"We didn't hire him," Bo said. "He works for Noble"—he checked his watch—"who was swinging from a second-floor banister five short hours ago."

Heller's eyebrows ticked up. He didn't know. He recovered quickly. "That's a problem."

"Why?" Bo asked. "Noble didn't do anything. He was half-dead already."

"It brings heat on Corner24. Not a good time."

"Cops think it was suicide," I said. "Given his condition, it tracks. I don't think they're looking at Corner24."

Still, Bo's words pressed a nerve. Had Adams been pulled off the case because Heller was already under surveillance?

"So, who killed my brother-in-law?" Bo asked.

"I don't know," Heller shrugged. "The locals, probably."

"I can't believe Radford or Cruz would kill anyone," I said.

"I don't mean them. I mean the yard dogs. The team that runs distribution."

"Zor and Ming," Bo said.

"Yeah. The Menendez brothers, without the excuses," he said, pouring another coffee. He waved the pot. "Anyone?"

We both held out our mugs.

"I don't mess with those two. They pay me, and I give them space in my warehouse. They're smart and savage. Feral fuckers who'll skin you just to hear you scream."

"That's very explicit," I said.

"Trying to make a point," said Heller. "Stay the hell away. You're making money. It's not costing Corner24 a dime. Everyone's banking. You decide to be heroes, you'll have to deal with those lunatics. If you get past them, then it's China and the Norks. And if you get past them, I'll kill you myself for burning my payday. Now, I'm not the killing kind, and I doubt it'll ever come to me. But I will piss in your urns for revenge."

He sounded like a bruiser from a '50s noir, every sentence carrying unnecessary weight. Bo sipped his drink; I followed his lead. Heller's eyes stayed steady. His smile was just a twitch at the corners. Within just a few hours, both a cop and a gangster had warned us to steer clear of Corner24. When did our chain of stores become Chernobyl?

"I can't just let Tadeo's murder go," Bo said.

"What are you going to do?" Heller asked. "Strap on a cape and go, Batman?"

"The cops aren't helping," Bo said.

I shot him a look to shut up.

"Let them work," Heller said. "If it was those psycho brothers, they'll figure it out. If it was the Asians? You're out of your league."

"You're losing me," Bo said. "This global stuff doesn't track. A few containers of fake cigarettes shipped to Portland don't bankroll black ops for China and the North Koreans. It's absurd."

"You're not listening. This isn't some fringe syndicate—it's a network with more scope than you can grasp. Portland's a pin on a map. Corner24 is a pressure point in a global artery. The Chinese and the Norks may not even know it exists. Think of it in drug terms: the cartel doesn't know the names of the street hustlers."

"And we're the street hustlers in this scenario," I said.

"Something like that." He set his mug in the sink and ran water into it.

He's neat.

"Hell, I didn't know much about your company until Radford and Cruz started buzzing like picnic flies. You're Zor and Ming's headache. They manage the outlets. The whole operation's compartmentalized—everyone in their lane. The Chinese and the Norks supply the product. I get it through the door, and the Mongolian disperses it. Your stores put it into consumers' hands. Everybody plays a role. You know yours?"

Bo and I shook our heads slowly.

"It's an easy one. Keep your heads down. Corner24's no different than one hundred and twenty corner boys slinging product for the local muscle—just a lot more professional. You're feeding a system you can't even see. If you fuck with that and jam it, you seize up the machine. And the people who own that machine? They don't send warnings. They send plumbers. And they fix whatever's broke."

"Who are those people?" asked Bo. "Who runs the machine?"

"Think of it as a franchise business. Jiffy Lube. Everybody runs their own store, but we all wear the same colors."

"But there's always one guy who writes the playbook."

"In this case, there's more than one, but yeah, I get your point."

"We're going to have to meet these guys," I said. "The Chinese—and *Norks*—that would be the North Koreans."

"What for?"

"Make friends," Bo injected, with a grin.

CHAPTER TWENTY-ONE

The Accident

AFTER BOB HELLER'S WAREHOUSE TOUR, Bo and I retreated to the office. Christine was gone; the place was empty. Through the window, I watched boats tie up at the dockside bar, people climbing out to chase happy hour. A preppy couple in their Sea Ray wrestled with a nervous dog that didn't want to make the jump. I caught myself smiling, thinking about Boomer—he never hesitated. Docks, decks, dinghies, he loved them all.

"I can't tell Katherine or my sister the cops aren't working the case. But if Laura calls on her own, finds out Adams has been pulled off—and I already knew?" His face showed the weight of the no-win situation.

"I know what Abbie would do. She'd demand answers from the PPB, and if she didn't get them, she'd run straight to the press— rattling cages from here to Salem."

"Katherine would do the same," he said. "And that's the one thing we can't afford right now."

He was right. We'd built this life carefully, brick by brick, until silence became its own architecture. Honesty traded for safety. That was the bargain.

Our phones lit up at the same moment. Bo's screen said *Katherine*. Mine said *Abbie*. We answered and walked to opposite corners of the office.

"Ali's been in an accident," Abbie blurted. "She's okay—no injuries—but she needs us."

"Where?" My heart kicked against my ribs.

"Del Prado. Dirt road, through the park. Take Mountain Park—"

"I know where it is," Bo snapped from across the room. Katherine had reported the same. He was already halfway to the door.

"Nat was with her," Abbie added. "She's okay, too. Everyone's okay." That last part was supposed to be reassuring. It wasn't.

The drive was a blur of red lights and tight corners. Bo muscled through traffic like it was Le Mans. Neither of us spoke.

Bo and I had met through our girls. On the first day of kindergarten, my daughter, Ali, had been sitting alone until Natalie Bishop— Bo's youngest—sat beside her. That simple act sparked a friendship that became a sisterhood, drawing our families into the same orbit. Katherine and Abbie became close friends, which bound Bo and me together. Eleven years later, that gravity still held.

Del Prado was a scar cut into the hillside—narrow, rutted, and walled in by trees that reached like they meant to catch you. I'm not sure who hated it more, Bo or his Mercedes, churning through the mud and deep ruts, a stubborn animal being dragged through quagmire.

We found the Jeep about half a mile in. It lay on its side, nose buried in brush, sludge slick on its exterior. Branches clung in jagged clusters. Mud swallowed the tires.

Ali sat on a flat rock, arms wrapped around herself, pale as paper. Her eyes tracked us, unfocused. Natalie wasn't with her.

Abbie and Katherine had arrived seconds earlier. Bo and I scanned the trees. A rustle—then Natalie stepped out from behind a dense thicket, hand lifted in a hesitant wave, unsure she was allowed to come closer.

Ali folded forward and vomited into the mud. Natalie ran to Bo and Katherine, pressing herself against them, and started to cry.

That's when the patrol car arrived, lights throwing slow flashes of blue and red across the mud and trees.

I leaned down to Ali. "Say you were alone. Natalie came with Bo and Katherine." She nodded, still in mild shock, and I murmured the same to the others. There was more to unpack in this wreck, but the most immediate was that Ali had had her license for only a couple of months. Oregon law allowed no passengers under the age of twenty for the first six months—a rule meant to stop kids from loading up their friends and showing off, which explained why Natalie had been hiding. They both knew they'd broken the rule.

"Anyone hurt?" called the officer, stepping carefully past our cars on the narrow lane, mud threatening his shoes. "Jesus! What a mess."

I wasn't sure if he was referring to the Jeep or his footwear. Katherine recognized him immediately. The school resource officer, assigned to Ali's high school. He recognized the Jeep.

Natalie leaned into Bo, trading silent cues with Ali the way Bo and I have for years. Neither had fallen far from the tree; they'd already learned the dance: when to lead, when to follow, that quiet rhythm we'd set long ago.

The officer spoke slowly, writing in a notepad no different from Detective Adams's. Ali explained she'd been heading for a friend's house from the Governor Hotel and decided to take a shortcut. I glanced at Abbie. Del Prado wasn't a shortcut to anywhere. My daughter's lying skills weren't as honed as mine yet. I hoped the officer wouldn't notice.

She spoke raggedly, breathless, as if holding back a scream. Abbie crouched next to her, rubbing her back with the flat of her hand. Ali said that as soon as she turned onto the muddy path, she saw flaring lights behind her.

"Did you notice them before the trail?" the officer asked, pencil moving.

No. But now the truck was right on her, impossible to ignore.

"Can you tell what kind of truck?"

Maybe a Dodge Ram. Black, oversized tires. Cars weren't her thing.

"How close?"

Close enough to fill the mirror. Close enough to see the chrome grill shaking. She pressed her palms to her ears, describing the horn—deafening, relentless, twisting her muscles and joints. The Jeep pitched violently; the seat belt tore at her collarbone. Mud splashed the glass, smeared by the wipers into a brown glaze. She rocked as she spoke, as if the horn was still crashing through her. Then the front left wheel dropped into a hole. The Jeep pitched sideways, branches whipped against the glass, splintering into shards.

She stopped. Breathing shallow and fast.

We didn't push. She needed the words to drain out of her on their own.

Bo met Natalie's eyes. Her story was locked inside her as well. He touched her arm, guiding her gently toward the trees. Katherine followed, and shadows swallowed them.

The officer didn't linger—just a few notes for his report, and he gave me a card for himself and one for a tow company. He'd concluded it was a typical accident. An inexperienced, young, and flustered driver was pushed by another, causing her to flip her car. He'd check on the tailing vehicle but had very little to go on. He told us that leaving an accident scene without reporting an injury is a Class B misdemeanor; if caught, the driver would receive a citation. Then he left, retracing his steps through the mud to spare his shoes. Abbie and I stared at the Jeep, on its side in mud—abandoned in battle.

I pulled Abbie out of hearing range. "What the hell, Abbie? What was she doing driving around?"

"Don't start with me, Martin," Abbie hissed. "You and Bo run around on your secret agenda, and Katherine and I are stuck with the kids and Tadeo's grieving widow in a hotel—because you'd rather play Dick Tracy than go to the cops."

She had a point.

"Why did you let Ali drive with Nat? You know that's illegal."

"She told me that Nat would drive. Nat got her license eight months ago. I let them go in our Jeep because Katherine's car is low on gas. We were going to fill up later and run errands."

"But Ali was *driving*," I pressed.

Abbie's lips stretched thin, and she let her eyes do the cutting.

"Call the tow company—I have a daughter to look after."

I called the dispatcher; he promised fifteen minutes. It would feel like an hour. I scanned the woods for the Bishops.

Ali sat on a flat rock, arms locked around herself, trembling as if on a block of ice. Abbie crouched before her, searching her face, already knowing more was coming.

"Sweetheart," Abbie said softly. "Was Nat the only friend with you?"

Ali crumpled, lurching forward and vomiting again between her sneakers, splattering Abbie's knees. Ali shook her head, small and desperate.

"Who else?"

Ali's voice split the air. "Anne … and … Courtney."

Abbie's hand moved to her mouth but held steady. "Where are they now?"

Ali explained. Anne and Courtney had been in the back seat. They climbed out through the window, then helped Nat and her out by forcing open the passenger door. Everyone was crying, all of them knowing how lucky they'd been—no one was seriously hurt. Ali and Nat stayed put, waiting because they knew we'd come. Anne and Courtney, too terrified to call their parents, said they'd walk home, it was less than a mile, and pretend nothing had happened.

Ali swiped her sleeve across her nose, murmuring it was her fault. She'd wanted to show off, to drive the stretch the kids had nicknamed Axle Alley. But then the black truck was there, pressing her, and she lost control.

There are moments in life that act like hinges—when everything swings a different direction. This was one of them. Someone had hunted our daughters—forced them off the road, four teenage girls boxed inside a rolling Jeep.

Someone was drawing lines and daring us to cross.

CHAPTER TWENTY-TWO

Breaking the Cardinal Rule

AFTER THE JEEP HAD BEEN TOWED AWAY, we returned to the Governor Hotel—two families, each reckoning with the immediate fallout. Abbie and Katherine stepped naturally into the role of moral sentinels, guiding the girls through accountability. They insisted Ali call the parents of the two friends who'd been with her, to confess and apologize. Ali chafed; her friends now faced their own punishments … their parents learning of their near-death experience.

Ali and Natalie were grounded from driving for three months, a penalty they both considered absurdly harsh. Instead of fracturing them, it bound them tighter—the perceived injustice forging their solidarity. Soon they were back in their shared room, the terror of only hours earlier already dissolving in the acid of adolescent outrage at their mothers' "unreasonable" decree.

Then it was our turn.

Abbie took over, and the room went quiet. She moved with calm precision, though there was an intimidating edge to her authority—anyone who resisted would pay for it. She laid out the plan like a casino heist: suitcases needed to be packed, tickets to be booked. She, Katherine, Laura, and all seven children would catch the 7 a.m. flight to Charlevoix, Michigan. She'd call her father, who would meet them with multiple vehicles.

His house, at the end of a mile-long private drive on Lake Charlevoix, was vast and solid—a place insulated from trouble.

As mayor of the Michigan resort town, he had resources, connections, and an authority no one questioned. It was like retreating to a military base minus the uniforms and the saluting.

The kids would love it. Sunfish and powerboats. A sandy beach for late-night bonfires and ghost stories. What had started as a terrifying mess now resembled a summer refuge at Grandpa's lake house.

Then Katherine turned to us. She insisted we report everything to the police, including the ambush. Bo and I admitted we already had—but for reasons we didn't yet understand, Detective Adams was stonewalling.

"Then call the FBI," said Abbie.

"I'm not sure that will help," I said.

"Let's find out," she said and pulled out her phone.

I threw up my hands in surrender. "Fine, I'll call. Put your phone away. I'll set up a meeting."

I called and scheduled a morning appointment, right after we dropped everyone at the airport. It was easier than I first thought. It seemed to ease the tension in the room.

Boomer would stay with me. He wasn't a good flyer. His seat would be in storage: no legroom, no window, probably jammed between two pit bulls in a middle crate. He'd flown once before, and then sulked for a week, assuring we understood the full indignity of it.

For Bo and me, it was the best outcome. No wives to join us at the table. No need to explain to the FBI what we hadn't yet explained to them. No need to peel back the lies we'd already told.

////////////////////////////////////

"I'll find a way to kill them," I muttered to Bo.

"Get in line," he whispered back.

We sat at the bar at Jake's Grill. A cluster of expensively suited financial types—masters of the universe—hovered near the reservation stand, waiting for tables to open. My gaze shifted from them to our bartender, Luke, gliding along the mirrored backbar, arched like a cathedral. He plucked bottles with a manic, effortless rhythm, poured, and slid drinks across the counter as if the motion were innate. Liquor labels shimmered in a kaleidoscope of color, and the din rippled with stray laughter and clipped instructions. It was crowded and loud, and the bustle made Bo and me feel safe.

I stared at Luke in his bartender's white shirt, crisp and plain. Clearly, an athlete when he wasn't pushing liquor. His movements were deft and precise—without thought, purely automatic. Alex came to mind—same build. From there, my thoughts slid to Natalya, and to what she'd said three years earlier when she first proposed our partnership: *You are men who solved a big problem without going to the police, which is very attractive to Dmitry and me.*

Back then, we took it as a compliment. Now, we take it as a curse. That sentiment had shaped every choice we'd made since then—some good, many not. And here we were, finally breaking it. I couldn't tell if it was fear, regret, or something darker: a hollow relief in breaking the one rule that had governed us.

"We're breaking the rule," I said, emptying my Glenlivet and signaling for another.

"I was thinking the same thing," Bo said. "Makes me feel weirdly … disloyal."

"It puts things in perspective," I said.

"How so?"

"When doing the right thing feels wrong—you've chosen a bad partner."

Bo downed his scotch, and Luke, ever observant, signaled he'd get him a refill.

"Luke's a good bartender," Bo said.

"He knows we own the place, and he's paying attention," I said.

"Stop being such a judgmental asshole," Bo whispered with a grin. "Just enjoy a man doing his job well."

I grinned back at Luke, reminding myself to leave a large tip and compliment him to the bar manager before the hotel and bar fell fully under Beaumont Enterprises and Natalya's control.

"Do we call Natalya and Dmitry?" I asked. "Tell them we're going to the FBI?"

"No," Bo said. "We handle this ourselves. Corner24 isn't theirs—and I don't think Dmitry knows about the smugglers."

"Natalya knows Tadeo's dead," I said.

"Sure. And Sokol knows the books are cooked. But Dmitry's either too busy or too disinterested to care. He's already checked out."

Luke slid another Glenlivet into place. Bo nodded. Luke allowed himself the faintest flash of pride—gone almost as soon as it appeared.

"More importantly," Bo said, "we do this right, and on our own."

I nodded, though I knew it wouldn't be easy for me. Bo had never been involved with Natalya. He wasn't haunted by her trace. I liked to think of us as ships that had drifted apart at sea—but our flags had never been lowered.

There's a simple truth about broken affairs: you can remain friends after love—but only if you learn to starve the memory.

CHAPTER TWENTY-THREE

The FBI

BO AND I WALKED INTO THE PORTLAND FBI FIELD OFFICE in the Crown Plaza building at First and Clay the next morning, right on time. Overhead light panels hummed, stale air wheezed through the vents, stripping away any pretense of comfort. It could've been the DMV for all I knew. I caught myself wondering if my plates needed renewing.

We emptied our pockets into gray trays and passed through the metal detector. A guard handed us numbered visitor tags, and we signed our names on a clipboard next to the number. The guard told us we'd need to sign out and return the badges.

Two agents sauntered up—one a tall, lean man in his late forties with graying hair and a dull suit; the other a woman, younger, perhaps in her mid-thirties, with light makeup and a rookie vibe. They flipped open their badges. I grinned—it looked odd. Security had already cleared us, so the gesture felt redundant, almost comical.

When I'd called for the appointment, I hadn't been coy. I told them we were reporting a smuggling operation inside our own company. I gave them enough to know this wasn't a waste of their time—enough to come prepared. They led us down a windowless corridor to a conference room with a rectangular table. Special Agent George Mueller asked if we wanted coffee. "Yes," we said in unison. He nodded to Special Agent Erin Cho, who slipped out, confirming my rookie assessment. A small recorder sat on the table.

"You gentlemen mind?" Mueller asked, pointing at it.

We shook our heads.

Bo and I took one side of the table; Mueller sat opposite, saying nothing. The silence pressed down. I studied his face; he studied ours. His nose and chin looked carved from a wooden post. I'd hoped for small talk to ease the tension, dilute the formality—but apparently, the FBI doesn't do idle chitchat.

My stomach tightened.

"Mueller," I said. "Any relations to Director Robert Mueller?"

"No," he answered, like he'd had to answer the question a thousand times. "It's a common name in the bureau."

Cho returned, smiling broadly. "Sorry to keep you waiting." She radiated a friendly, earnest energy. I guessed she'd been assigned the good cop role, which explained Mueller's stone face. I slapped my own thoughts aside—calm down, Marty. Stop seeing phantoms where there are none.

Mueller pressed the record button and asked us to give our full names. Then: "This is a voluntary interview. Neither of you has asked for an attorney to be present. Can you both confirm that?"

We nodded.

"No, you need to answer out loud for the recorder."

"Yes," we said in sync.

The moment hit me—we'd made a mistake. We hadn't brought counsel. We'd walked in unprotected, exposed. My stomach clenched. I wanted to bolt down the corridor, slam through the turnstiles, rip open the doors, and gulp the cold, clean air outside. We were bare, handing over our story with no idea of the consequences.

What the fuck were we thinking?

"How would you like to proceed?" asked Cho.

"How would *you* like us to proceed?" echoed Bo.

Embarrassing. We'd started dancing before the music even began. I could practically see "guilty" stamped across our foreheads like a gang tattoo.

"Let's start broadly and work toward specifics," said Mueller, his face still carved and unyielding.

I glanced at Bo. He touched his chin. *The signal.* Tadeo was his brother-in-law—he would take the lead here. I exhaled and sat back.

He started talking—and didn't stop for almost half an hour. The agents never interrupted, just scribbled notes, parking questions they'd circle back to later.

Bo steered clear of anything sensitive—no Natalya, no Dmitry, no mention of the company's divestiture. He stuck to ground already broken: the smuggling in Corner24, how we discovered it, Tadeo's murder, Jeff Noble's apparent suicide, and our recon with Bob Heller at his warehouse. Enough detail to keep them busy, but nothing that would open doors we couldn't close.

He named Altan Ganzorig and Zhao Ming, spelling both. He included Alisandro, last name unknown. He gave them Nate Radford, Ed Cruz, and Kennedy Johnson.

When he named the company's controller, Cho smiled at the name. "Really?"

I raised my eyebrows and smiled back.

"Really."

It was my only contribution.

//////////////////////////////////////

Agent Mueller reviewed his notes—three pages of them.

Their questions were surprisingly light. They didn't dig, almost as if they didn't want to intrude. It felt unnatural, utterly different from being grilled by Adams. I'd been scared stiff at the start of the interview, but the fear drained away, leaving me wary of how easily it happened.

Bo told our story, and they listened—too politely. It felt like theater, and I couldn't shake the sense that they weren't the audience. They were the act.

Suddenly, Mueller clicked both his pen and the recorder, then jerked his thumb at Cho.

"Mind if we step out for a moment? I want to confer with our security folks and see about getting some protection for you and your family."

Bo and I nodded, caught off guard. The meeting had begun to lurch and stall—a stick-shift awkwardness that kept us off balance. Already … protective custody?

"Everyone is on a plane to Michigan," I said. "They left an hour ago."

"Everyone?" Agent Cho asked.

"Everyone but Boomer," I said.

She cocked her head.

"The dog," I added.

Both Cho and Mueller wrote Boomer's name.

"Golden Retriever," I clarified, and Cho jotted it down next to his name, as if she needed a reminder when she read her notes later.

"Where exactly is this … Charlevoix?" asked Mueller, referencing his note.

"It's a resort town in northern Michigan. More boats than people. Affluent but also homey. My father-in-law is the mayor. I'm sure he'll talk to the chief of police, to keep their eyes open."

"I think we can help in that regard," Mueller said as he and Cho made their way to the door.

"What is happening here?" I asked as soon as the door shut. "I feel like I'm on a date and the girl can't figure out if she likes me or not."

Bo put his finger to his lips. "Not so loud, they might be listening."

"I know," I said. "I want them to hear me."

He leaned in, whispering. "I agree. It's like an alternate reality."

"They're acting like we're delivering old news. Barely curious."

"Maybe that's how they work. There's a cop level and an FBI level."

"You mean crime is divided like floors in a building?" I whispered, my voice drenched in sarcasm. "Local cops operate on the ground floor, getting into the weeds, and we've taken the elevator up to the FBI floor, where they only handle big-picture stuff, like executive management?"

"How the hell should I know?" Bo hissed. "How many times have you talked to the FBI?"

I shrugged; he had a point. "Ironically—never."

"Maybe it's not old news," he murmured, staring quizzically. "Maybe it's us—*we're* the old news. What if they've been watching us for a while, investigating us, and our connection to … " Bo trailed off.

We sat in silence for ten minutes. Paranoia, coupled with guilty consciences, had become almost reflexive for us. They say your life flashes before your eyes at critical times. Trust me—it doesn't. It lingers on the frame in front of you. In my case, a small, dull room the color of damp paper.

When Mueller and Cho returned, they carried the expressions of people who'd just argued. Cho smiled, but tension pinched behind her eyes—the kind of tight smile you give when you can't tell the whole story.

Mueller began, "Gentlemen, our immediate concern is your families' safety. I'll need a full list of everyone who traveled to"—he glanced at his notes—"Charlevoix. Names, ages, and the exact address of the residence."

Cho added, "We'll notify local police so they're aware, but coordination will come through our Detroit Field Office. They'll likely send an agent from Traverse City to keep watch and check in with your families. It won't be intrusive."

"What does that mean—*intrusive*?" Bo asked.

Mueller said, "Traverse City is a resident bureau—smaller than a field office like Detroit. The SSA there will be looped in, and they'll assign a case agent to work with local police and your families. That agent will check the house, recommend any quick fixes, and make sure they all know to call the agent first—then 911—if anything looks suspicious."

"SOP," Bo said with a dimpled grin.

"We don't use that expression," Cho replied evenly. "We say 'protocol.' But yes—same idea."

I raised my eyebrows, figuring Bo had a new favorite word. "I'll text Abbie to let her know what to expect," I said.

"The agent will also go over communication etiquette," Mueller continued. "We don't want anyone posting their location or sharing details with outsiders."

"Can they confiscate the phones?" I asked. "There are six teenage girls and one teenage boy. It was easier keeping D-Day under wraps."

Bo nodded aggressively.

Mueller snorted. "Welcome to my world. I've got three myself. No—we don't take phones unless you agree, or there's a court order. But we'll ask them to treat them as off-limits—no email, no texts."

He leaned forward, hands clasped. "Now, regarding your own activity—you need to maintain normal routines. No contact with the subjects. No side investigations. And no interference at Corner24."

I blinked. "Wait—you're saying you don't want us to join our families?"

Cho tilted her head. "Correct. Stay here. Conduct business as usual. Avoid the smuggling, avoid the suspects. That's the best way to protect your families. If you change your pattern, it could spook them and jeopardize the investigation."

Things weren't going as expected. Bo and I had figured they'd spend a few days verifying our story, making sure we weren't cranks. But after a cursory interview, here they were—fully engaged, assigning protection to our families and issuing instructions like we were already part of it.

"We know it's uncomfortable," Cho said. "But any sudden change could blow the case. The smugglers could vanish or relocate. Your normalcy—your routine—is the safest course. And it buys us time."

I exhaled, rubbing my neck, feeling the invisible leash.

We covered a few more details before Mueller left. We entered their direct numbers into our speed dial. They advised us on how to act normally around criminals, which carried its own bizarre humor. They suggested we manage our other companies and steer clear of Corner24.

Cho lingered after Mueller's exit. In a low whisper, she said, "The SAC was part of our discussion. He's very interested in this case. Follow instructions and don't do anything stupid."

Bo and I blinked and exchanged a look.

"Special Agent in Charge," she clarified. "Top guy here."

"You think we might do something stupid?" Bo grinned.

"No," she said with a grin of her own. "Special Agent Mueller does."

CHAPTER TWENTY-FOUR

Breaking Trust

"IF I TELL YOU SOMETHING, CAN I COUNT ON YOU TO KEEP IT BETWEEN US?"

Natalya paused slightly, then said, "It depends, Martin. I keep many of our secrets. They fill my heart and memories. Why do you ask?"

"Do you tell Dmitry everything I tell you?"

"I tell Dmitry about our business together. I don't talk about our personal lives. He isn't interested in hearing about it, and I am not interested in talking about it. I am not a teenage girl."

"You told him about our affair," I reminded her.

Her hand drifted across the table, the back of her fingers brushing mine in a gesture that probably said more than she wanted it to.

"I hate that word."

"Entanglement," I corrected with a half-smile.

"Involvement," she countered with a full smile.

We sat at a window table on hard wooden chairs, at Mother's Bistro overlooking SW Stark. The air was thick with the aroma of coffee and bacon, conversation fragments pulsing through the room like hail on a tin roof. The place was packed as usual, waitresses weaving through the obstacle course with invisible maps in their heads, plotting the most efficient routes from table to kitchen. The din made us lean forward to hear each other. I liked any place that pushed our faces closer together.

I'd chosen the spot on purpose. I didn't know if the FBI had put someone on me—or on Bo and me—but better safe than sorry. Trying to eavesdrop in Mother's would have been hopeless. Natalya had flown in the night before. Today marked divestiture day for Paladin Holdings—the day the hotels and the Naples foundry would be spun out.

After the FBI meeting, Bo and I had spent time unpacking its oddities, speculating on what it all meant, and then shuttling between our legal and diligence teams to review and sign documents. Natalya had sent me her resignation letter as Paladin's chairman, then called to share her travel schedule. I told her I wanted to see her privately this morning before the signing and the post-closing reception. We agreed on breakfast at Mother's, and then to walk down Broadway to the attorney's offices, where Marek Sokol and Bo would join us.

"I want to tell you what's been happening at one of our companies, and what Bo and I are doing about it."

"Let me guess," she said, grinning. "Bo doesn't want you to tell me, and that is why you wanted to have breakfast with me."

"Correct."

She sipped her coffee and nudged the plate away, her mushroom omelet half-eaten, cooling in place. Natalya never finished a restaurant meal. I could never tell if it was a cultural convention or simply a quirk, but she always left something behind, as if the last bite belonged to someone else. At home, it was the opposite. Meals were rarely formal. She preferred to *perekus*—snack—often without clothes. She devoured every small portion, chasing the remains with a spoon until the plate was so clean I'd wonder if it even needed washing. The contradiction fascinated me, and I never mentioned it, preferring that this private little oddity remain hers alone, observed only by me.

"I'm sure it's about Corner24," she acknowledged. "I've heard there are problems—bad ones."

"What have you heard? And from whom?

"Would you like me to list my sources, Martin?" She stretched her lips into a straight line. "My secret informants are you and Marek."

"And what did Mr. Sokol *and I* tell you?"

She looked around. The tables close to us were all filled with babbling breakfasters.

"Well, *you* told me that Tadeo, Bo's brother-in-law, who worked at the company, was shot at my stepson's dance club. *You* also told me that Jeff Noble committed suicide." She lowered her eyes. "Poor man. I only met him twice when we were buying his company, but he seemed a good person. *Marek* told me the books are crooked. They don't add up." Then she raised her eyes to mine again. "Would you like me to say more here, or do you think we should talk outside?"

I signaled the waitress, paid the tab, and we strolled west on Stark for three blocks to Waterfront Park, along the Willamette, pretending to study the bridges. She slipped her arm around mine, and I kept an eye out for weird-looking guys who might be FBI agents. I had no idea what they'd look like. Maybe someone in shorts, a T-shirt, and sunglasses—wearing a fedora.

The weather was a perfect summer day in Portland, low eighties, with a clean, crisp breeze sweeping down from the still-snow-covered Mount Hood in the distance.

"We went to the cops about Tadeo."

"I know. Alex received a call from a detective while visiting me in Florida. It upset him. He's always afraid he might say something wrong. For him, words are birds he cannot catch once they fly out."

I told her about the smuggling ring operating in the company. I explained that Bo and I were confident Jeff Noble hadn't committed suicide, and that the local police seemed oddly incurious about investigating either his or Tadeo's murder. She listened the way a card shark takes a hand—without reaction. That was Natalya—steady, composed, calm. It's a quality I'd always admired, as, I suspected, did Dmitry.

I left out the warehouse tour with Bob Heller. Any mention of

China or North Korea would instantly push the problem out of our small bubble and into Dmitry's world. The bigger it got, the harder it would be for her to avoid passing it on. I wanted her to feel we could handle it ourselves, without burdening her with information that might force her into an impossible choice—breaking faith with Dmitry or with me.

And then I screwed up.

I said too much. I told her about Ali and Natalie joyriding with their friends and getting hit by a truck—the same kind used in Tadeo's shooting. Her eyes widened, and I kept talking, words tumbling in a rush, slipping past me as I spilled that Bo and I had gone to the FBI.

"You talked to the FBI?" she interrupted for the first time.

I knew then I'd stepped in it. In one verbal blur, I'd broken three separate trusts. I'd promised Bo to stay silent. I blindsided Natalya by confessing we'd gone to the FBI—the one thing she trusted I would never do. And Dmitry … I showed him that Bo and I were weak links in the chain.

Regret hit like I'd plunged through thin ice.

"I shouldn't have said that," I mumbled, shaking my head slowly.

"Shouldn't have said that because it's not true, or because it's true but should not be?"

"Because it's true."

There was a park bench a few feet away, and she detoured to it, slumping onto it, head bowed, letting the world contract around her as her thoughts raced.

"Oh, *Milyy*, I wish you had not done that," she said. "Or at least not told me."

"Natalya, there's a smuggling ring running through Corner24. Two people are dead. Our girls were attacked. We have three families staying at my father-in-law's for their safety. The lead cop's been yanked off the case, and the PPB acts like they don't care. What do you want us to do?"

"I don't know," she shot back, anger creeping into her voice for the first time. "But we've had it worse, and we never went to the federal police. You do not pull a spider out of its hole. If you need help with these smugglers, I can remove them with one phone call." She gave a flick of her wrist like a monarch dismissing an annoying subject.

"And what, Natalya? Fill the Governor Hotel with *gopniks,* as we did at the Raphael Hotel in Rome—end up having a gang war here in Portland? Last time I checked, the final tally in Italy was over two hundred and twenty dead."

Without hesitation, she snapped, "*Da*—yes, if that is necessary," and I knew then that Bo and I had done the right thing. Natalya's world had no room for perspective, only extremes. Anything else was weakness. She was like Dmitry in that way.

"We said almost nothing about Paladin to the FBI. Dmitry's name was never mentioned. For that matter, neither was yours. We were careful."

"The FBI isn't like the local police," she said. "They are more dangerous. They dig deeper. They will look at Beaumont Enterprises, which holds the Chiurazzi foundry, and my ownership records are not as guarded as Paladin's."

"You're being unreasonable," I said, frustrated at the sudden collapse of her stolidity. "The FBI is investigating the smugglers. They aren't interested in our other companies or our equity partners." I paced back and forth in front of her, like an apologetic spouse seeking forgiveness. "Besides, we're signing the papers in a couple of hours that will officially separate your world from mine."

"When did this smuggling start?"

"Maybe six months ago. I don't have an exact time."

"I was chairman for last six months. On paper, I was in charge."

She stared at Mount Hood for a while and then, without looking at me, she said, "When Viktor, my first husband, was assassinated and lying in the driveway of our *dacha,* outside of Moscow, I made the mistake of letting the *militsiya* deal with it. Naturally, they were corrupt monkeys, and soon the FSB took over investigating the death of *Moskva's vory pakhan*." She looked at me. "The FSB was the new chapter of the old KGB, and *pakhan* means leader of the Moscow mafia."

I nodded in understanding.

"They took me to a *SIZO*. It is a detention place with cells, where FSB keeps people before trial, before they declare them guilty. I was accused of planning Viktor's murder. I was an easy target. Viktor was most powerful *vory* in Moscow, and the FSB needed to find his killer quickly so the … arrangement … between the *bratva* and the *siloviki*—the power elite, was not put out of balance. The *Cheka operativnik*—FSB agent—his name was Igor Petrovich Morozov. I will never forget it because he made me call him *Starshiy Ofitser Igor Petrovich Morozov* every day to remind me that I was nothing and he had my life in his hands."

I stood utterly still, not daring to move. After our time together and countless stories, she'd never told me this one. If it were possible to hear a pin drop in an open waterfront park, then this was the time. Her accent always became thicker when she told Russian stories.

"He never raised his voice. It was always dull and quiet, like a priest forgiving the dying—only I was not dead. His eyes were cold, black glass. I stayed in cell that smelled terrible—like vomit and cigarettes." She wrinkled her nose as if the scent still clung to her.

"They gave me shapeless brown dress, rough and itchy. They let me keep my underwear, but after few days, it was foul. The food was brown mush. It looked like diarrhea. That was on purpose. It was tasteless, with the stink of metal from the bowl. I was afraid they spat in it, but in the end, I was too hungry to care. I closed my eyes, swallowed fast, and tried not to gag.

"Every day, *Starshiy Ofitser Igor Petrovich Morozov* had new questions, different approaches. He told me if I cooperated, things would get easier. So, I cooperated. I answered every question, but I did not confess for something I did not do, and so nothing changed. Most days, he left me alone. There was no beating, no torture, nothing like in the movies—it is worse. If you are beaten, you have pain to focus your mind. When there is nothing, you are left with fear, suspicion, the cold, brown *gavno* to eat, and no future. That is more painful."

"*Gavno?*"

She shrugged. "Shit."

I let a few seconds pass. "What happened?" I finally asked.

"Dmitry happened. I do not know how much it cost him, or what favors he paid, but one day, eight weeks after I was arrested, *Starshiy Ofitser Igor Petrovich Morozov* said his investigation was over, and I was free. The next month, I was on a plane with Vasili to America. My papers were already done when I came out. Dmitry promised the FSB I would leave and never return. They were afraid I would take the place of my dead husband in the *vory*. His real killer did not want competition from me, and Dmitry convinced him I would not come for revenge."

"Dmitry knew who killed your husband?"

"Even back then, Dmitry had great power. Yes. No one would dare kill the *pakhan*—the leader of the Moscow *vory* without permission from *siloviki*, the ruling elite."

I shuddered, realizing how small I was in her world. A world so benignly dangerous that love and death sat side by side, like casual friends. Some truths are not meant to be understood. They're meant to be survived.

She reached out her hand, and I helped pull her off the bench. We started toward our attorney's office on Broadway. She slipped her arm around mine and said with a firm, unwavering voice, "Since that day, Martin—*milyy*—I have never again spoken to a government officer.

"Not once."

CHAPTER TWENTY-FIVE

The Divestiture

"NEGOTIATION IS JUST A POLITE WAY OF TAKING WHAT'S YOURS."

Tom Barnes had said that to me once over a casual scotch, while discussing the art of negotiating breakups of marriages and companies. He was a close friend, and the only one outside of Bo I trusted enough to confide about my relationship with Natalya. He'd been visibly upset, and I quickly realized he was a closer friend to Abbie than to me, so I swore him to secrecy and never brought it up again. From time to time, he would feed me little moral bromides, subtly reminding me that he knew and was quietly peeved at my infidelity. To my credit, I always felt guilty for ever burdening him with the knowledge. I'd wanted someone other than Bo to talk to about it since Bo wasn't much of a fan, but I'd chosen badly. It had been selfish—and unfair.

Tom specialized in family law, but the firm he worked for also had the M&A attorneys we needed. Steering our business their way was my way of apologizing to him. His corporate colleagues did the heavy lifting—tearing Paladin Holdings apart and stitching the pieces into Beaumont's portfolio.

We sat around the long oak table in the conference room, twenty floors up, a wall of glass stretching before us with a sweeping view of downtown Portland. From my chair, I could see the huge vertical, iconic PORTLAND sign, a retro monument to the city's sawdust past, now leaning confidently against its polished modern skyline.

The final document review and signing was civilized, professional, almost genteel. Still, it felt to me as if the blood had been wiped from the blade while everyone pretended they hadn't been cut. It had gone more smoothly than we'd expected, but it left its own kind of wound.

I could see the agitation behind Natalya's eyes. She wanted it over so she could talk to Marek, and, I suspected, Dmitry, about what I'd told her an hour earlier in the park. In her mind, the dissolution of our company and the transfer of millions in assets—from luxury hotels to Italy's oldest foundry, with its vast inventory of Renaissance art—paled beside the greater cataclysm of confessing to the ever-evil, monolithic FBI.

I could tell by her body language, a dialect I'd learned to read and interpret like a UN translator, that she wasn't paying much attention. She'd just increased the size of her company, but it meant little. It was a *fait accompli*, and she had a crisis to attend to—or at least a crisis as she saw it.

Tom stuck his head in the door and asked, "How are things going?"

He stepped in. His eyes were friendly and perpetually amused, the kind that put you instantly at ease and made it impossible not to like him. He moved with an easy confidence, seemingly unaware of the quiet charm his presence carried. He avoided eye contact with Natalya, as if looking at her would betray Abbie.

"Beaumont Enterprises is much bigger, Paladin Holdings is much smaller," I said. "Sort of like your last divorce settlement."

Nobody laughed.

"Are we done here?" Natalya asked, standing. "If so, I'd like a room for a private conversation with Mr. Sokol." She nodded toward him.

"Yes, follow me," said one of the four fresh-faced lawyers who had guided us through the signing.

"I also need to make an international call. How is your signal here?"

She didn't need to ask; she could've checked her phone. The question was for my benefit. She was still pissed and wanted to make it clear she'd be reporting to Dmitry.

I turned to Tom. "Can I borrow your office?" I asked. I now needed to come clean to Bo, and I knew it wouldn't be pretty.

◢◤◢◤◢◤◢◤◢◤◢◤◢◤◢◤◢◤◢◤◢◤◢◤◢◤◢◤

"What is wrong with you, Marty?" Bo's face was red, his fists balled. He paced back and forth like a sentry. "You're still in love with her, aren't you?"

"No, I'm not," I said. "It's complicated."

"No, Marty. A Rubik's Cube is complicated. Nuclear physics is complicated. Understanding my three daughters is complicated. You and Natalya? Not very complicated. You can't stop talking to her about things that don't concern her. You're like a fifth grader desperate to share a secret with your first-ever crush."

"She's our chairman, for crying out loud."

"She resigned!" he yelled back. "At this point, you're not even trying to find a good excuse; you're just winging it."

"Are you done?" I hissed. "Or do you need another minute?"

"I'll keep going until you promise to never talk to Natalya again about our business. Not one word." He was breathing hard, but I could tell the anger was fading. "It's not Natalya—it's Dmitry. She's a conduit. A frictionless funnel to the most dangerous man on this planet without nuclear weapons—and I doubt even that."

Bo's wrath was like his road rage—furious, but fleeting.

"I promise."

He stared out the window for a good minute.

I tried to break the ice. "What if someone held a gun to my head and ordered me to talk to Natalya?" I said.

"Take the goddamn bullet," he snapped back.

{{

Back in the conference room, an hour later, Natalya, Marek, Bo, and I talked casually while the receptionist brought us coffee. This was the extent of our post-divestiture ceremony. No music, no dancing, no scotch, just coffee and frowns all around.

"I need to tell you about Refco Inc.," Marek said as soon as the receptionist left.

"Refco?" Bo asked.

"They're still your new banker, right? They replaced my client as your money source."

"Yes. The $100 million we just paid you to settle with Dmitry came from them. You were here when it happened."

"They're in trouble."

"What do you mean?" My eyes darted to Natalya beside him. She already knew. Likely, Dmitry had briefed her.

Marek pulled a printed financial bulletin from his briefcase and began reading it aloud.

"The SEC has determined that Refco's CEO concealed approximately $430 million in bad debt by transferring it to a company he controlled shortly before their recent IPO. As a result, investor confidence has deteriorated significantly, and the company is now under substantial legal scrutiny. While the full impact is still developing, Refco's stock has already experienced a sharp decline."

He paused to allow us time to absorb the news. "I know you guys have been busy, dealing with Corner24, and from what Natalya just told me, so much more. But you're in trouble."

"You just said '*they're* in trouble,'" I said.

"Which means *you're* in trouble."

Bo sank back in his chair and let out a stunned sigh. "This day is just not turning out the way I expected."

Natalya found her voice and softly said, "We just spoke to Dmitry. The $100 million was transferred to our Beaumont account, and he moved it out immediately. It is gone … it is in the wind."

"Fuck me," I said.

"*Da*," she replied.

Another time, she might have said something funnier.

"Well, they loaned us the money. It was a legitimate transaction. If Refco's in trouble, they can't just ask for their money back," I said.

"Correct," Marek replied. "But their loan to you is recorded on their books as an asset. It's worth $100 million plus interest because you intend to repay it. You used Paladin's assets to collateralize it. It's a class A loan. If Refco's problems continue to spiral out of control, they may decide to sell their assets to rebalance their portfolio. They could sell your loan to another bank or institution at a discount. There'd be a lot of eager buyers. You could end up with a new note holder who's less accommodating."

He didn't tell us anything we didn't know. Bo was right. The day wasn't turning out the way we'd hoped.

"Keep the faith, gentlemen," Marek said. "Pray for their recovery."

"Ha," Natalya sputtered. "In Russia, we say prayer is hope; vodka is certainty."

She wasn't wrong.

We were neck-deep in trouble—and sinking. Smugglers, FBI, Refco. Prayer offered relief, alcohol offered oblivion. Two sides of the same coin. Bo drank to drown risk. I drank to drown regret. Bo prayed because he believed.

I prayed because I was too scared not to.

CHAPTER TWENTY-SIX

Boomer

IT HAD BEEN TEN DAYS since we flew the families to Michigan. Eight since Natalya boarded her Hawker 800 back to Miami, taking with her whatever scraps of our relationship remained. Seven since Alex Danilenko reopened Shangri-La before the competition poached his dancers.

And six since Boomer had a stroke.

Six and a half days to be exact—it happened in the middle of the night. I'd fallen asleep on the couch, Boomer sprawled between my legs, his head on my thigh, my hand idly stroking behind his ears until we both drifted off. The TV woke me. We were about to go upstairs, the house glowing with every light on—my belief continued to be that predators shun the light, preferring to hunt in the dark, so I gave them none.

We stopped in the kitchen for a drink of water. His back legs slid out behind him, like he'd stepped on ice. His head cocked at a strange angle; his breathing was shallow and fast. Then his front legs gave way. He collapsed onto his side, tongue lolling. My chest seized. I, too, began to breathe shallow and fast. I called 911. The dispatcher and I debated briefly what counted as a family member—two-legged or four. When my voice hit official shriek levels, she connected me with an emergency vet clinic, and I told them we were on our way.

The Jeep was in repair. The Z8 had no back seat. I slid him into the sedan and drove as if I were Bo. Boomer stayed down—no curiosity, no head out the window—just panting. I reached my arm back to hold his paw, told him he wasn't allowed to die, and cried. By the time we arrived, he was sitting up, blinking at the new surroundings like he'd forgotten ever getting into the car. The vet saw him immediately. She crouched beside him, hands gentle on his golden head.

"Walk him for me," she said.

His steps were slow and deliberate, nose tilted to the ceiling, ears twitching. She checked his pupils, tapped his paws, listened to his heart, and muttered to herself. Pinched him. Studied his chart. Then leaned back.

"TIA," she said. "Transient ischemic attack. A mini-stroke. Happens sometimes. They usually bounce back fast. He's nearly there already." She scratched behind his ears, and he leaned into her, panting. "You're a brave fella," she said in baby-talk, and then in adult-talk, "Just keep him calm and watch him."

"Will he have another stroke—something more serious?" I asked, my voice begging her to tell me no.

"It's possible," she said, "but it's also possible he'll never have another. The blood flow to a small part of Boomer's brain was blocked—probably a tiny clot in a vessel. When that area didn't get enough oxygen, he lost coordination, stumbled, and got disoriented. The good news is, unlike a full stroke, the blockage clears on its own fairly quickly—sometimes within minutes—and his brain tissue isn't permanently damaged."

"He can still do math?" I asked.

"Balance his checkbook," she played along.

I nearly hugged her. She sensed it and hugged me instead.

On the way home, Boomer sat up front and was more himself, sticking his head out the window. I talked to him. Told him he scared me half to death. At one point, he looked at me, as if to say, I'm the one who had the stroke, and you're typically making it all about yourself. I agreed with him and drove carefully, mindful that he had no seat belt and might bang his head. It was two in the morning, and the streets were empty except for a pair of lights following in the distance.

By the next day, Boomer was fine. I was more shaken than he was. I could tell he'd dropped into a lower gear. When his somber eyes met mine, he'd look away quickly, like my gaze was too heavy for him now.

I called around and found a girlfriend of my daughter willing to come to the house and stay with him during the day while I worked. Abbie and I discussed putting him on a plane to Michigan, but we worried about the pressure changes. I suggested paying someone to drive him to Michigan, but four days in a car had its own risks. In the end, we agreed to hire a Boomer nanny until the family came home—someone paid to walk and pamper him all day. Boomer loved it.

Bo and I spent the next week attending to business, meeting with the executive teams of the companies still inside Paladin, and listening. One by one, each team came to our office to walk us through their performance and their three-year plan. We weren't worried about uncovering additional corruption; the odds of that were near zero. But Corner24 had taught us what happens when attention drifts.

The meetings helped Bo and me reconnect with all the company managers and soften the "absent parent" vibe we'd unintentionally created. They also gave us a read on how the remaining companies felt about the breakup. Because Paladin was private, we hadn't made a show of the divestiture. Avoiding publicity had left the other companies blindsided and annoyed that we hadn't looped them in. The meetings were informal—more about morale-boosting and ego-stroking than holding anyone's feet to the fire.

Nate Radford called daily, sometimes twice. Christine ran interference, promising we'd call back. We never did.

We called the FBI a few times before realizing they were avoiding us, just as we were avoiding Corner24. So, we stopped trying.

In our spare time—now that our families were gone—we dug through everything we could find on Refco Inc. The financial behemoth was in full damage-control mode. Most of what we found was rumor and speculation. The SEC was quietly investigating potential CEO fraud. Investors were jittery, pushing the stock lower day by day.

At night, the house remained bright enough to host Game Seven of the World Series. After paying Boomer's nanny and sending her home, I never let him out of my sight. If he sauntered to a different room, I'd follow. I could tell it started to annoy him.

I spoke with Abbie every night. From her reports, being exiled to Charlevoix wasn't exactly a hardship: kayaking in the mornings, water skiing by day, bonfires by night. The kids ran wild, as if summer had been invented for them. Their evacuation had turned into a vacation, and that dulled the edges of my guilt.

I could tell by the lift in Abbie's voice that, with each passing day, she was letting go of the anger she'd aimed at me for getting us tangled in this mess. She didn't blame me for criminals operating in Corner24; she blamed me for owning a company where something like that could happen—for not having done enough homework before acquiring it. It was as if I'd moved us all into a new house, only to discover the neighbor beat his wife and children. She needed a target for her anger, and although the fault line was tenuous, it was still a line.

CHAPTER TWENTY-SEVEN

The Request

THAT MORNING, BO CAME INTO THE OFFICE AND ANNOUNCED, "FBI Agent George Mueller wants to meet with us."

"Why?"

"I'll let him surprise you," Bo said cheerily, though something in his eyes sparked my curiosity.

"Really? You're not going to tell me?"

"Nope. I want to catch your reaction in real time."

"I'll be that surprised?"

"Like one of your kids walking in on you and Abbie."

"Speaking from personal experience?" I asked.

Bo smiled. "I'll never tell." He took a beat and then said, "Mueller won't come to our home or office. Said it was too risky. He wants to meet us in Salem."

"That's a full hour's drive."

"Yeah. He said it'd give them time to see if we were being followed."

An hour later, we were barreling down I-5, Bo checking his rearview, me angling the door mirror for a better view of the traffic behind us.

Bo drove the way he always did—like the car had been stolen.

"At this speed, nobody's following us," I said.

"SOP," Bo deadpanned.

"Protocol," I rebutted.

We both laughed.

///

We sat in a black leather booth against a red brick wall, our backs to the door, Mueller and Cho facing it. Mueller wore the same suit and face as at our last encounter. Cho went casual—khaki pants, a dark-blue T-shirt tucked in, her black hair in a short ponytail, as if it were her day off.

The restaurant was The Wild Pear. Bo had received a text to drive there as we neared the outskirts of Salem. Mueller and Cho were already in the booth, so clearly they hadn't been tailing us. I wondered if all the cat-and-mouse surveillance was just a game—an adrenaline rush for them, and a way to keep us twitchy.

Bo and I made small talk with Cho while Mueller studied the menu. I was reminded that "Joe Friday" Mueller didn't blather.

"Is the FBI picking up the tab today?" I asked mockingly.

"It's Dutch," he said back.

We all ordered burgers except Mueller, who went for the four-cheese mac—no bacon bits. Apparently, he was vegetarian. He just kept hemorrhaging points in my book. Bo sensed it and slapped my knee under the table.

"How is the investigation going?" I asked after the waiter left with our order.

"I can't tell you," answered Mueller. "We don't discuss ongoing investigations."

"Of course you don't," I said. "Neither do the cops. But I'm not asking." I leaned forward and lowered my voice. "I'm demanding. Our families are cooling their heels in Michigan, and our company is under assault by murderous smuggling scumbags. So, I don't give a rat's ass about your 'protocol.' I want to know what the fuck is happening, what progress you've made, and how much longer we're all in jeopardy."

No one responded as the waiter brought our four iced teas.

"Your families are fine—in fact, they're enjoying themselves. We have an agent visit them every day, and the local police have stationed a car at your father-in-law's." He took a sip of his drink. "The two of you are in no immediate danger as far as we can tell. Both the PPB and our office are monitoring your homes and your office. I've been told your power bill must be astronomical."

Bo looked at me, puzzled. He didn't know about my odd security strategy—that my house could be used to rescue ships at sea.

"Your company is fine. All one hundred and twenty stores are fully stocked and operational. What else would you like to know?"

"How close are you to arresting the Mongolian and the Chinese guy?" asked Bo.

"That is not as easy as you might think," said Mueller.

"Why not? If you can't arrest them on murder, then arrest them on smuggling. We saw them do it. We will testify. We're your eyewitnesses."

"It's more complicated than that," said Agent Cho, and Mueller gave her the universally recognized look to shut up.

The waiter brought our food, and our conversation came to a halt. Once alone, and with a steaming pile of creamy pasta in front of him, Mueller continued. "Let me break it down for you. The murder of Tadeo isn't within federal jurisdiction. We'll help the PPB close the case, but our focus is the smuggling network. That's federal. We're interested in its scale and scope. We don't want to rush in and cut off one Hydra head while the others survive."

"Our priorities are not aligned," said Bo. "Marty and I want you, or the locals, to get Zor and Ming off the street. They probably killed my brother-in-law, and maybe our business partner, Jeff. As long as they're running wild. ..."

"I'm keeping the lights on at night," I injected. "And yeah, I'm sending my power bill to the FBI."

"The investigation is ongoing," said Cho, carefully separating the meat and toppings from the bun and setting it aside. Then she ate her burger—sans bread—with a fork and knife. "We've obtained the grainy video from that night and have shipped it to Quantico for enhancement. We're hoping it might give us a better definition of the vehicle. We're also exploring a forced-deportation angle; it looks like both of them violated their work visas."

"I'm overwhelmed. It's more than I can stand," I sneered, taking a proper bite of my burger. "Can't you help the cops find actual evidence that they killed Tadeo?"

"It doesn't look good," said Mueller. "From my vantage, the best we can do is indict Zor and Ming for conspiracy to distribute contraband cigarettes across state lines."

"I'm with Marty," said Bo. "I'm all tingly with excitement. These goons will get what? House arrest and six months wearing an ankle bracelet?"

"No," said Cho, cutting another bite from her burger. "They'll get five to ten, followed by immediate deportation."

"How much longer before we get our company back?" I asked. "I want to fire the pricks working for us. Declutter the place."

"Nate Radford and Ed Cruz?" Mueller clarified.

"Among others."

"You won't need to fire them. Radford, Cruz, Johnson, and several others will be arrested along with Zor and Ming."

"And Heller's entire operation?"

"All of it. One clean sweep."

"So, these a-holes will get a few years for killing two people, not to mention smuggling, embezzling, and nearly destroying our company," Bo said, pushing his half-eaten burger aside. "It's wrong. More than wrong. It's criminal."

"And when will all this *justice* finally happen?" I added.

"That's why we wanted to talk to you," said Mueller, both he and Cho laying down their forks and knives. Lunch was over.

"We need to ask you something highly irregular … ," Mueller said, tilting his head, " … to *do* something highly irregular."

Bo tapped my leg under the table. Here it comes.

"We'd like you to meet with the head of the entire smuggling network at Heller's warehouse and talk to him."

Bo was right. I stared at them as if they'd just stripped naked and were about to do something obscene.

I'll spare you the next ten minutes of standard *you've got to be kidding me* parley.

Even during the back-and-forth, I could tell something wasn't quite right. Maybe it was Mueller's tone, maybe his body language, but he came across as a man selling someone else's plan. His words were professional but empty, like he was pitching a car he'd never driven. Clearly, he was under orders to make it happen.

Cho, on the other hand, was enthusiastic as ever. She reminded me of Boomer when I said the word "walk."

"Do we invite ourselves to this meeting?" Bo asked.

"You'll get a call," Mueller said. "Bob Heller will ask you to meet."

"How do you know …"

"We're monitoring Heller's phone," Mueller replied, shifting in his seat. "We know the top guy told him to set up a meeting with you two. We figure he'll call."

"He doesn't have our number," I said.

"Then Radford will call. Take it."

Cho leaned forward before I could ask the next question. "We don't want you to say no. Especially since we already told you not to contact them."

"What's the guy's name?" I asked.

Mueller exhaled. "I don't want to tell you more than necessary. We're in a tough spot. We know more than we're sharing, but we don't want you up to speed. This has to unfold naturally—organically—so you don't accidentally telegraph that you know more than you should. That would make Heller and the others suspicious."

"Do we wear a wire?" I asked.

Mueller shifted again, looking cramped in his half of the booth. "No. Too risky. Just debrief us afterward."

"But wouldn't anything we tell you just count as hearsay?"

"You're mistaking investigative intelligence for prosecutorial evidence," Cho said. "We're gathering operational intel—size, structure, relationships. What you tell us, even without a wire, helps us understand the scope of the operation."

"Anything in particular you want us to find out?" Bo asked.

"No," Mueller almost shouted, then caught himself, making it more of a grunt than speech. He shook his head and, with his straw, played with the ice chips at the bottom of his empty iced tea. "I'm not sure this will even work. You guys don't know what you're doing."

Cho stepped in quickly. "You just have to be yourselves. Don't push, don't pry. These guys can smell a setup from across the room."

"Smell it?" Mueller huffed. "Hell, they'll *reek* of it. Like a fart in an elevator."

Cho gave him a look but pressed on. "Which is why you need to be yourselves. Anything that sounds rehearsed could put you in danger."

"Just take the damn meeting," Mueller said. "My advice is avoid saying anything that might get you killed—but that's just me."

"What if Radford never calls?" I asked.

"He'll call," Mueller said confidently.

"Are you nearby?" Bo asked. "Will you have eyes on us?"

Mueller shifted again, restless.

"I told you, we're not going to tell you more. It's not that we don't want you to know—it's that we *don't* want you to know."

Someone at the back of the restaurant set down a tray of dishes, and it rattled loudly, like a punctuation mark to his comment. Then we turned back to Agents Mueller and Cho and agreed to be under-cover agents for the FBI.

CHAPTER TWENTY-EIGHT

The Invitation

NOTHING HAPPENED FOR SEVERAL DAYS.

Bo vanished, claiming golf, which made sense. With Katherine and the girls in Michigan, a round of golf wasn't stolen family time anymore—it was a gifted indulgence.

I spent the days in the office, taking Boomer with me. He loved the lake and dove in at every opportunity. Our office wasn't set up for wet retrievers, but Christine would dry him off in the lobby, and he'd get plenty of attention from everyone else. At times, I'd explain a company's business model to him while he flopped on the leather couch with half-closed eyes. Maybe he liked the drone of my voice—maybe business bored him.

Finally, Nate Radford called.

Christine patched him through to my office phone, then dialed Bo's mobile and added him to the conference.

"Nate," I said, loud and casual, like we hadn't spoken in months.

"Jesus, you're impossible to reach," he said. Polite, but his tone carried a bite—something that could hurt if I cared, but I didn't.

"We've been up to our eyebrows in company review meetings," I said.

"I heard. When do you want me and my team to come in?"

"Not necessary, Nate. Bo and I have a pretty good handle on things," I said, keeping it neutral.

A pause. Then the faint click of Bo joining. "Hey, Nate," he said, a little too casually, like it was deliberate.

"Hey, Bo. You in the office?"

"I'm driving there now. Be there in ten minutes."

Agent Mueller's warning echoed in my head: *don't telegraph you know more than you should.* I kept it light. "How's the store?"

"Kind of on autopilot," he answered. I could almost hear him shrug. "Everyone knows what they're doing. Jeff wasn't a hands-on manager, so we all learned to be self-reliant, competent at our jobs."

"Yes, we know that about your team," Bo said. "We'll have to get together soon to talk succession. Marty and I have been looking at potential candidates."

Nate didn't respond, but I could feel his spine stiffen through the phone. Bo's words were a chess move—letting him know he wasn't taking over and signaling we weren't letting things stand.

"Yeah," Nate said. "We need to meet about that. There are things to review. I was hoping I could convince you guys to promote me to CEO. Keep the team together since we're doing a good job."

The conversation had a strange rhythm—like passing a hot stone. Words about business, succession, operations. But everything unsaid carried weight. Nate knew we knew everything. He'd arranged for us to meet Heller. And still, here we were, pretending to talk like colleagues reviewing org charts, while the subtext vibrated with threat. I suspected he was on his best behavior because he worried we were recording him. Tadeo had planted that bug in his mind. We, in turn, were on our best behavior because we weren't sure if the FBI was actually recording us.

"I think before we discuss promotions, we need to talk operations," I said.

"Maybe look at some internal projects," added Bo.

"How did your meeting go with the warehouse man?" Nate asked, abruptly changing the subject. He meant Bob Heller, so perhaps he *did* think we were recording him.

"It went as expected," Bo said. "Did he say anything to you?"

"He thought there was room to negotiate a continuation of the partnership."

"That seems very optimistic," I said.

"He's willing to negotiate a different profit structure," Nate said. "More in our favor."

He was slowly guiding us toward a meeting.

"That's a positive sign," Bo said.

"He wants to meet again. Introduce you to someone else," Nate added.

"Who?"

"Someone I've never met. Important—top of the totem pole."

"Have him call us," I said.

"Not necessary. I have all the particulars right here."

The meeting was set for Heller's warehouse the following evening, 8 p.m. sharp.

CHAPTER TWENTY-NINE

Wilton and Lian

BO DROVE, BUT HIS USUAL CALM HAD A CRACK. He stayed silent, answering my questions with a nod, a grunt, or a single word. He'd been unavailable all day: missing from the office, not returning calls, offering nothing but a vague, "I was busy."

His right hand lifted casually, adjusting something in his coat pocket. A gold Cross pen.

"Nice pen," I said.

"Gift from Katherine, years ago. Found it this morning."

"Planning to take notes?"

He gave me that "stop the annoying questions" look.

The highway stretched empty in the late July light, the sun low and gold, casting long shadows across the barren landscape that smelled of dust and grass. Ahead, the warehouse looked worn and dark, like a foreboding apparition in a scary movie—everyone in the theater knowing it was where all evil lurked, and no one in their right mind would ever enter it.

Bo and I headed straight for it.

"I don't see Agent Mueller and the gang anywhere," I said.

"You wouldn't," said Bo. "They get paid not to be seen."

The dust cloud we kicked up on the gravel road toward the bleak, almost fatalistic structure hung in the air, hazing the fading light. We pulled up next to a dark gray Lexus. I assumed it belonged to the "top of the totem pole" guy.

As before, Bob Heller's car was nowhere in sight—he must have a back door or some side entrance. No one came out to meet us, so we trudged toward the dented side door and yanked it open.

I braced myself, half-expecting guns to be trained on us. But there was nothing. The place was unsecure—casual, inadequate, almost careless. I thought about how reality was often less sinister than it looked, yet somehow more threatening.

"Did we get the time wrong?" asked Bo.

"Did Radford set us up?" I added, sounding panicked. "Is this an ambush?"

Bo reached his hand into his jacket pocket. Until then, I hadn't noticed the weight pulling on it.

"Did you bring the gun?" I asked.

Bo raised his finger to his lips, and I heard someone call, "Over here."

The place still looked like a barn that had been muscled into a warehouse more by determination than design. High rafters, cheap corrugated walls clinging to the timber frame. In the center of a truck bay, five stools formed a kind of council. Heller sat on one; a man and a woman on the next two; the rest were empty, waiting for us. Bo took his hand out of his pocket, and we slowly walked over. I made a point of straightening my back. So did Bo.

As we neared them, Heller stood and, grabbing the cane that leaned against his stool, tottered toward us. He looked the same—a gaunt man dressed more for campfires than cocktails. He stretched out his free hand, palm out, signaling us to stop.

"Arms up, gentlemen," he said, flicking his fingers like he was trying to dislodge something sticky.

"What?" said Bo, his voice betraying his indignation.

"Nothing personal, guys. I gotta check you out. My guests don't know you, and they want to be sure they can talk"—he cocked his head—"openly."

"I've got a .38 in my right pocket," said Bo.

"Okay—just relax," he said. "Take it out with your left and give it to me. I'll give it back when you leave."

Bo handed the gun to Heller, who slipped it into his coat pocket. I stared at the man and woman perched on low-back barstools with metal footrests. They looked out of place in the warehouse—their black clothes, the stools beneath them, the way they sat. I figured the stools were meant for the guys loading and unloading trucks; these two had never moved anything heavier than a suitcase. They looked as divorced from labor as a pair of silk gloves in a machine shop.

Heller handed his cane to me to hold and moved his hands loosely over my frame, patting my pockets, quick and impersonal. He did the same with Bo and stopped at the pen. He pulled it out and studied it. Bo looked annoyed.

"I might take notes," Bo said, and I huffed.

Heller pulled off the cap and drew two ink lines on the back of his hand. Satisfied, he recapped it and slid it back into Bo's shirt pocket.

"I prefer Bic," he said, smirking.

"I'm not surprised," Bo returned.

"This is Wei-Lin Kao-Su and Lian Hua Chen," Heller said, ignoring Bo and extending his hand like a porter. They stayed roosted on their stools, as if climbing up had been punishment enough, and neither wanted to repeat it. We shook hands, nodded, and took our place in the players' circle.

Heller spent a few minutes introducing them.

He noted that Wei-Lin went by Wilton—the English version of his name—"because, as he often says, 'it's just misleading enough for Americans to underestimate me.'"

Both he and Lian came from Rosemead, in the San Gabriel Valley, also known as the Chinese Beverly Hills. Wilton had made his early money in the eighties, when import-export still passed as a legitimate answer to dinner-party questions. He conveyed the relaxed confidence of someone who'd been rich a long time and had never been asked to explain how.

Along with a short, superficial history, Heller pointed out that Lian was Vietnamese, raised in California, and added that her previous Taiwanese boyfriend had been arrested for carrying two million counterfeit California cigarette tax stamps from Xiamen—an odd detail to share, as if he were proud of it.

Heller then turned to Wilton, outlining his activities out of the Long Beach Port complex. That enterprise, compared to the Portland operation, was older, more sophisticated, and far larger. Heller's role there was similar: he provided dock access and a warehouse for unloading and redistributing shipments.

"I live in LA," said Heller. "I come up here only when a shipment is scheduled. My contacts in Long Beach lined me up with the right dock crew up here. We process only two shipments a month."

We listened politely. This was not what I expected or what I had steeled myself for. It felt like a meet-and-greet for eager interns looking to enter the world of global contraband. I kept looking at Bo.

Me: *What the fuck is happening?*

Bo: *How should I know?*

Wilton Kao-Su flashed his eyes between us. His square, fleshy face hinted at the movie-star handsomeness he might've had decades earlier—prominent chin, broad nose, dimpled lines running from eyes to jaw. A wave of black hair swept across his high forehead, and I noticed a thin, perfectly applied layer of makeup on his skin. He wore a loose-fitting black cashmere polo, black khakis with cuffs, and black shoes without socks. Everything about him was soft, feminine, almost maternal. He reminded me of an older Asian woman whose beauty had aged into quiet authority.

Lian Hua Chen, by contrast, was young enough to be his daughter—thin and sharp, with black hair falling to her shoulders, wide-set, inviting eyes, a pointed chin, and red lips stretched over perfect teeth. Her black dress hung from her neck, leaving her shoulders bare and angular, but in a deliberately elegant way. She was a touch flirtatious, letting eye contact linger a second too long, smiling in a way that felt personal. I caught myself thinking that today we'd call her forward rather than a tease.

"Forgive me, Wilton," said Bo finally. "Why are we here? Why did you want to meet with us?"

Heller stopped talking and leaned back while Wilton leaned forward. His voice was as soft as his features.

"I asked Bobby to arrange this visit because I'm looking for good partners," he said. His English was excellent, with only a trace of an accent. "Bobby told me about you. You're businessmen. Your company, Paladin, has just separated from one of its founders—a Russian woman, Natalya Danilenko, who took several major assets with her. You're looking to rebuild. I may provide that opportunity."

"You have excellent sources, Wilton," I said. "Much of that information isn't just recent—it's also confidential."

"People talk," said Lian, in flawless English. She'd clearly grown up here. By *people*, I assumed she meant Radford and Cruz.

"I think there's been a misunderstanding," Bo said. "We're businessmen, but we tend to stay in our lane. And no disrespect, but what you're describing sounds well outside of our comfort zone."

Wilton smiled faintly, more amused than offended. "Comfort is a luxury," he said. "So is staying in one lane." He glanced down at his cuffs and bare ankles. "Yes, it's true. I import restricted product. I bend rules. Bobby assists with that. In my world, these are not moral distinctions. They are logistical ones." He looked back up at us. "But what you're circling is much larger than me. The syndicate I belong to is international. My associates operate at a scale you can't possibly imagine."

He took a beat. Lian looked bored. "The annual market exceeds forty billion dollars."

Bo and I expressed our surprise with raised brows.

"You all get together in board meetings and compare revenue?" I asked, sarcasm gushing unchecked with every word.

Wilton's smile didn't move. "Amateurs brag—professionals measure," he answered.

Lian shifted on her stool and tilted her head toward me. "Those numbers come from government estimates. Black-market contraband. Cigarettes. Alcohol. Pharmaceuticals." Her eyes stayed on mine. "They tend to underestimate."

Wilton nodded once, pleased. "Success is not celebrated loudly," he said. "It's simply … expected." He paused, then added, "People who stay in their lane rarely get to choose where the road leads. People who expand their comfort zone do."

The meeting had slid into the surreal. Bo and I were sitting there, listening to two international smugglers lay out their operation as if it were a corporate pitch, with us as potential investors, complete with a few homespun platitudes about humility and success. Bo paid them the kind of attention he'd give a chirping smoke alarm in an empty building—aware something's wrong, but not convinced it's his problem.

Then Wilton said, "Your former chairman of Paladin, Ms. Danilenko, is a known associate and close friend of Dmitry Chernyshevsky."

Bo and I stiffened. So did Heller. The pause that followed had a gravity that pulled us all forward, leaning into each other.

"Mr. Chernyshevsky was your main investor," said Wilton. "He helped you build Paladin Holdings."

"Is that illegal?" I asked flippantly.

"Certainly not. But you went out of your way to keep it a secret."

"Secret is the wrong word," said Bo. "It implies something criminal. It was *confidential,* which is not *illegal.* And it's what Mr. Chernyshevsky requires in all his transactions."

"I understand," said Wilton. "I mention it because I'm familiar with him—by reputation, not personally—and I was wondering if you could arrange a meeting with him."

And there it was.

Wilton didn't care about us. He wasn't looking to threaten us or recruit us. He wanted access to our former business partner, like a celebrity fan asking an agent for an introduction. With the Russian billionaire backing him, Wilton Kao-Su would have a gateway into Russia—or Europe. Dmitry controlled much of the Russian *vory v zakone*. A nod from him could open markets that would expand Wilton's operation a thousandfold.

I thought about Agent Mueller and the briefing he expected. Should Bo and I tell him that the "top of the totem pole" wasn't some shadowy kingpin but a San Gabriel businessman angling for a backstage pass to our previous benefactor?

It was almost satirical. What this well-fashioned, well-mannered black-market profiteer didn't know—but Bo and I did—was that Dmitry Chernyshevsky tended his world the way a spider tends its web: patient, effortless, and lethal to anyone who mistook civility for safety.

We didn't have to tell the FBI about Wilton's overture, because without even glancing at Bo, I knew we would never do it—not for our sake, but for his.

Heller suddenly stood and, without his cane, limped toward the distant side door we'd come through. His expression tightened, like he'd caught a sound. Before he could reach it, the door slammed open, and Zor's bulk filled the frame, Ming close behind.

"*Blyad!*" Zor roared, his voice rolling the length of the warehouse. "The gang's all here."

Wilton's smile vanished. Lian's eyes went wide. Heller halted mid-step. Bo and I stood stunned, mouths half-open.

They hadn't been invited.

They were intruders.

And just like that, the uneasy tension I'd carried into the meeting—lost somewhere in the comfort of Wilton's mild, mellifluous voice—came roaring back.

CHAPTER THIRTY

The Intruders

THE WAREHOUSE CHANGED the moment Zor and Ming entered it. Our meeting space suddenly felt more like a cage, and we were the next fight on the card. The air thickened. The exits shrank.

Bo and I stood without speaking. The shift in the room was palpable—the kind that happens just before a clash or a confession.

Heller's arms stretched forward, palms extended. Wilton's expression held a note of curious surprise. Lian didn't move at all.

Zor, with Ming behind him, looked comfortable inside the storm he'd clearly come to unleash. He wore a grungy leather jacket zipped halfway, blue jeans, and heavy black boots that looked military. His bony partner had on a gray windbreaker over a black T-shirt, snug black pants, and brown loafers—casual criminal chic.

"All right—everyone, stay put," said Heller, his tone firm but strangely measured. "No one needs to do anything stupid. It's under control."

Control of what? I thought. We hadn't moved an inch.

"I want to meet our new friends," the Mongol said in a low baritone, stepping farther into the bay.

"Stay the fuck where you are," Heller shouted, loud enough to freeze even the rats in the rafters. "Nobody here is your friend." He jabbed a finger at Zor; Ming moved an extra step, flanking him.

"Why are you here?" Heller asked.

"We follow them," Ming said, pointing at Bo and me like that settled the matter.

Zor and Ming crossed the wide bay toward us at a slow and deliberate pace, like they were pushing through water. Wilton's soft lips stretched tight in curious anticipation. Lian stayed completely still, coiled and ready, waiting—a snake before the strike. Bo and I balled our hands into fists.

They brushed past Heller, who wanted to frisk them the way he'd frisked us, but he never got the chance. They stopped three feet in front of us, ignoring Wilton and Lian entirely. Either they were unfamiliar with them, or too familiar, to bother with courtesy.

"Did you T-bone Ming at the warehouse?" Zor asked, eyes locked on Bo.

"Maybe," Bo answered.

"Could've broken his back."

Bo didn't answer. His eyes never left Zor's.

I watched Ming instead. He stood motionless. Expressionless.

"You know me?" Zor continued.

"No," Bo said. "But I've heard of you."

"What did you hear?"

"That you're a dangerous prick."

"Good." Zor's lips curled slightly. "You on our side or not?"

"Is this an interview?" Bo's eyebrows rose slightly.

I stood directly in front of Ming. He was wiry, but I had about twenty pounds on him. I'd have to punch him in the Adam's apple first, then knee him in the balls.

"Either—or," said Zor.

"I'm not," Bo continued, leaning forward just enough.

"That's a problem," Zor said.

"For you, or me?"

Zor's right hand slipped slowly behind his back—everyone saw the move; he wanted us to see it. Heller's eyes narrowed. Despite the limp that tugged at his step, he moved with surprising speed.

He came up behind Zor, drew Bo's .38 from his pocket, and in one fluid motion pressed the barrel into the soft tissue under Zor's chin. Zor, a head taller, went rigid as Heller finished the circle and cocked his wrist, locking the gun in place.

He bared his teeth and snarled. "If you find whatever the fuck you're reaching for, we're gonna find out if your brain matter can reach the rafters."

Slowly, Zor brought his hand forward. There was nothing in it. Heller patted the rest of him down, never moving the barrel from under his chin. From Zor's waistband, he pulled a short, curved blade—a six-inch *bichak* in a worn leather sheath, riding flat along the belt. Heller held it up for a moment, then glanced at Ming and raised an eyebrow.

Ming shook his head. He carried nothing.

"Well," said Lian, her eyes bright with near-delight, "that was interesting."

Heller lowered the .38 but kept it visible. "I'm disappointed in you, Zor," he said. "You know better."

"I would have to agree with Bobby," said Wilton.

"They gave us shit at our last delivery," said Ming. "I cracked a rib. Still hurts."

"Radford told us they would be here tonight," added Zor.

"Did you know they were eager to meet you?" Wilton asked, looking our way.

"We have a regular fan club," I quipped.

Heller retrieved his cane but didn't sit. His nerves were still buzzing. He nodded toward the chair for Zor. Ming took it first.

Bo didn't bother easing into it. "Why'd you kill my brother-in-law?"

Zor didn't hesitate. "I didn't."

Bo looked at Ming.

"Not me."

"You killed Jeff Noble," Bo said.

Zor shrugged. "Should have. Didn't."

"Not me," Ming echoed.

Oddly, they answered with conviction. Either they were excellent liars, or we were still at square one.

"What kind of truck do you drive?" I asked.

"What're you? My mother?" Zor sneered.

"I'm guessing you never had one."

He stepped toward me. Bo slid between us.

"Oooooo," Lian cooed. "I like this—a proper cockfight."

Wilton shot her a look. "Enough. Just answer him, Zor."

"White Ford F-two-fifty," he said.

Ali and Natalie had said the truck was black.

Bo eased back half a step. Not much—but enough.

"You'll have to forgive Zor," Wilton said smoothly. "He's from northern Mongolia. Near the Russian border. Cold country. Wind off Siberia. It breeds a certain … durability."

That explained the Russian. And the Chinese.

He gestured to Zor, then to Ming. "Altan Ganzorig and Zhao Ming were recruited by someone other than me. An administrator out of the American consulate in Shanghai. I was informed after the fact. We met in Los Angeles. My people trained them."

An operative at the US consulate.

Mueller would salivate.

"You've got diversity covered, I'll give you that." I nodded to each in turn—Chinese, Mongolian, Vietnamese, American.

"I can see why this feels confusing," Wilton continued. "Our network is complex. The US isn't even among our top three markets. China comes first. Then Russia. That's why I want to meet your friend—Mr. Chernyshevsky."

"You're telling them too much," Zor said.

Wilton didn't argue. "What would you suggest we do?"

Zor's answer came fast. "Kill them. Burn their house down while they sleep."

Ming smiled approvingly.

Bo took a step forward. "You come near my family, and I *will* break your back."

Heller moved instantly, the .38 back up. "That's enough, Bishop."

"Then tell your dog to stop barking."

Wilton exhaled, almost patiently. "Gentlemen, Zor is simply clarifying our problem. Your chain of stores moves serious volume. Losing it will create gaps he won't enjoy filling."

"You run a business," I said. "Nobody wants an unhappy vendor in the mix. Tension. Constant worry that they'll screw things up. Adapt. Partners change. Supply lines shift. Find another distributor. Someone who'll actually appreciate the bonus to their bottom line."

Lian cocked her head at Zor. "How long would you need?"

"Maybe two months," he said.

Bo looked at Wilton. "We can live with that." I knew Bo was figuring that in two months, they'd all be in jail.

"Will it affect anything else?" asked Lian. "Our other shipment?"

Zor leaned forward. "What other shipment?"

Wilton's voice sharpened. "Nothing to do with you."

What other shipment? Another nugget for Mueller.

Zor scowled. "I don't trust 'em. They'll sniff around. Talk to the Feds. We need insurance."

"Zor's concern is legit," Wilton said mildly.

"We're not here to wreck anything," Bo lied. "We just want to clean our house and rebuild. I don't care if some idiot smokes a shitty cigarette occasionally. I just want to find the dirtbag that killed my brother-in-law and almost killed our daughters. That's it. Leave us alone, and we'll stay out of your way."

Zor huffed. "Bullshit. I say we put them down."

I didn't raise my voice. "We can hear you, asshole."

Zor closed the distance. Two slow steps.

Heller blocked him, solid as an oak door. "Not now."

I didn't move. I wanted him to see I wasn't impressed.

"I trust them," Wilton said. "They built their company with Dmitry Chernyshevsky. They understand discretion."

"Dmitry who?" Zor started.

"You don't need to know," Wilton cut in. "It means they're not interested in us."

"Not interested in making a citizens' arrest," added Lian with a smile.

"I'd still rather bury them," Zor muttered.

I smiled thinly. "Still hearing you."

The argument sagged into an ugly hum. Threats lose their edge when you repeat them. Wilton and Heller seemed to agree. Lian looked entertained.

We stood. Bo reached out to Heller, and Heller let the .38 drop neatly into his hand. Zor froze—not because of the gun, but because now it was Bo holding it.

"I don't want to see either of you again," Bo said, looking at Zor and Ming.

Nobody had a comment.

We backed toward the exit, careful, eyes locked, and didn't turn around until the door was closed.

We got in the car.

"That Mongol asshole won't let this lie," I said, adrenaline pumping.

"I know," Bo answered.

"Mueller won't be able to put him away. He doesn't have enough on him." I felt the words scrape my gut. "He'll be a threat to us forever."

"I'm not so sure," Bo said.

"Heller said, 'Not now' to him when he came at me. What's that mean? Later? Alone? Asleep? With our families?"

Adrenaline ramping.

I could feel the tough guy inside me trying to punch his way out.

"Maybe I have to put the bastard down—and his mutt."

My voice went flat. Adrenaline now mainlining fury into my brain.

"Stop it, Marty," Bo said. "You're getting stupid."

"I'll put a bullet through his head the way I did Vasili," I hissed.

"Jesus Christ, Marty—shut the fuck up. Just stop." Bo gunned the engine, gravel spitting. He steered one-handed and slapped his chest with the other like he needed to cough.

"You having a heart attack?" I asked.

He kept hitting his chest and hacked. "Just stop talking already."

"I mean it, Bo," I pushed. Rage muscling out reason. "I shot Vasili through his fucking eyes. Natalya will help me dump their bodies—like she did before. She knows what needs to be done. Jesus—I killed her nephew, and she still slept with me. She's good that way. I'll need to borrow your rifle. I'll bury that Mongolian motherfucker next to Vasili Bobrov and call it a day."

"Shut up!" Bo screamed. He yanked the gold pen from his shirt pocket and threw it out the window, wild-eyed.

And then everything narrowed.

The pen.

It wasn't just a pen.

Bo was wired.

CHAPTER THIRTY-ONE

The Wire

CONFESSION, WHEN IT ISN'T PRIVATE, BECOMES EXPOSURE—one of my rules.

And in that instant, I'd broken it spectacularly.

I sat next to Bo, listening to the two of us pant from our rhetorical sprint. I heard my own voice, furious and foolish, replaying in my head. The car felt smaller than it should, the air damp and heavy, almost humid, every word settling on me like mist turning to sweat. Nothing had changed, and yet everything had. I couldn't move, couldn't think clearly, and for the first time in a long while, I understood the cost of words that could never be taken back.

"What happens now?" I asked in a tone stripped of emotion.

"I don't know," said Bo, hesitating, and then slammed his fist on the steering wheel. "Goddamnit! I just don't know."

We said nothing for several miles. The sun had set, and we headed toward the city shrouded in gloam. Bo drove slowly, staying in the right lane. Cars passed us, and I tried to recall the last time that had happened. His expression was so stiff and controlled it reminded me—fittingly—of how he looked right after I killed Vasili.

"Why were you wearing a wire?" I finally blurted the obvious.

"Mueller asked me to."

"And did he tell you not to tell me?"

"No." He took a deep breath. "I did."

"What the …" I started.

"Back up, Marty," he said, presenting the palm of his right hand. "Remember when I told you the FBI wanted to meet with us, and I said, 'Wait till you hear why?' Well, Mueller called me—not just to tell me about meeting the top guy with Heller, but also to ask if we would both wear a wire."

I twisted sideways into my door and stared hard at Bo's profile. "Okay."

"I told him I'd wear the wire, but you shouldn't, and he shouldn't ask you to."

"Why?"

"Because you tell Natalya everything. You can't keep your mouth shut around her. It's a damn disease. I figured you couldn't be trusted."

"You've never said that to me."

"And I never thought I would."

We drove in silence another mile. More cars passed us.

"You could have told me today, a couple of hours ago, when we drove to the barn—before going in. You could have said, 'I'm wearing a wire, so don't say anything stupid.' Did you think I was going to slip away and call Natalya? Let her know you're playing Maxwell Smart?"

"That's harsh. James Bond is the better analogy."

"It's not funny, Bo."

"It's a little funny."

More silence. Our friendship had suffered a serious rupture. Neither of us knew where it would lead.

"Please tell me you didn't tell Mueller about Natalya," I said, striking my head into the headrest.

"No. I just told him you're not good with secrets."

"Christ, Bo. That's a shitty thing to tell an FBI agent."

"Yeah—he dislikes you even more now."

"You think Mueller will call us?"

"I don't know anything, Marty. But if he does call, he'll likely call me. I'm his new boy."

"Where was he? I saw nothing near the barn. No car, no van, not even a bicycle."

"Don't know that either. He said the pen had a half-mile range. He has a team. They could've been in the surrounding woods or a side road on the other side of the freeway."

"You think they heard my tirade?"

"Marty—the f'ing dead heard your tirade."

"What do I do?"

"I told you to stop talking."

"I was on a fucking roll, dammit. Why would I stop talking? Why would I think your pen was a wire? Even Heller didn't catch it—he tested the damn thing, fingered it like he was gonna steal it, scribbled on his hand with it—*for Christ's sake*."

"I know. I nearly crapped my pants."

"I'll call Mueller tomorrow. I'll tell him I was just spouting nonsense."

"You're not calling anyone. Right now, Vasili Bobrov is just a name. There's no body, no police reports, no missing persons reports. Nothing."

"Bo—it's the *F-B-I*."

"You're paranoid again. It's your nature. We don't even know if they heard anything. Maybe the signal was weak. Maybe all they got was static. We say nothing unless they bring it up. Until then, we don't know what they're talking about."

"And if they bring it up?"

"We cross that bridge when we come to it—*if* we come to it."

I tried again to remember exactly what I'd said—my chest-thumping rant, my macho soliloquy, my inner assassin. What a royal screw-up. I imagined my reckless words, printed on a folded piece of paper, passed silently from jury to judge. *Guilty as charged.*

Bo dropped me off at home. Typically, we would have gone to a bar and had a scotch and talked about the motley crew of gangsters we'd just dealt with. But things had changed, and we instinctively knew it. It was still early in the night. Our houses were empty, our families gone, and we both wanted nothing more than distance between us. I thought about how sometimes the strongest friendships can also be the most fragile.

"I'll call you if I hear anything," said Bo as I exited the car.

"If I don't answer, call back later. I was probably telling secrets to Natalya."

I slammed the door.

CHAPTER THIRTY-TWO

The Department of Justice

OVER THE DAYS THAT FOLLOWED, I talked only to Abbie and the kids. I called in the morning and again at night. The rest of the time, I walked Boomer and sat in the TV room, flipping channels with the mute on. Boomer and I had lengthy discussions about politics, friendships, and betrayal. He wasn't much of a talker, but I could tell by his eyes that, except for politics, he agreed with me. I ignored calls from work. Bo didn't call either. We have an instinct for distance—we both know when to keep it.

I didn't dare tell Abbie about anything that had happened. It had all erupted in that insane outburst, and the thought of her ever learning of it filled me with a terror greater than anything else—including the constant, malignant shadow of Zor and Ming.

Finally, Bo texted me to say he was going to call. It was an odd gesture—usually he'd just call—and I couldn't tell if it meant we were on the mend or the opposite.

"Mueller called," he said after a perfunctory greeting. "Something's clearly up."

I skipped any preamble and went straight for the bleeding wound. "Did he say anything about the wire? What had he heard?"

"Marty, Jesus Christ. Slow down. I told you, I won't bring it up unless they do. You, too. Don't draw attention to it. Pray they either heard nothing, or didn't understand it if they did."

"Easy for you to say. It's not your life—or your marriage—on the line."

"Stop feasting on fear, Marty. Your ghosts will kill you."

"It's because you set them loose, Bo."

"We can fight about it for an hour, or we can talk about the meeting with Mueller."

"What meeting?"

"Mueller wants us at the Multnomah County Court building at 10 a.m. tomorrow."

"About?"

"Didn't say. Just said if we want to bring an attorney, we could."

"You're serious."

"Afraid so."

"They heard it all," I said. "I'm totally fucked."

Bo didn't answer. He didn't have to.

///

We hit the steps of the Hatfield Courthouse, a block-long tower that made every other building downtown look small, well before our scheduled time. Revolving doors swallowed us into a lobby so polished it could've doubled as a showroom for marble. The air carried the chill of formality. A guard waved us toward the metal detectors. Bags scanned, IDs checked, we slid toward the elevators. Seven floors up was the US Attorney's office. Key cards and escorts only. I let my eyes roam the shrinking lobby below. It looked like the kind of place where a confession on a wire could echo long after you'd left.

On the seventh floor, another guard checked our names off a clipboard and handed us badges on lanyards reading "Guest – Rose Smoke Task Force." We were directed down a long, narrow corridor—the length of a basketball court—to the double doors at the end. Our escort looked like a high school student doing a summer internship. Halfway along, a wooden door bore a bronze Department of Justice seal and the words *"United States Attorney, District of Oregon."*

"I'm officially nervous now," I whispered.

"You and me both."

We came to the double doors and knocked. Someone inside yelled, "Enter," and I swung the door open.

Both Bo and I leaned back as the room slammed into us. It was packed—almost a dozen people: suits, uniforms, tactical polos, each with a badge clipped to a belt or hanging from a bead chain. Some wore empty holsters at their hips or shoulders, dark, intimidating barnacles suggesting their guns were close. Sleeves were rolled. Jackets lay abandoned over chair backs. Styrofoam coffee cups crowded the long conference table, some full, some empty, none of them anonymous.

Along the side wall, a rolling cart stood loaded with coffee dispensers, lined up like sentinels beside boxes of bear claws, donuts, and muffins. Above it hung a giant mid-century pictorial map of Oregon, bright and optimistic, presiding over a room that was neither. At the far end, between an American flag and an Oregon State flag, a whiteboard still rocked slightly, as if it had just been spun around—evidence we were late to something already in motion.

It felt like we'd suddenly stepped onto a stage with an audience waiting for our performance. Bo and I had worn suits that morning, expecting to confer with someone important. We were overdressed. No one spoke. The door clicked shut behind us. I caught the faint smell of baked goods and stress.

Whatever this was, it wasn't just a meeting—it was destabilizing.

A tall man near the head of the table stood, lifted his arms, and said, "Ah, you're here." He glanced at the clock above the doors behind us and added, "And on time. Fantastic," as if that were a rare thing. Black wavy hair cut in a 1950s style, a chiseled square face—the very definition of clean-cut. His white shirt sleeves were rolled to the elbows. No gun, no badge, just authority radiating from every pore. He looked like he'd fallen out of an FBI recruitment brochure.

"Mr. Bishop, Mr. Schott," he said, crossing the room with an easy stride. "Derek Hayward, deputy assistant director, FBI. I oversee the bureau's criminal investigative division." He shook Bo's hand first, then mine—firm, not cocky. "Please—call me Derek. Mind if I call you Bo and Marty?"

We nodded, still trying to absorb what was happening.

He guided us toward two empty chairs at our end of the table—the only clear space left. Each seat had a notepad and a pen.

"Before we get started, I'll ask everyone to introduce themselves," he said in a calm, steady tone, clearly used to rooms filled with people who answered to him. He walked back to his seat at the far end, stayed standing, and said, "Let's keep it short—name and agency, please," nodding to his left.

"Evelyn Price, US Secret Service."

"Marcus Keane, ATF."

"Rosa Delgado, Homeland Security."

"Tom Irons, Customs and Border Protection."

"Claire Bouchard, RCMP."

"Excuse me," I interrupted. "Did you say RCMP—as in Royal Canadian Mounted Police?"

"The same," she answered, her voice carrying a slight French-Canadian lilt.

Bo hesitated. He was next. "Uh—Bo Bishop—Paladin Holdings."

Then me. "Marty Schott, Paladin Holdings."

"John Kunitzer, Multnomah County DA."

"Autumn Flener, Multnomah County deputy DA."

"Linda Barrett, captain, Portland Police."

"George Mueller, FBI." Half smile. "We know each other."

Derek looked around. "All right. Now that we've got names to faces, let's get to why you're here."

I can't speak for Bo—I didn't even dare look his way—but I felt like a beetle trapped in a jar. Never in my life had I sat at a table stacked with so much firepower. I set my pen down. My notes looked like wriggling worms. I pinched my bladder, hoping it would hold. My hands shook.

"Five days ago," Derek started. "You were involved in an FBI operation code-named Rose Smoke at our Rivergate District warehouse."

He paused, knowing the word *our* hit us like a slap.

"I want to apologize for that. It should never have happened. It seriously violated bureau policy. Civilians are not placed inside a live federal investigation." He took a breath and scanned the room. "That decision was … misguided … to say the least. The personnel responsible have been reassigned and are no longer attached to this task force."

I noted that Agent Cho was not in the room.

Derek sat, put both elbows on the table, and shifted his tone from formal to friendly. "You two were put at risk—without informed consent—and without legal authority. That's unacceptable, and I'm here to fix it." He nodded at George Mueller. "Agent Mueller has been reassigned to lead the task force moving forward."

"It was Agent Mueller who asked us to participate," I said, confused.

"Yes," Derek answered, "and he opposed the operational decision to include you. He was forced to comply by his SAC—Special Agent in Charge. I've reassigned the SAC."

"Where? To Alaska?" I asked.

A suppressed snicker rippled through the room.

"No," said Director Derek with a thin grin. "Biloxi."

"I did three months at Keesler Air Force Base, just outside Biloxi," I said. "Air Traffic Control school."

"How unfortunate for you," said Derek, grin intact.

"I got shipped to Vietnam right after."

"Probably to make up for Biloxi," he replied. The room went from a snicker to a full laugh.

"Agent Cho?" asked Bo.

"A little too enthusiastic about the policy breach," Derek said. "Returned to Quantico for remedial training."

"Can I get some coffee?" I asked before the humor thoroughly drained.

Agent Mueller jumped out of his chair toward the airpots, asking, "Milk?"

"Yes," said Bo, indicating one for himself.

Derek watched him go, then turned his attention back to us. "How much do you know about tobacco smuggling?"

"Only what a few lowlifes have told us," answered Bo.

Derek leaned back, folding his hands in front of him. He looked almost regal with the two flags framing him.

"It's a white-collar crime with blue-collar logistics," he said. "All the product is manufactured overseas. Nothing domestic. Ninety percent comes from China. The rest from North Korea. One syndicate alone managed to funnel a billion sticks into Los Angeles and New Jersey."

"A billion cigarettes!" The words fell out of my mouth.

"Yes," he said. "In the trade, they're called loosies or sticks."

I saw Bo's eyebrows rise, like he was calculating just how many cartons that would be.

"Same in Europe. Eighty percent of their counterfeit supply comes from the same sources. In 2001, Chinese shops were turning out eight different Marlboro knockoffs. According to PMI, counterfeiters later ramped that up—producing tailored versions for about sixty different markets. I mean, down to the tax stamps, regional health warnings, and country codes. Everything tailored to fool regulators and consumers."

"And the Chinese don't stop it?" Bo asked. "Doesn't it screw up their market as well?"

Derek nodded to the woman sitting next to him. I looked at my notes. Evelyn, US Secret Service. She leaned forward. "The largest market for counterfeits is China. It's so big there that many Chinese prefer fakes to the real thing. They've gotten used to the taste."

Derek jumped in, "These damn things aren't just fakes, they emit eighty percent more nicotine and carbon monoxide, and carry crap like insect eggs and feces."

"And they taste it," I added, bringing back the cynical vibe from before. "Are we feeling bad for smokers now?"

"I used to smoke like a street hooker between johns," said Evelyn. "Thank God for nicotine patches." She smiled and continued with her insight. "To understand where it starts, follow the trail to Yunxiao."

I frowned. "Yunxiao?"

"Small town in China," she continued. "Most factories are underground, beneath ordinary buildings. Even the village temple hides a factory below. The mountains around the town are high, and government oversight is minimal. Local officials can be bought—sometimes for as little as a few thousand bucks."

I gulped my coffee. It was too strong. Mueller hadn't put in enough milk.

"It's more than business," she said, almost reverently. "It's a brotherhood. Only families with roots in Yunxiao are allowed into production. Territories are divided and fiercely respected. Families don't compete; they cooperate."

The RCMP woman spoke up. I looked at my notes, Claire Bouchard. "Once the cigarettes leave Yunxiao, the distribution network goes global. Anywhere with a strong Chinese migration, you'll find them. Major hubs are New York, Vancouver, Le Havre, Valencia, Hamburg, Rotterdam."

Bo tilted his head. "Rotterdam?"

"Yes," she said, a faint French accenting her words. "It's one of their key ports in Europe. And the people running it … not amateurs." She paused, then lowered her voice a notch. "Take someone like

Altan Ganzorig. Mongolian by birth, but part of the Fujian diaspora. Raised in Rotterdam, speaks half a dozen languages fluently. Knows the ports, routes, and shipping lines. He's been around the network for years."

"We're familiar with him," Bo said. "Goes by Zor, and has a Chinese sidekick named Ming."

"Bo and I think they're responsible for killing Tadeo Ramírez and Jeff Noble," I added. "Not to mention scaring the shit out of our daughters by playing bumper cars with them."

"We've all read the reports," said Derek.

Rosa from Homeland Security took the floor. "Zor and Ming have been monitored for years. Everything points to organized smuggling and related criminal activity, but there's never been any evidence connecting them to violent acts—no homicides, no assaults, no use of lethal force."

"Bullshit," spat Bo. "You just haven't caught them. Those cretinous fuckers killed my brother-in-law. I'm sure of it."

A dozen eyes snapped to Derek—maybe swearing in a room with this much rank was like throwing a match.

"Jeff Noble told us they threatened to kill his daughter. He sent her to Europe. They threatened us—twice. You need to get them off the street," I said, remembering the rant I'd let rip over the live wire.

"Or what?" said Police Captain Linda Barrett.

"Why are you looking at me?" My voice pushed up a full notch. "You're the police. Do something about it. My whole family's holed up in Michigan because these two assholes said they'd hurt them if we didn't cooperate." Rage boiled up and I stood, chest tight, words firing out of me. "Figure it out, for Christ's sake."

Derek stood when I did, pointed his finger at my head, and said firmly, "Sit down, Mr. Schott."

Bo pulled at my suit jacket. I sank back, breathing heavily.

"We heard your intentions. You've been very clear about them," he said.

And there it was.
The wire *was* hot.

CHAPTER THIRTY-THREE

Operation Rose Smoke

FOR A MINUTE, THE ROOM HUNG IN STASIS. Images captured in a photograph. The only movement came from dust motes drifting like smoke in sunlight. A dozen people, all locked in a mutual knowledge recursion—I know … that you know … that I know.

The quiet was the kind that made me reconsider speaking.

"So, what happens now?" I asked softly, afraid of my own voice.

"We're shutting it down," said Derek, his full bravado in effect. "The operation. It's getting to be a problem."

"Wait, what?" said Bo, suddenly. "The *operation*. It's getting to be a *problem*. That doesn't sound like something we brought to you just a few weeks ago."

People started to play nervously with their pens, doodling.

"Hmmm … yes," said Derek. "Are you gentlemen willing to sign some paperwork before you leave? If not, I'm not authorized to proceed. If yes, we can continue."

"I already carried a wire for you to meet with a guy who runs a global smuggling network," said Bo. "Why wouldn't I sign some papers?"

"Ditto," I added.

"It's just a cooperation and confidentiality agreement. It lays out roles and risks, and ensures you won't talk to the press." He looked squarely at me. "It won't stop a court, however, or a subpoena, or an investigation. Given all the eyes we've got on this"—he searched for a word—"fuckup, we need to be sure to dot all the I's and cross all the T's."

"Director, I can give a brief overview," said newly promoted Agent Mueller, who'd been a sphinx up to that point.

Derek nodded.

"We've had this syndicate under investigation now for over a year. We've had Corner24 under surveillance well before Ganzorig and Ming put the squeeze on Mr. Noble several months ago. We've had you and Paladin Holdings under review since that time."

My bladder began to hurt.

"We've got extensive documentation on you, your company, and your investment partners. You are not, however, under investigation. This task force, code-named Rose Smoke, is focused on the contraband cigarette trade, not on the specific activities of Corner24 or Paladin Holdings."

"Rose Smoke?" I scoffed. "Should have called it Dead Smoke— it's more appropriate."

"The FBI doesn't like to use fatalistic words in its code names," said Derek. "Most of the cases end up in court, and judges hate fatalistic-sounding names—they can prejudice the jury."

"Well, there *is* that," I replied.

"We knew who you were when you called to make an appointment," Mueller continued. "Agent Cho and I were assigned to interview you, but we already had most of what you told us—everything except your daughters being attacked."

"Jesus H. Christ," Bo whispered.

"Our job was to ensure you didn't compromise the operation, and that our suspects remained unaware. The investigation is almost wrapped up, so your part was supposed to be quick—just a brief interlude. We were supposed to manage the disruption and move on."

"We were the *hiccup*," clarified Bo.

"In a manner of speaking," said Derek.

Mueller nodded toward the police captain. "Captain Barrett has been with the task force since day one. When Detective Adams entered his homicide report on your brother-in-law, she flagged it for us, and we asked her to allocate extra resources. When his follow-up came in, logging Jeff Noble as an apparent suicide, we pulled Adams off the case and assigned our team to provide protective surveillance for your family."

"You've been watching us?" I asked.

"Yes. It's how I know your dog went to the emergency vet at two in the morning." He paused. "I trust he's bounced back."

Suddenly, I felt a warm liking for Agent Mueller.

"You've had eyes on Zor and Ming?" Bo asked the police captain.

"Yes and no," she said. "We don't have the resources for continuous coverage, but we run spot checks, share intel across agencies, and collect CI reports—that kind of observation net."

"Rose Smoke also has UC assets in the field providing intel."

"And you got nothing on Zor and Ming murdering Tadeo or Noble?" Bo pressed.

Mueller leaned in, patient, like he was explaining a homework assignment to one of his kids. "That's the point, Bo. We know where they both were the night Tadeo was shot, the morning Noble was found hanging, and the afternoon your daughters were sideswiped. They weren't anywhere near any of it. We're confident. In Tadeo's case, they were under direct UC surveillance."

"UC?"

"Undercover."

Bo stared at his notepad. "Then who killed Tadeo? Why?"

"We're pretty sure it ties back to the smuggling," Captain Barrett said. "Your brother-in-law started digging, and somebody shut him down."

"Radford and Cruz?" I suggested.

"They're on our radar," Mueller said, "but there's no history of violence."

"Jesus! George!" I exclaimed. "These guys are scum—they define the word. Look up *scum* in Webster's and their photos appear."

"Marty," Derek said, "scum's a moral judgment, not an evidentiary one. Calling someone scum is therapy. It's not probable cause."

"If scum were chargeable," Barrett added, "we'd need bigger prisons."

I sat back in surrender. They'd made their point.

"Heller—Bob Heller?" asked Bo, not willing to let it go. "He's got a bum leg, but he could have done it."

"Naw … we're pretty sure it's not Heller," answered Derek. "It's not his style."

"But they're all getting arrested for *something*—right?" said Bo, frustrated.

"Them and a whole bunch more," said Derek.

"It's not just about contraband cigarettes," said the man who had been silent until now. He sat between Rosa from Homeland Security and Claire from the RCMP. Bo and I looked at our notepads. Tom Irons, Customs and Border Protection. Big guy. Big hands. Knuckles like doorknobs. Perfect name for the job.

"The network also moves *yaotouwan*—what the Chinese call 'shake-head pills.' Ecstasy. Manufactured in Amsterdam, routed through Montreal, moved across the northern border, distributed in Los Angeles. We're also seeing crystal meth in the pipeline."

"Talking to Wilton and Heller," I interjected, "I got the impression they were only into fake cigarettes. Drugs were too messy and not worth the risk."

"It was Jeff Noble who told us that," Bo reminded me.

Derek leaned forward, hands steepled. "You're missing the larger picture. The value here isn't a bunch of bad cigarettes." He paused for effect. "It's the apparatus. Once a smuggling network is built, staffed, paid, insulated, and invisible, it becomes priceless. You can move anything through it: drugs, cash, people, weapons. The product doesn't matter." His eyes scanned the table. "We don't care about what's moving *through* the pipe. We care about the *pipe*."

Tom jumped back in.

"This pipeline starts in China, moves through Singapore, and Dubai. Container origins are masked, and shipments can linger at sea for up to three months. Manifests declare the contents as wicker furniture, toys, or rugs—the rugs are used to move the money."

"Let's not get into that right now," Derek said, cutting him off. I could see Tom had let a cat out of the bag—maybe just a kitten— but Derek made sure the bag was resealed before any other critters escaped.

Derek glanced at the wall clock above the door, then checked his wristwatch as if he couldn't believe the time.

"Marty, Bo, I'm going to have to cut this meeting short. This team still has a lot to do, and I have a plane to catch this evening. You'll need to sign some paperwork, and Agent Mueller wants to speak with you privately, as does Deputy District Attorney Flener. I appreciate you coming in, letting us explain the situation, and allowing me to thank you personally for your assistance in the investigation."

He came around and shook both our hands. "I also need to ask you to stay out of this investigation and your company until we've made the necessary arrests and can make sure it's safe for you and your family."

"When can we ask them to come back from Michigan?" I asked.

"Not until Agent Mueller says so. He will serve as your liaison."

"Will they continue to receive protection?" Bo asked.

"Yes, until the operation concludes. There are details I can't discuss right now—you'll learn them soon enough—but until Rose Smoke is closed, your family will remain in Michigan."

"Can we go join them there?"

"From the FBI's perspective, yes. I can't speak for Deputy DA Flener."

I looked at her. She had been so silent I'd almost forgotten she was there. Her features were striking, classical, with deep-set eyes and a sharp, straight nose that cut her face with perfect precision. Her hair was pulled into a tight bun, the color somewhere between brown and blond.

I nodded, and she returned it. Agent Mueller leaned in and whispered something to her that sounded like, *"I'll bring them to you,"* then steered us toward the door, arms out like a parent herding children.

Once we were in the long corridor, Mueller said, in a total non sequitur, "I never thought Director Hayward would ever approve this—maybe someone leaned on him."

"What?" I asked.

"You'll see," he said, opening a door marked with the DOJ seal. He guided us to a small room just off the reception area. A single metal table and a few chairs sat under bleached light. It looked like an interrogation room from a cop movie.

Mueller stepped in first. We followed … and that's when I saw him.

A man leaned casually against the wall beside the door, hidden 'til I stepped inside. My jaw went slack. I checked his wrists instinctively. No cuffs. No chains.

"You've been arrested," I blurted, eyes locked on his face.

"Sadly … no," he said calmly.

Bo glanced at Mueller, waiting for an explanation.

Mueller's eyes danced between us. "You've met—Bob Heller.

They shook hands."FBI agent—Bob Heller."

CHAPTER THIRTY-FOUR

The Sting

IN BO-SPEAK, MY BRAIN DUMPED THE CLUTCH and stripped the gears. I'd been blindsided before—more times than I cared to count—but this wasn't shock. This was rewrite-your-entire-reality-in-under-a-second shock.

The mental whiplash from criminal to cop hit so hard I had to plant both hands on the small metal table to stay upright.

Bo pulled out a chair and slumped into it, running a hand through his hair.

"Jesus Christ," he whispered.

"Fuck me," I added.

"Yeah," said Heller. "I get that a lot."

"We never pull UCs out of the field," said Mueller, taking a seat at the table. "But when the D.A.D. flies in and wants to talk to everyone involved, we break protocol. When Bob learned you were going to attend, he insisted on speaking to you."

"You wanna hug?" I muttered.

Heller grinned. "Hayward didn't want me in the briefing. Too much interagency clusterfucking. Plus, I'm still livin' the lie. So they gave me this room."

"Lucky us," said Bo, mirroring my sarcasm.

"I wanted the opportunity to clarify a few things."

I immediately thought of my rant and intuitively understood what he meant. "Yeah, I should do the same."

I sat next to Bo, and Heller sat next to Mueller. For the first time, I noticed his ID in a clear plastic sleeve, swinging slightly from a black lanyard around his neck. He'd traded his retro lumberjack look for a more formal "meet-the-boss" version. The plaid shirt still fit snugly, the pearl-front snaps gleaming like tiny moons. The jeans were cleaner, the belt newer, and his cane absent—although the limp remained, a reminder that some truths held firm.

"I've been working this crew for about three years now," he said. "You guys tripped into it just as it was coming to a head."

Mueller jumped in, catching the earlier contradiction. "Rose Smoke has been active just under a year, like the director explained, but the larger smuggling operation in Los Angeles and other ports has been running much longer."

"Nobody wanted the network to expand," Heller said. "Too many moving parts. Our focus has always been on mapping its structure— its sources, internal hierarchy, and the who and the what. So, when Wilton decided to open a small node in Portland, I volunteered to be the point man here as well as in Long Beach. That way, we conserve resources and still gather the intel."

Bo sat straight. His eyes told me he'd had an epiphany. "Rose Smoke isn't an investigation into smuggling. It's a sting. A full-scale undercover takedown."

Mueller didn't flinch. "I thought that was obvious."

"No, it wasn't," Bo said. "Marty and I thought we were handing *you* the smuggling case. We didn't hand you shit. You delivered this package to *our* door, and our gremlins happily opened it. We thought you were investigating contraband cigarettes, and the associated murders of Jeff and Tadeo, but that's not your gig at all." He pointed at Heller. "You're running the warehouse because it's a bureau front. Wilton thinks you're bribing customs and the port crews, but they're probably bureau. You're a cat toying with rodents—baiting them."

Bo's epiphany became mine. "*Our* gremlins—Noble, Radford, Cruz, Johnson, the other flunkies—have no clue they've been folded into an FBI sting. We bought a clean company, and then it got swallowed up by *your* operation. We're not being investigated because we're suspects. We're being investigated because we're collateral."

Mueller and Heller exchanged a look. Neither spoke. Perhaps they were starting to regret our little get-together.

"Is Bob Heller your real name?" I asked.

"No … Bob is. I like to keep things as close to real as possible …" he trailed off.

"How in hell does an average guy like you get close to a Chinese smuggler like Wilton Kao-Su?" asked Bo.

"He trusts round eyes more than Asians. Don't ask me why. It's weird but true."

"Why meet with us?" I asked. "You told Radford to bring us in that first time."

"Because you came out of nowhere and were one spark away from torching three years of my life," he said. "You scared the shit out of me. The op's almost over. One last piece to lock down. You two appear suddenly, and I thought you'd create enough friction to make Wilton twitch. Maybe piss off Zor, or worse, get him arrested. I needed to see if I could get you to back off without blowing my cover."

"That explains all the '*they're gonna kill you*' crap," I said.

"If Tadeo hadn't been shot, we wouldn't know any of this. We would have slept through it and showed up one morning with the entire Corner24 management team arrested for tobacco smuggling."

Mueller frowned and nodded his head. "That would be true."

"And Tadeo's killer would—what? Get away with it?" Bo asked.

"Zor and Ming were with me that night. In the warehouse, fixing a stamp machine. I don't come to Portland often, but chance put us together that night. I've got the tapes to prove it." Heller shrugged. "They talk tough, but I've never seen them go hands-on."

"Bob, in our meeting, you said it was probably them," I said.

"I lied. It's what undercover agents do. I figured they were scary enough to get you to back down—to keep you from doing something stupid. I hoped PPB would find the perp and get you to focus elsewhere."

"Zor pulled a knife on me," Bo said deliberately.

Heller exhaled. "Tried to—but yeah, that was a fiasco. I'm trying to keep the op open long enough to catch a specific shipment. Wilton hears something's going sideways in Portland. I'm not feeding him comforting news, so he calls Ganzorig—which he never does. He hates him more than you do. But two people are dead, and two others …" he pointed at us, "… are strangers.

"Zor tells him what he knows. Wilton does some checking—he's got serious reach—Chinese and North Korean intelligence. He finds out about your silent partner—the oligarch. I don't know much about him, but Wilton gets excited. You guys are sudden celebrities, and he wants a 'meet-and-greet.'"

Heller shook his head, shifted his butt, and grimaced. "Believe me, the last thing I wanted was you anywhere near Wilton. I called Mueller, and he said, 'No way.' But Wilton was about to go around me—have Zor and Ming use Radford and Cruz to set it up. If that happened, we'd be blind to the discussion."

Mueller picked up the thread. "I went to my SAC. The guy who's now in Biloxi. He'd already approved keeping you two local instead of flying you to Michigan—thought disappearing you would spook the targets. I was against it, but Cho pushed me to loop him in. The SAC doesn't just approve it—he thinks it's a great opportunity. The warehouse is ours—wired like a recording studio. But there are dead zones, so I was told to fix you up with a wire."

Mueller shot a brief glance at me—Bo's warning about not connecting me didn't need repeating.

"We set up two sites. Surveillance van about two hundred yards out and a foot team in the brush."

"I had an earpiece, full comms with both teams," said Heller.

"But they're telling me they're not getting audio from the pen—zero signal."

My heart stuttered. *It wasn't working.*

"So, I improvised the frisk," Heller continued. "I don't frisk people—I was trying to kick the pen on. Then you said you're carrying a .38—my earpiece nearly detonated. Everyone started yelling. I told them all to relax. I wasn't talking to you. I was talking to agents who were seconds from storming the castle."

"And the pen?" I asked, fingers crossed under the table.

"The cap wasn't secure. It needs to click into place to turn on. It worked fine."

Shit.

"And when Zor and Ming showed up?" asked Bo.

"We saw them coming," said Mueller. "The gravel spat up a cloud. We told Heller."

I remembered how Bob had started for the door well before they'd come in.

"Everything I said was for the benefit of the cover team. They had no eyes inside the warehouse, only ears. They were going nuts. When Zor got too close, I pulled your gun on him to let everyone know I had it under control. The SAC was freaking out. He kept yelling in my ear to shut it down. Make an excuse. Set the goddamn place on fire if necessary. He knew it would be reported, and his job was on the line. No one expected Zor and Ming to show up. Even if I know they're probably not dangerous, the SAC doesn't. For him, the big opportunity went from manageable to intolerable in a second."

"So, when you said, '*Not now*' to Zor …" I started.

"I wasn't talking to him," he said. "I was talking to the agents about to breach the door—armed with M4s."

"But why all the bad movie dialogue from the Mongol? All that, 'We need to bury these guys?'" asked Bo.

"Probably how he's survived all his life—empty threats. He

plays the bad guy. Pretends he'll eat your liver off the floor. It scares civilians and gets compliance. Maybe he *is* a monster—I don't know. He's never had to prove it to me. From what I've seen, he's a barking Rottweiler: loud and scary as shit, but not a biter."

"When will he and the others get rounded up?" I asked.

"Soon," said Mueller. "Activity is already slowing down."

Heller looked at our curious stare. "Okay, I'll go off script a little, but I can only give you generalities." He looked at Mueller, who frowned. "Have you read about the suicide bombings in London—blew up the underground trains, the bus?"

"On 7-7? Yes—of course," said Bo.

"DHS bumped up port security from routine to hypervigilant," said Heller. "More spot checks, more random inspections. Wilton and his crew are anxious. They're thinking about mothballing the operation for a while. That's our cue to close it down."

"I thought you were waiting for an important shipment?"

Heller looked at Mueller. "Is this room bugged?"

"It's not my room," said Mueller, scanning all four corners. "But I don't think so. It's a side room for the DA to talk court strategy with his team, so I doubt it. I'm also bringing them a 312 to sign."

"Okay—this doesn't leave this room. I'll stay off script, but only 'cause you've been dealt a shit hand and you should know what's at stake."

Mueller stood up and said, "Not sure Director Hayward would agree with you."

"What's he gonna do? Fire me?"

"No, but he might fire me—so I'll go check on the paperwork," and he left the room.

"You guys ever heard of a supernote?"

Bo and I shook our heads.

"Also called greenback. Supernotes are counterfeit $100 bills—so perfect they're nearly impossible to detect, even by our own people. They're so good, rumor has it the CIA makes them to fund its own operations, but it's not true. They're made in North Korea. Part of Room 39's strategy to fund nuke and missile development."

"Room 39?" I asked.

"Secret agency inside of North Korea responsible for bankrolling the regime. They handle slush funds and generate fake foreign currency to pay for the little dictator's ambitions. It's not a code name, it's an actual office on the third floor of the WPK building in Pyongyang."

"Now I understand why the Secret Service was in the meeting," said Bo.

"Evelyn? Yeah, she's good," said Heller. "These damn notes have been floating around since '96. We've tried to outwit the counterfeiters twice with different designs, but the Norks kept pace." He paused, knowing Bo and I were processing as fast as possible. "Any idea how much of the US currency is located outside of the US?"

Again, we shook our heads, getting good at the bobble-head routine. "About half. The world is flooded with dollars. It's what makes supernotes so damn dangerous. They're not found in the US. The Norks distribute them in Asia, Europe, the Middle East; it's easier to pass them outside the country."

"What makes them so much better than standard counterfeits?" asked Bo.

"Everything. The paper is a cotton-linen blend produced on a Fourdrinier-style machine. It's printed with optically variable inks, microprinted on an intaglio press, so the design sits off the surface. Security threads and watermarks are perfectly matched. You can't tell the difference between real and fake, even with a microscope. Only our Washington lab can tell them apart. They're laundered through ATMs and casinos in Eastern Europe."

"I thought money-making equipment was strictly controlled," I said.

"It is. How the Norks got hold of our machinery is murky—personally, I think they bought it from the Russians during the collapse of the Soviet Union. We had no idea Wilton's network could deliver supernotes. Lian played a significant role in that. From a national security perspective, a billion cigarettes doesn't compare to several million in supernotes. It's the mother lode, and we've got a chance to pull in a big delivery."

"The value of the pipe," I said, repeating Hayward's words earlier.

"Yeah. It took me three years to prod Wilton to open the pipe to other merchandise, not just cigarettes. We know the Norks funnel supernotes through the Russian Embassy in Beijing. We know Wilton's got contacts at the highest levels of the Chinese government and the North Korean military. We think his North Korean connections come through Lian.

"Born in Vietnam, her father is North Korean, and her mother is Vietnamese. She has an uncle who is a *daejang* in the KPA. We think that's how Wilton gets his Nork juice."

"KPA?"

"Korean People's Army. *Daejang* is like a four-star general over here."

"She's a looker," I said.

"Wilton's girlfriend?" asked Bo.

"Not sure. She likes guys. She flirted with me, but it felt forced, like she was looking for an ally. Her problem is she's more of a source than a partner. Wilton lets her circle the table but never sit at it."

"But you said she's his North Korean asset."

Heller paused, looking for the right words. "Lian is valuable the way a key is valuable—but you don't confuse it with the house."

"How big is the shipment?" I asked.

"Six million. I got it for thirty cents on the dollar."

"You paid $1.8 million in real money for $6 million counterfeit?" I blurted.

"No one at the FBI fronts that kind of money." He teased a grin. "You think we're the CIA? No one was willing to sign off on the approval for the spend. First, I had to get Lian to supply a few notes so I could get them tested. Then I had to prove to Wilton I had the money. We used a controlled account. I deposited $1.8 million of forfeitures into it."

"Forfeitures?"

"Yeah. Seized money, mostly from drug deals."

"The container is somewhere on the water now. Will arrive any day. After that, we shut down the operation. I can't go into detail; there are other operations. Portland is a small outpost. You already know about my Long Beach warehouse. But there's another. We've got to let the bad guys run around leash-free for a while so we don't spook 'em. If we arrest one group, the other gets on a plane and disappears."

"So, we're part of a national sting," said Bo.

"Did you catch all the agencies in that room?" said Heller. "It's not just national, it's international."

My bladder began to pinch again. Did I just confess to killing Vasili Boborov and having an affair with his aunt to the entire federal octopus—the national security community? Who was going to see the wire transcript? I couldn't take the not knowing anymore, and although Bo had insisted we not bring it up unless they do, I finally burst out.

"Have you heard anything about my rant after we left the warehouse?"

Bo glared at me.

Heller frowned, thinking. "Nope, but they tend to keep noise off my radar, so I don't get distracted."

The door opened, and Agent Mueller stepped in. "Guys, I've got some paperwork for you to sign," and he laid two manila folders in front of us. At that point, Bob Heller pushed himself up from the chair with a faint wince. He brushed a hand over his thigh, letting the osteomyelitis ache know it wasn't welcome.

"Gotta go, fellas," he announced.

"When does it end for us?" asked Bo, shaking his hand. "When do we get our lives back?"

"I can't tell you, but it's not weeks, it's days, and you'll read about it in the papers."

"Wait a minute," I said, remembering something. "Didn't we find a couple of hundred-dollar bills in Tadeo's fake humidor?"

"Yeah," said Bo. "I forgot. I thought it was stash money to buy more cigars."

"Or boner pills," I added.

Heller and Mueller grimaced at the inside joke.

Bo reached into his pocket and pulled out his money clip. "I'd meant to give these to Laura but kept forgetting. I never spent them—no one ever has enough change."

The bills were at the bottom of the stack, and he handed them to Mueller, who held them up to the light.

"Don't bother," said Heller. "They're called supernotes for a reason."

"How would Tadeo have supernotes?" asked Mueller.

"He couldn't have," said Heller. "I only got a couple from Lian as samples, and it wasn't easy. She holds onto them like hens' teeth. No way Tadeo could have had any. Get them checked by the bureau. I'll bet they're the real thing. Probably just like you thought—cigarette money."

I shook his hand, and we smiled at each other. It was easier for me, knowing he hadn't heard my rant.

As we signed the 312 documents promising we would never reveal a word spoken that day, I asked Mueller the same question I'd asked Heller. His response wasn't as satisfying. His face went tight, almost like he was embarrassed, and then he said, "I can't talk about anything regarding the wire, but the Deputy DA is waiting in the office next door and wants to see you after signing the papers."

"I'm almost done," said Bo.

"Not you, Bo. Only Marty."

Mueller looked my way. "The door has Flener's name on it. No need to knock."

I left the small, dull room and walked into the larger, more official office. It looked formal and imposing, meant to make people like me—guilty people—feel small. District Attorney Autumn Flener sat at a meeting table away from the main desk, her dark suit matching her even darker eyes. There was great beauty in her stone-sharp angles if she chose to offer it. She didn't. She didn't smile.

A single file lay in front of her, aligned with the edge of the table like it had been placed there using a carpenter's square. I approached. She rose, offered her hand but not a chair. Her posture said this wasn't a conversation. It was a judgment.

"Mr. Schott," her voice was razor sharp, "my office has received a transcript of an exchange you had with Mr. Bishop upon exiting the FBI warehouse in the Rivergate District several days ago."

She slid the file an inch toward me with one finger, as if it were infected with misfortune.

"I strongly advise you to retain an attorney. My office will be in contact soon to discuss the matter."

She didn't blink.

CHAPTER THIRTY-FIVE

The Conflict Waiver

WE MET IN A PRIVATE ROOM AT THE BACK OF JAKE'S GRILL. It wasn't my restaurant or my hotel anymore, but Natalya was back in town putting her stamp on things, and she'd brought Marek to settle some post-divestiture legal work.

"Martin, you look … *zhizn' tebya pobedila* … like life beat you," she said, seated at a table already set.

"I didn't know it was a competition," I said with a slight bow and let the heavy mahogany door click behind me, sealing off the hum of the main dining room. The air hinted of furniture polish and steak fat. I was sure she'd had every inch of the rich woodwork buffed the day she took possession. She wore jeans, a cream satin shirt, and her soft, well-worn lambskin jacket, molded to her frame by years of wear.

After we hugged and brushed cheeks, she slipped it off and draped it over the back of her chair. I loved that jacket. She'd worn it that day, three years ago, when she came to make us the offer that changed our lives. At some point, I'd told her it was my favorite piece in her wardrobe, and sometimes she'd tease me by wearing only it—and nothing else. She once made dinner for us in just the jacket and heels. I shook the memory out of my head.

"Well, if it is a competition, you've come in second," she said.

"I've had a rough couple of days."

"Is Boomer all right?" she asked. I'd told her about the stroke.

"He's good, but I'm not."

I sat and reached for the short glass of scotch on ice opposite her goblet of pinot. She had Glenlivet waiting for me—as she always did when I visited her in Miami. It was her small ritual of keeping our past present.I drank most of it in one long swallow, reached for her hand, and started talking. There was much to say, and to her credit, she interrupted only once, asking me to repeat verbatim what I'd said on the wire. The words were embarrassing, and repeating them felt like reciting pornography to a nun. Her eyes never held anger, only a quiet sadness, like I was a kid recounting a *"terrible, horrible, no good, very bad day."*

When I finally ran out of words, two more scotches were gone, and her pinot was empty. We sat quietly. Our hands were close but not touching, each of us silently weighing the consequences of what I'd done.

"When will Marek show up?" I asked.

"Soon," she said. "I thought you'd want to talk first, so I asked him to come an hour after you."

She poured more pinot. I switched to water. The Glenlivet was making itself known—either sharpening or easing the edge.

"I'm sorry," I said.

"I know," she said.

Silence.

"Martin, you made a mistake in anger. I cannot be upset about that. In anger, I made the mistake of bringing Vasili into your life. I set him on you. My mistake was worse than yours, but you might end up paying for both."

"I have to find a way to contain it," I said. "I'm less worried about the legal fallout than I am about Abbie finding out about us. I've worked hard to fix my marriage. I can't lose it now."

"I don't think you can keep the shooting of Vasili from her," she said. "Abbie will learn at least that much."

"I can live with that." My fingertips tapped hers briefly. "Murder's easier to accept than betrayal."

"Ouch."

"Sorry. But it's true. Just like murder, infidelity has no statute of limitations."

Before she could answer, the door opened, and Marek Sokol came in. Natalya stood, touched my face lightly, and mouthed, "I know, Martin … I know."

"I like what you've done with the place," Marek said—loud, or maybe it just sounded loud after we'd been conferring in murmurs. "Martin and Bo kept it in perfect shape. I just polished the wood."

I knew it.

Marek's white hair had that practiced disarray that said he didn't care. But the suit was expensive, because, like me, he enjoyed dressing well—another reason I liked him, and, oddly, trusted him. The more someone mirrors you, the easier it is to lean in. He'd stopped at the bar, a Manhattan in his right hand, so we shook with our left.

"Please tell me you haven't eaten yet—I'm hungry enough to eat a small country," he said.

On that note, we flagged a waiter, ordered the Seafood Tower, and attacked oysters, lobster, crab, creamed spinach, mashed potatoes, and whatever else the chef decided to serve the new owner of his restaurant. Suffice to say, the meal probably shaved a couple of years off my life.

Shortly after Marek ordered a second Manhattan, I started to retell the story. I covered everything, with Natalya jumping in whenever she thought I'd skimmed over a detail. When I got to the wire—and my idiocy—Marek threw up both hands, bits of crab meat flaking from his fingers.

"Stop. I represent both Dmitry and Natalya. There's only so much you should tell me. I'll need a conflict waiver before you go on."

"I'll sign anything you need—so will Dmitry. Just hear Martin out," Natalya said.

And he did.

By the time I finished, we were past dessert and into coffee.

"Does Dmitry know about you two?" Marek asked—a natural question for anyone suddenly learning about us.

"Oh yes, Marek," Natalya said. "I don't keep secrets from Dmitry. He's fine with it. He has his entertainments; I have mine."

Both Marek and I raised our eyebrows.

She almost laughed. "You know what I mean."

"I'm telling you all this because I don't have an attorney who handles this kind of mess," I said. "You've got business and criminal experience. I need someone tough—an ass-biter—to help me navigate it. I'll pay whatever you charge."

"Money isn't the problem," he said. "I need a private meeting with Natalya and Dmitry to go over their potential liabilities. I can't represent you without their permission, and I'll need it in writing. I've already crossed a line by hearing all this. You told the FBI Natalya helped you bury a body—that's a problem for her. It might be suppressible, but I don't know how eager the DA is. They'll squeeze you for something; I just don't know …"

"Can't I just say I was spouting nonsense?"

"That's what you *will* say. But I don't yet know their strategy. I suspect they'll try to pry out more about your relationship with Dmitry—that's why I'm worried about conflict."

"I don't understand what their case would be," said Natalya, sipping her decaf latte and sounding very casual. "There is no Vasili to be found. He is a name Martin said on a tape recorder. He could have said, 'I shot the Easter Rabbit between his eyes, and Natalya helped me eat his basket of eggs.' This makes no sense to me."

"Natalya," said Marek, looking at her intently, "The whole thing is either a pebble or a landslide. I'll stop talking about this now. I will confer with you and Dmitry individually, outline the possibilities, and you'll need to sign a waiver before I proceed. Once you do that, I can go talk to … what was the DA's name?"

"Autumn Flener."

"I'll find out her intentions and what she has on you. Then I'll have a sense of how hard she'll push. We'll go from there."

"Okay," I said, relaxing my shoulders.

"Is there anything you've told me that Bo doesn't know?"

I shook my head.

"And his wife, Katherine, and your wife, Abbie??"

"They know about the smuggling operation and the FBI investigation. Nothing else. I'll tell Abbie everything except my relationship with Natalya. The affair has to stay secret."

Marek smiled. "*Affair* and *secret* are redundant by definition."

CHAPTER THIRTY-SIX

A Pebble or a Landslide

THE FOLLOWING DAYS BLURRED into a haze of phone calls, worry, work, and half-hearted distractions. I spoke to Abbie and the kids every morning and evening, sounding cheerful while holding back a storm. None of them knew about our little powwow with half the US intelligence community, and since I hadn't spoken to Bo, I knew he hadn't spilled to Katherine either—or Abbie would have been all over me. I'd have to say something eventually, but until Marek figured out whether the DA threat was a "pebble or a landslide," I decided to keep my mouth shut—for a change.

Boomer and I went for walks. He noticed I was spending more time at home and with him. He didn't seem to miss Abbie and the kids, though that may have been my ego talking. He belonged to all of us, but in my heart, he was mine, and I merely loaned him out to the rest of the family. I think he felt the same way, though he never let on. We explored the forest across the street, then settled in front of the TV—usually on mute—while I sifted through emails and the demands of work. He lay on the couch next to me, positioning himself close enough so my hand could rest on his head and stroke his ear when I wasn't using it to type.

I avoided Bo, mostly out of anger. He did the same. I was pissed that he didn't tell me about the wire, and he was pissed that I was pissed. Eventually, he texted me: "Come in. We need to talk about Refco."

I'd been following it on TV. It was national news. Refco Inc. had declared bankruptcy. It took decades to build the financial behemoth and a couple of days to bury it. The CEO hid hundreds of millions in bad debts; the books were meaningless; clients pulled their money; trust evaporated; liquidity froze; and within days, the giant came crashing down.

Creditors moved to claim whatever they could, while secured and unsecured obligations shuffled through the courts like a bad poker hand. For Paladin Holdings, the disaster didn't just shuffle the deck—it served up aces and eights—spades and clubs—dead man's hand.

Bo sat on our office couch, staring out at the lake, the surface flat and catching the August sun. He was unshaven, tired, and somehow lighter.

"You lose weight?" I asked as I stepped into the glass cage.

"Maybe. Nobody's home. I'm not eating well."

We caught up for a few minutes—surface-level stuff—before I asked, "How bad is the Refco thing?"

He drew a breath, twisted open a bottle of Pellegrino, and said, "Our loan's just one asset in the bankruptcy estate, buried in the middle of Refco's portfolio. The court's liquidating everything to pay creditors. Our attorneys are working the phones, but information's tight. Nobody wants to give anyone an edge, especially the casualties—and we qualify. Discounts in these auctions range from ten to forty percent, depending on how ugly the loan looks. My guess is a few banks will bid, and one ends up owning our debt for less than face value."

"But we're secured and financially solid. It's a class-A loan. If there's a discount, maybe we can renegotiate better terms."

"On paper, we're fine," he said. "But the court's moving fast. Too fast. With almost no time for due diligence, our loan looks messy—layers of collateral documents, cross-company pledges, and potential legal issues. Banks get jumpy. That pushes the discount up."

"Bottom line," I said, "whoever buys it, we keep going."

"Unless the new owner calls the loan," he said. "Then we're liquidating."

I nodded. "I see why you've lost weight."

"Have you been contacted by the DA?"

"No. But I've hired an attorney to help me deal with it—Marek Sokol."

"Jesus, Marty was that wise?"

"I don't want to drag new people into this," I said defensively. "He's not a friend, but I don't have friends lined up for this kind of shitstorm. Natalya and Dmitry trust him, and he's been ferreting through our closet of secrets for a while now."

"I'll hire him, too."

"You can't," I said. "He was barely able to represent me, given he represented Natalya and Dmitry, but he got a waiver, and he represented them on business matters, not criminal. He can't represent you or Natalya on this. You all have to get your own attorneys."

He gestured for us to leave the glass cage and go outside. Standing outside at the water's edge, he said, "I don't trust our office anymore. Anywhere, really. The house, the car, Starbucks—Christ, even the grocery store. I check out the pockets of the people shopping around me. I search for shiny gold pens."

"I know what you mean. When I had dinner with Marek and Natalya, I told Natalya to scrub the private dining room. She sent in a whole maintenance crew. They even exchanged the wall plugs."

"Find anything?"

I shook my head. "Polished the wood nicely."

"How much did you tell Marek?"

"Told him everything."

"You told him you shot Vasili."

"No, Bo. It doesn't work that way. I told him what I said on the frigging wire. Every humiliating word. But he didn't ask me if it was true. I think he'd prefer not to know."

We watched a couple of kids on a bright yellow raft across the lake, their laughter carrying over the water.

"The case, if there even is one, is weak," I said. "Marek thinks he can get it tossed. It's the affair that worries me. If Marek can't make this go away, I'll have to tell Abbie … *something*."

The silence between us hardened into a wall I wasn't willing to climb.

"Anything I can do?" he asked.

"You've done enough."

"Jesus, Marty, I get it. I didn't tell you about the wire, but you're the one who shot his mouth off. Call it even already."

"It's not even for me," I said. "I shot my mouth off to my closest friend—who's never lied to me, and who I trusted with my life."

"I didn't betray you," he said quietly. "I've never broken a promise to you. You can't say the same. We're in this because of your choices, not mine."

He was right. That was the worst part.

"*We* are not in this, Bo—*I* am."

"Whatever happens to you—happens to me," he said.

"Even you don't believe that."

I kept my eyes on the lake. Neither of us looked at the other.

Finally, the words formed and settled in my throat—not a lump but a stone—and I let them sit there for a few breaths while we watched the kids splash around, as if the world were simple. Then I let them out. "It's time for me to do something else."

He snorted. "Cut the theatrics. We'll figure it out."

"You don't understand, Bo," I said. "Whatever happens—good, bad—I'm out. There's a decent chance I've wrecked my marriage, my life, my friendship. You're just standing in the fallout."

Then, I turned and looked at him.

"I'm doing this for both of us."

"I don't need saving, Marty."

"I'm not saving you, Bo. I'm saving me."
I walked back inside.

CHAPTER THIRTY-SEVEN

Grim Math

THE NARROW TRAIL WAS FAMILIAR, but I still felt off balance, even days after talking with Bo. Boomer led the way, needles crunching under our feet, the loudest sound in the woods because neither of us wanted to be the first to speak.

Marek had called that morning: the waiver documents had been filed, and I was officially his client. He'd already reached out to the DA's office, and we were scheduled to meet with Flener the morning after next. My job was to hold still while the world rearranged itself around me.

I didn't like it, but fear is a potent inhibitor. I spent hours talking to myself—or to Boomer—replaying mistakes and, worse, marveling at how brilliant I once thought I'd been. I have the bad habit of collecting regrets the way some people collect stamps: quietly, obsessively, and uselessly.

I counted the people I'd killed—one.

The people I'd watched die—seven.

The people whose deaths followed from the choices Bo and I'd made—two hundred twenty-three—and counting.

A casualty census. Cause and effect. Grim math.

Marek rented an executive suite downtown, in the pink tower. It was more than he needed and expensive, but I'd never counted pennies in my life and wasn't about to start during the undoing of it. After my morning constitutional with Boomer, I drove to his office to talk strategy. I was aware of Bo's absence. It was the first time in a decade I'd faced something significant—personal or business—without him.

"You're going to plead the Fifth," Marek said, settling behind an empty desk, its bare surface reflecting the ceiling lights. He hadn't even brought his desk calendar.

"Why?"

"Marty, the DA has almost nothing. She has a handful of angry words you said on a wire during an FBI sting you were never supposed to be a part of. She has no body, no missing person report, no corroboration, no crime scene, no physical evidence, no witnesses, no timeline. Her only evidence is your uncorroborated statement, and even that is suspect because you were never Mirandized."

He lifted a hand. "In formal prosecutorial parlance, this is what we call a premium shit sandwich. No DA with a functioning brain would file a murder charge on it."

"Then why bring it up at all?" I asked. "Why scare the shit out of me?"

"My guess? The FBI has no jurisdiction over you. They're not investigating you—they're investigating the smuggling syndicate. Their unauthorized wiring of Bo caught collateral dirt. Protocol forces them to hand it over to the locals. Normally, it might have died quietly—but this sting is huge, and everyone in the bureau with a title after their name is paying attention. So, they ship it to the US Attorney and wash their hands. But murder is a state crime, not a federal crime, so it lands on the county DA—he passes it to his deputy. Now she's stuck with it, and it's got more fingerprints than a public bathroom stall. You're the duck in the crosshairs."

"I'm not a duck," I said. "I'm a goddamn pigeon."

"Not if we handle this properly."

He paused, then offered me a coffee from a portable Starbucks container, which I gladly took. "These suites come with nothing. Not even a coffee machine."

"It's uncivilized," I said.

"You give her nothing. You plead the Fifth on everything except your name and number. No other word. Any question she asks puts you in legal jeopardy. She'll ask if you know Vasili Bobrov. What was your relationship? Whether you put a bullet between his eyes. Every question is another shovel to dig your hole deeper. Don't dig." His voice flattened. "This is where you shut the hell up."

"What about Bo and Natalya? Flener will question them, too."

"I can't talk to them, but I can talk to their attorneys. I'll tell them our strategy and recommend the same approach. They're competent. They're probably already thinking it, but I'll confirm."

He took a sip of coffee, then asked, almost casually, "How's the FBI investigation going? Any updates?"

"No. They don't call me. I'm persona non grata—the mess they didn't mean to kick loose. If they call anyone, it'll be Bo. Their boy scout." My bitterness surprised me; I'd never aimed it at Bo before.

"We're barred from going anywhere near Corner24," I continued. "Nate Radford still calls every day, but I keep it strictly operational. The poor bastard has no clue there's a building with the FBI logo on it about to fall on top of him. I almost feel sorry for him. As far as our company is concerned, it's basically on autopilot. I don't talk to Ed Cruz or Kennedy Johnson. They don't reach out either."

"You're sure they don't suspect a thing?"

"I think Heller keeps them in line. He's assured them that Bo and I are fully on board. He just has to keep the music playing a few more days."

I'd told Marek about Heller. I knew I shouldn't have, technically, but if he was going to keep my life from detonating, giving him the full picture felt like the bare minimum. The only thing he didn't know, and didn't want to know, was if I actually killed Vasili Bobrov.

It felt like a fair compromise.

CHAPTER THIRTY-EIGHT

The Evidence

THE CONFERENCE ROOM IN THE DISTRICT ATTORNEY'S OFFICE felt colder than necessary, as if the HVAC was angry and wanted everyone to shiver. Marek and I took the near side of the long table, the blinds behind us half-closed so the city outside was sliced into gray slats.

The far side was already occupied.

A young man in a Brooks Brothers suit—gelled hair, lazy eyes, slightly crooked teeth—gave his forgettable name and sat with a legal pad open, an expensive pen displayed like a prop. I wondered if it was the pen his parents had given him when he passed the bar. An even younger man, probably a paralegal, sat next to him, looking grateful just to be allowed in the room. In the center of the table, a small digital recorder blinked red, already running.

The paralegal offered coffee and bottled water. I took the coffee; Marek took the water. Nobody said anything important unless weather counts. It wasn't so much a meeting as a controlled burn. Marek had prepared me: hands in my lap, eyes locked on a fixed point.

After a fifteen-minute wait that felt intentional, Autumn Flener arrived. She didn't walk—she glided, all economy of motion, a folder tucked under her arm. No handshake. No smile. She slid into her chair, pulled the recorder closer, and said, "Multnomah County Deputy District Attorney Autumn Flener. Present with me: DDA

Investigator Michael Warren and paralegal Daniel Ruiz. Interview with Martin Schott. Counsel Marek Sokol present."

She clicked the folder open and pushed it toward Marek with a soft, deliberate motion that conveyed more threat than charity.

"Let's get right to the point. Here's our preliminary findings."

I didn't move. My mantra repeated silently: *She doesn't have anything.*

Flener spread her documents as if laying out tarot cards. Travel records with blacked-out lines. Phone logs with highlighted time-stamps. A grainy grayscale photo of Vasili—washed out by toner, but the eyes still carrying violence like a birthmark.

Her gaze never tracked the papers; it tracked me.

"Mr. Schott, you said something on a federal wire," she began. "Your exact words were: 'I shot Vasili through his fucking eyes. Natalya will help me dump the bodies—like she did before.'"

"That was anger," Marek said smoothly. "Not evidence."

She ignored him.

"Mr. Vasili Bobrov immigrated to the United States from Russia about fifteen years ago, accompanied by his biological aunt, Ms. Natalya Danilenko, listed as his legal guardian. Mr. Bobrov was a known associate of Florida's Russian organized crime network, the Miami Bratva. Ms. Danilenko has a stepson, Alex Danilenko, who lives locally. He owns the dance club Shangri-La, where Mr. Bishop's brother-in-law, Tadeo Ramírez, was murdered seven weeks ago."

I didn't move. My face stayed a mask.

Flener consulted her notes. "In October 2002, Vasili Bobrov flew to Portland from Miami. According to the PNR," she hesitated, "that's the Passenger Name Record—it's the airline's official booking file—he traveled with a Mr. Brody Lynch."

She let the name hang, then added, "Mr. Lynch shares the same bratva association as Mr. Bobrov. Upon arrival, they rented a car. Three days later, Mr. Bobrov purchased a ticket to Las Vegas. You and Bo Bishop were on the same PNR. You and Bishop returned the following day; Mr. Bobrov came back on a later flight. Since then, he has not been seen. No bank activity. No phone activity. No tax filings. He apparently never returned home.

"In that same time window, a man named Albert von Baltruschat and his wife, Crystal, were found murdered in their residence, which was then destroyed by arson. Portland Police recorded your presence at the Baltruschat home on the evening before the murders."

She took a breath, checking her notes as if the list were too long to memorize.

"Also, during that same period, your business partner, Mr. Nico Scava, went missing. His wife, Charley Scava, filed the missing-person report. Neither you nor Mr. Bishop reported him missing. Mr. Scava's name was quietly scrubbed from your company's public filings. No financial activity. No phone usage. No confirmed sightings. No tax records. His wife has since petitioned the court for a declaration of presumed death and is now living with Mr. Scava's brother, Dante Scava, a known business associate of both you and Natalya Danilenko.

"Shortly after the disappearance of both Mr. Bobrov and Mr. Scava, Ms. Danilenko joined your small company, Paladin, as partner and chairman. Several months later, you renamed it Paladin Holdings, and it has grown exponentially."

Her words left bruises. She had more than I thought.

"Taken together, Mr. Schott, it is all very suspicious."

I didn't look at her. My eyes stayed pinned to a scuff mark on the table—the spot I'd chosen to fix on.

"My client will be invoking his Fifth Amendment rights."

The silence that followed settled like a verdict. A hairline fracture showed in her composure—small, but visible.

"You're hiding behind the Fifth?" she demanded. "I bring you in to explain a recorded confession, and your strategy is silence?"

Marek drank from his water bottle. Slow. Deliberate. Provocative.

"Your evidence is entirely circumstantial. My client is not required to help you build a case against him."

Flener pushed her chair back, inch by inch, her anger rising with her. Her assistants didn't know where to look—at her, at me, at Marek, or at the scattered papers. The display felt practiced, almost calibrated, as if she'd decided the moment required heat. I'd spent years negotiating contracts, where anger—real or manufactured—was part of the dance. Maybe she thought I wouldn't recognize the move. The language was different. The tactic wasn't.

"Walk out without answering my questions," she said, "and I'll assume you're guilty as sin. I'll use every tool I have to tear you open—you'll be a piñata."

Marek smiled. He'd achieved his objective.

"You can't assume anything," he said softly. "It's my client's right. I guess in anger, we all say things we regret." For emphasis, he tapped the recorder.

Her eyes betrayed the look of someone who'd misstepped. She stood. Her team rose. The meeting was over.

Back in the car, where we could speak freely, Marek asked, "How the hell did Flener get all that in just five days?"

"The cop," I said. "Detective Adams. He's been mining for gold for some time now. He did the legwork. Flener just glued it together."

"Well, she's pissed now."

I didn't need the reminder. I knew it wasn't over. We hadn't ended anything.

We'd lit a fuse.

CHAPTER THIRTY-NINE

Corpus Delicti

THE MEETING WITH FLENER STAYED WITH ME—her certainty, the way she said my name, flat, formal, as if she were calling it out in court. I kept telling myself that Marek could keep the mess behind a curtain. But pressure was building everywhere, and sooner or later I'd have to tell Abbie something.

But what? How much?

Telling her everything was impossible. Telling her nothing was worse. So, I took the coward's path—partial truths wrapped in the soft cotton of concern. I told her I had legal issues tied to the FBI investigation, fallout from Adams's obsession with Nico's disappearance, and the Baron murders. I let her connect harmless dots, even though I knew I was covering a shark bite with a Band-Aid. I told her I'd hired Marek "as a precaution."

Bo and I synced our stories. He had no incentive to tell Katherine anything, either, so even though we were "quarreling," we were chained together—forced to move in step.

Abbie accepted it—or pretended to. Fatigue has a way of settling in. She'd been in self-imposed exile for weeks, checked on daily by the local FBI agent. Every time she spoke with me, I added another thread of concern. I was stacking bricks on a wall of disaster—after a while, each new piece of bad news barely registered; it was just another brick.

Meanwhile, Marek worked the phones, trying to keep the

temperature down. It didn't help. Bo went in and invoked the Fifth. Natalya refused to come at all—her attorney told the DA she wasn't cooperating and was leaving the country "for an indefinite vacation." The phrasing alone could've started a fistfight.

Flener took it personally. She told Marek we were stonewalling as a unit—acting in concert, building a conspiracy. Then she said the words neither of us wanted to hear—*grand jury.*

When Marek told me over the phone, my legs gave out, and I had to sit down. Not because of the charges—because of what a grand jury touches once it starts moving.

I kept my voice low, as if the house itself were listening. "A grand jury doesn't need proof, Marek. It needs momentum. A story. Flener has that. If there's an indictment, everything breaks the surface—press, headlines. I don't get to decide what stays sealed." I swallowed. "Abbie will know everything."

"Yeah. Which is why I'm trying to settle."

"Settle what?"

"A plea. Something small. Something survivable."

"You're joking. Did Natalya put you up to this?"

"Marty," he said, calm as a pilot in turbulence, "you're spinning into shock. Breathe. In—out." He took a beat. "Listen. The DA has a *corpus delicti* problem."

"A what?"

"She can't prove a crime occurred. She can't sell that to her boss or anyone else. So she's going to keep digging until she finds something that will stick to you. It's the digging I'm worried about. Sooner or later, she'll find enough to make the story compelling enough for a grand jury."

"Like what?"

"That's what we can steer. We nudge her toward a charge you can manage—something I can shave down to the minimum. A Class C felony."

"What's a Class C?"

"Perjury. Obstruction. Accessory. Tampering."

"Fuck me."

"I'm trying to keep it to one count, contained. That gets the case off her desk and stops bugging her. Everything else dismissed. No public trial."

"What do I tell Abbie? The kids?"

"I don't know yet, Marty. I haven't proposed anything. I'm still looking for her pressure point—something she can accept and walk away. Tell me what you remember from the interview you had with Detective Adams about Baron Albert Von Baltruschat."

"It was three years ago."

"Do your best."

I did.

CHAPTER FORTY

Suspicious Cargo

BOOMER SNORES LOUDER THAN I DO. He'd stolen Abbie's empty side of the bed again, his warm spine pressed against mine. The ringtone carved through the dark, and both of us lifted our heads. It was a minute past two. Given my superstitions, my thought went straight to Abbie and the kids. I answered too loudly.

"Yes."

"Mr. Schott?"

The voice was unknown. "Yes."

"Officer Lawrence, Portland Police Bureau. Badge number five-four-one-three-two."

"Yes?" My voice pitched higher. Boomer rolled upright, and the mattress bounced.

"I'm sorry to call this late, sir, but I'm at your Emerson Street warehouse with a delivery driver who reported a suspicious routing change. You're listed as an executive contact on the company record, and we need access to verify the load."

Not Abbie. Not the kids. Thank God.

"Suspicious how?"

"The route he was given doesn't match the bill of lading. He won't enter the lot until we clear it, and we can't do that without a keyholder."

"Why are you calling me? There must be half a dozen people who can deal with this."

"Yes, but I don't have their contact information."

"What about Ed Cruz?"

"I called Mr. Cruz twice—no answer. Your name came up in the property records as a contact, so you're on our call-down list."

"You have the property records?"

"I had my dispatch pull them. It's two in the morning. Everyone's tired."

"Can't you just force entry?"

"Not for a property check. This isn't a warrant situation. We need someone with authority to open the bay so we can confirm the seal and release the driver."

My mind was starting to clear. Did Wilton slip something past Heller? Deliveries don't show up at 2 a.m.

"Tell the driver to wait till morning and call his company."

"He can do that," the cop said, "but he called us because he thinks his load is suspicious, and now it's my problem. I can't just leave him here."

"Let me talk to him."

A new voice came on, low and gravelly, every word rolling in marbles. Heavy accent, struggling with English. I asked the basics again, and all I got were soft "yes … *sí* … yes" answers, nothing useful, nothing clear.

"Put the officer back on," I said.

Nothing about this felt normal. Then again, normal had been off the table for a while. If this was a syndicate shipment, it needed to be controlled. Heller's warning rolled through my head—keep the sting intact. Random cops reporting random deliveries at 2 a.m. was the kind of noise the FBI couldn't afford. If it was harmless, fine. If it wasn't, I could try to contain it. First, I had to know what I was dealing with.

"What delivery company is it?"

"Pacific Evergreen Logistics. Standard container. I can read you the manifest number if you want."

"No, that's fine. I'm on my way."

"Appreciate it, Mr. Schott. We'll meet you at the entrance."

On the drive over, I called Nate. No answer—not even voicemail. I called Ed. Same thing. The time at night was one explanation. But I didn't buy it. Nate and Ed were crooked, but they were careful. I thought about calling Bo, but pride and anger stood in the way, and I wasn't in the mood to fight either of them.

I thought about the one date on the schedule sheet that had been underlined. 8-5—2—1407. Today.

I pulled up to the Emerson Street warehouse half an hour later. The lot was empty except for a white van and a single container truck idling near the gate. No flashing lights. No patrol cars.

I rolled down my window. "You the driver?"

He nodded. "*Sí, señor*. I wait. Gate … you open?"

I got out and punched in the code. The padlock clicked, the chain sagged as I pulled the latch free. The driver eased the truck into the lot and parked in front of the warehouse bay, the container doors facing the building. The lot lights cast long shadows across the pavement.

No sign of Officer Lawrence, badge number five-four-one-three-two.

While I worked the lock on the side entry, the driver backed the trailer tight against the dock, the black container looming like a steel vault. I hit the bay-door switch. The doors rattled up, and a thin wash of diesel and dust drifted out of the dark.

"Where's the police guy?" I called to the driver.

He didn't respond. He started working on the container doors, ignoring me.

"Hey, buddy? What happened to the cop?" I repeated.

"I sent him home," said a soft female voice behind me.

I turned.

Lian Hua Chen stood there, hands in her pockets, eyes calm and unreadable. A thin, insincere smile creased her face.

"Glad you could make it, Mr. Schott," she said, her tone steady and even.

I threw on a half-hearted grin, "Where'd *you* come from?"

She tipped her head. "The truck—back of the cab." She still oozed that brazen flirtatiousness, but this time it felt more creepy than calculated. I slipped both hands into my jacket pockets and looked over her shoulder, scanning the lot.

"Are you looking for someone? Perhaps Wilton, or Bobby?"

A new voice rose near the container. I turned. Another man—bald, tattoo sleeves, thick around the middle, more bulk than brawn—was helping the driver crank the doors open.

"No, I'm looking for Zor and Ming," I said.

"They're not here," she said, as a tall, handsome Mexican man with close-cropped hair and a trim beard walked up behind her. I recognized him. He wore a gray coverall and carried a Glock 19 in his left hand.

"Wow, how many people can you fit in the back of that cab? It's like a circus clown car."

"Lian said you were a funny guy," said Alisandro, his lips curving upward.

Jeff Noble's watchdog.

And then it all fell into place with a brutal clarity.

"Holy shit," I said.

They didn't respond, but Alisandro's left hand twitched a little.

"You killed Tadeo and Jeff." I paused and glared. "You almost killed my daughter."

"I did not," said Alisandro. "I tried to scare her. She was all over the road. She hit a hole and rolled. She's a shit driver."

I decided to kill him then and there, but while the decision came easily, the doing did not. Alisandro waved the Glock, ordering me deeper into the warehouse, and I backed up slowly.

"Your phone," said Lian. "Where is your phone?"

"In my pocket."

"Give it to me."

I pulled it out, showed it to her, and threw it onto a nearby crate, which seemed to satisfy her.

"You're not delivering cigarettes," I said.

"I'm not," she said.

Alisandro walked up to me and put the Glock to my chest.

"Put your hands behind your back."

He cinched my wrists with thick, black zip ties. Told me to sit, then did it again to my ankles. My bladder began to hurt.

"Is this necessary?"

"Shut the fuck up or I'll beat you to death with a tire iron," barked Alisandro. Given what he did to Noble, I believed him.

Lian watched the two men working in the container. They had started to pull boxes.

"It's in the back, go deeper," she yelled, her voice echoed through the hollow dim. "Look for large bolts of fabric and rolled rugs. The rest is filler."

"It's the supernotes. You're picking up the greenbacks," I said— and a crushing pain blew through my ear and cheek. Heat streaked down my face; a metallic tang flooded my mouth. The pain spiked so hard that everything pitched sideways. I swallowed to keep from retching.

"I told you to shut up," Alisandro said, close to my face, his breath stale and sour. Not so handsome anymore.

He'd driven the butt of the Glock into my cheekbone just in front of the ear—split the skin, maybe tore something deeper. My ear burned as if he'd struck a match inside it. I shut my eyes to stop the vertigo.

"I'll go help 'em," he said to Lian. "Keep an eye on him."

A minute later, the spinning eased. I cracked my eyes open.

Lian stood a few feet away, holding the Glock indifferently, almost carelessly, her gaze deliberate, sliding between me and whatever was happening in the container behind me. She saw my eyes open and took a moment to study my bleeding face with a kind of quiet, predatory satisfaction.

"You were a Hail Mary," she said.

The roar in my ear was deafening, but I caught enough. "What?"

She spoke louder. "We diverted the delivery. It was supposed to go to Bobby's warehouse. He's probably still sitting there waiting for it. I paid their driver to walk. My driver brought it here, where Nate and Ed were supposed to unlock it, open it, and help unload it. We got here three hours ago—waiting, calling, nothing. Both those bastards got cold feet."

I let blood drool past my lips, which I couldn't feel anymore.

"We had a problem," she continued. "How do we unload a forty-foot container without equipment? You can't do it by hand—it'd take hours. Meanwhile, Wilton and Bobby are searching for their missing truck."

All the bones in my face began to throb in sympathy with my cheekbone. Even my scalp screamed in agony.

"It was Alisandro's idea. He does a bit of acting—mostly community theater stuff. Played a cop once. Said he could call you, pose as a cop on-site, and get you to come out and unlock the place. Everything he said was bullshit, but you wouldn't know …"

"You couldn't just break in?" I mumbled, spitting blood. "It's a warehouse. Emerson's dead at night." I made a herculean effort to pronounce my words as best I could.

"And trip the alarms? Too risky. You were a last resort—and you showed up."

"Happy to help," I said, trying to sit up. "What if I hadn't?"

"Probably would've started to drive it out of town, figured something else out, but it wouldn't have been easy. So, I'm glad you got out of bed for us."

"Your *f*oyfriend has a *f*oor way of showing his *aff*reciation." My ability to enunciate was directly correlated to the amount of blood in my mouth.

"Yeah," she grinned wickedly. "I'm the lover—he's the killer."

My wrists burned in the zip ties. My face was swelling; my eye was slowly closing. Cold crept up from the concrete.

Through the gap beneath the pallet—the one under the crate where I'd dropped my phone—I watched a forklift shuttle rolled up rugs and bolts of fabric to a white van. Alisandro and the driver stacked them, grunting with each one.

It looked exhausting. I was glad they hadn't put me to work.

Pain does strange things to your thinking.

Lian stood near the edge of the light, Glock hanging loose in her hand. She glanced at me occasionally, tilting her head as if wondering if I was still worth her attention.

My ear and face pulsed with the rhythm of my accelerated heart. Blood continued seeping into my mouth. Someone swore—they'd dropped a rug or a bolt and had to chase it as it rolled away.

The van filled fast.

I caught a thin trace of smoke, or maybe it was just the floor grit my body had stirred. I wasn't even sure my nose was working anymore, but then the next breath told me through the blood in my mouth, at the back of my throat—smoke was threading through the air.

"Wha' are you doing?" I asked, as if I were complaining to a clerk behind a counter.

"Just a little distraction. With a dozen fire trucks hosing the place down, Wilton and his crew won't find the container. They'll keep searching. It'll buy us a day or two."

I coughed. Gasoline stung the air. Someone was dousing crates and cardboard. I couldn't feel the flames yet, but I heard the sizzling and spitting over the roar in my bleeding ear. Smoke came fast.

Lian approached me and tightened her grip on the Glock. I tensed every muscle in my body. She stood directly in front of me as I tried to straighten. For a moment, I thought she might lift me up, maybe cut my leg ties, and let me run. But she didn't. Instead, she crouched down like she would for a child she wanted eye contact with. She pressed the gun against my belly. Neither of us blinked.

"Before I go, I have to tell you something," she said with a slight, melancholy frown.

My tongue was floating in too much blood for me to respond. I just returned her frown, tightened my stomach muscles against the muzzle, and shifted my torso slightly to the left.

"When I said I'm the lover and Alisandro the killer …" She paused. "… I lied … he's the lover."

I heard the shot before I felt the pain—a deep, ripping heat that tore through my gut and erased everything happening in my face. I drew in a lungful of smoke and coughed, and the pain intensified, if that was even possible. I barely saw her rise as I fell to my side, feeling nothing except an all-consuming, searing heat.

I started to go. My brain was shutting down, every thought sharp and separate. There was nothing left but the fact of it.

This is how I will die.

CHAPTER FORTY-ONE

A Fortunate Man

I'M WARM. I CAN'T MOVE, AND DON'T WANT TO. I can't see, and don't want to. The concrete feels soft. Almost comfortable. I'm dying, but I'm toasty—it's probably the fire. I hope it doesn't hurt to burn—but I don't feel pain anymore. I guess I'm past feeling things.

///

Quiet voices. Lights behind one eye, black behind the other. A foul taste was in my mouth—did I drink sewage? Something soft closed around my left hand. I wanted to sleep. Maybe death is sleep. I remembered it was warm. Abbie's face floated up—lovely, unmistakable. I wanted to tell her that I love her, but I was too tired. Death does that to you—makes you tired. I hoped she would carry me into her future. Give my love to Andrew and Ali. I wanted to slip back to sleep, back to my death.

///

I stared at Abbie's face. It's a great face. My eyes were open this time—correction—my right eye was open; my left eye was wrapped in gauze. I wasn't dead, obviously, but I felt like it. Even with the meds, every molecule in my body felt abused—vodka in a martini shaker.

I'd woken up lucid for the first time in the middle of the night. Abbie was sleeping in a chair by the bed. She'd been holding my hand, but sometime during the night, hers had fallen into her lap. I wanted to say something, but didn't. I let her sleep. She probably needed it. A thin, continuous tone whined in my ear. Ignoring it, I drifted back under.

When the sun broke through the next morning, a nurse was injecting something into my IV on one side, and Abbie was holding my hand on the other.

"Morning," I mumbled.

"Yes, it is," she said, smiling.

She'd caught the first flight out of Traverse City without even packing. Everyone had been incredibly helpful, and she'd come straight from the airport. I'd been out for twenty-four hours. We spent the next hour talking, pausing for nurse checks and chewing ice chips. I explained everything that had happened, starting with the fake phone call.

"Did they get them?" I asked.

"I don't know," she said. "I haven't left this room."

"Where are Andrew and Ali?"

"In Michigan. They wanted to come, but absolutely not. All I knew was you'd been admitted with gunshot wounds. I thought I was flying into a war zone. They're safe and sound with Katherine and the rest of the family."

I closed my eyes.

A few minutes later, Bo came barreling in—agitated, panting as if he'd sprinted from the parking lot.

"Jesus H. Christ, Marty," Bo said, chest heaving. "You scared the hell out of me. They wouldn't let me in until now—only Abbie. I told them I was your brother. No go. I even tried, 'he's my Don't Ask, Don't Tell partner,' but they still shut me out."

"Don't make me laugh," I groaned.

The nurse swapping out my saline bag cackled.

"I guess you got my call," I said, looking at Bo.

Abbie frowned. "What call?"

"My phone was in my pocket. I managed to call Bo's number before Lian made me ditch it. I assume it stayed live."

Bo nodded. "At first, all I heard was muffled noises. But you don't butt-dial at 2 a.m., so I knew something was wrong. I practically shoved the phone into my ear canal. Then there was this thud, and suddenly I could hear you—and maybe a woman? Couldn't be sure. It sounded like you were outside. Then somebody threatened to beat you with a tire iron, and that's when I launched out of bed."

"And?" Abbie asked.

"I never took the phone out of my ear. Heard her feed you that cop story. Figured it had to be one of our warehouses. Then you said 'Emerson'—*thank you very much*—I called 911, told them to get there on the double, and drove like hell. Funny part? Cops chased me half the way. I hit one-twenty on the freeway, and three cruisers lit me up. I called Mueller."

"You called someone while driving a hundred and twenty miles an hour down the freeway?" Abbie said.

He shot her a look—as if a lecture was the last thing he needed.

"It was almost three in the morning. The freeway felt like a race-track after hours. The cops never caught me—not until I landed. Then they took my license. Thirty days. I had to take a cab to get here."

He stared at me. "I thought you were dead."

"Only on the inside."

It's an old joke, but he laughed anyway.

"Mueller must have called the cavalry because by the time I got there, maybe twenty minutes, there were firetrucks already pulling into the place. I screamed that you were inside, and they told me two guys were already searching for you. The cops were on me like I was a serial killer. I wrestled them—not a good idea, by the way—and they took me down and cuffed me. I managed to see them carry you out like they do in war movies. Scared me to death. But then an EMT put an oxygen mask on you, and I figured they don't do that to corpses."

Abbie's face was pale. "My God," she whispered.

"Mueller showed up about ten minutes later. Talked to the cops, and they uncuffed me. They didn't look happy. They turned me over to Mueller's custody. Cited me, took my license, and I've got a court date in thirty days."

"I'm confused," said Abbie. "How did you dial Bo's number in your pocket?"

I tried to shake my head. Vertigo hit, and I shut my eyes to let it calm.

"I didn't," I finally said. "You know the cheap Nokia I have bedside?"

She nodded.

"I keep it there instead of my usual Blackberry because it's simpler. Each button's programmed to speed-dial someone in an emergency at night, in the dark. Bo's zero. You're one. I brought it with me because the BlackBerry was charging. When I saw Lian, I knew I was in trouble. I reached in, felt the keypad, pressed zero, held it a few seconds—it dialed Bo."

The doctor entered a few minutes later, a chart in hand.

He greeted everyone with a brisk, hurried hello and introduced himself as Dr. Patel, the trauma surgeon who'd operated on me. He looked older—or maybe just tired. The bags under his eyes were the most prominent feature. Eastern, possibly Indian, but no discernible accent. I hoped he was a Harvard grad who'd written books about my condition—but I didn't ask. When our eyes met, I think he sensed my thoughts, and he smiled wryly.

"Mr. Schott—Mrs. Schott. Let me tell you what we found."

He ignored Bo, who leaned against a corner.

"First, the gunshot." He glanced at his clipboard. "Entered right flank, just below the liver, exited in the back. Passed through muscle and soft tissue only. No organs." He smiled again. "Very fortunate.

Had the trajectory been different, we'd be having a very different conversation—if at all."

"I twisted to my left just before she pulled the trigger," I said. "I figured it was going to hurt, so I angled to prepare for it."

"You did more than that. That twist changed the bullet's path away from your bowel, liver, kidney, stomach—even the major vessels. You lost blood, but not catastrophically. We irrigated the entry and exit, removed debris, repaired torn muscle, and placed a drain. You'll be sore for weeks, but it will heal."

"And his face?" Abbie asked.

"That's trickier than the gunshot. You were struck hard with …" he looked at me.

"Butt of a Glock 19," I said.

"Ah. Yes." He jotted on his paper. "Zygomatic arch fracture—cheekbone. We're treating it conservatively. Not displaced, so no surgery. Expect swelling, pain, difficulty chewing or speaking comfortably for a bit."

"The bleeding from my ear?"

"Blunt trauma that close can injure the canal or middle ear. You likely have a labyrinthine concussion—shockwave injury to the inner ear. You'll feel vertigo, a sense of imbalance, maybe ringing. Could last a week or two—or linger. An ENT consult has already been arranged. No skull fracture, no brain bleed, hearing largely intact."

"Why did my mouth fill with so much blood?"

"Soft tissue along the cheek and gum line was torn. Nothing needed stitches. Sore for a week or two. Eat soft foods. Barring complications, you'll be walking in a day or two. You'll be fully recovered in several weeks. Cognitively and neurologically, you're already there. Given what happened, Mr. Schott, you are a fortunate man."

I mustered a tight smile.

Tell that to my lawyer.

CHAPTER FORTY-TWO

The Sweep

THE FOLLOWING DAY BROUGHT TWO VISITORS—FBI agent Mueller and excoriating pain. One shook my hand; the other shook my swagger. The doctor had said the bullet had taken a clean path through my flank, but my organs and muscles were pretty pissed over the intrusion, and their protest had devolved into a riot. Any movement lit my nervous system on fire. I could move my one good eye, but that was about it. I begged for more morphine, but the nurses just smiled and said they'd check with the doctor. I knew they wouldn't—in my mind, they'd all turned into malevolent goblins watching me suffer.

Abbie went home for a few hours to shower and change out of the clothes she'd slept in for two nights. I took long calls from Andrew and Ali. When Ali cried, I cried along with her. Boomer needed some attention too; he'd been staying at his sitter's place, and Abbie called to check on him. She said he was a little mopey, probably missing home and family. I took that to mean he missed me—of course.

Bo refused to leave. He was afraid they wouldn't let him back in. I finally ordered him to get some sleep. He returned well before anyone else—he'd always been an early riser.

"What have you told Abbie about the DA?" he asked after helping me spoon green Jell-O into my mouth.

"Just general stuff," I said, and winced. "Marek is negotiating. But sooner or later, I'll have to tell her about Vasili. It's Natalya I can't have her know about. I'm orbiting a black hole, trying to keep her from getting pulled in."

"She'll forgive you, Marty," he said sympathetically. "You nearly died." He put on his coaching face. "I read somewhere once that when God made death … he gave it a smile."

I gave him a crooked grin—the best my face could manage. "He did that just to fuck with us."

///////////////////////////////////////

Abbie and Agent Mueller arrived almost simultaneously. They met in the hospital hallway, so I dispensed with introductions. He was in the same suit I'd always seen him in—I wondered if he bought them in bulk. However, unlike his suit, his face had changed. It was less strained, almost affable.

We went through the obligatory "That was a close one" discussion, then I asked, "Did you get those assholes?"

"The bureau put out a BOLO—be on the lookout—APB immediately. My gut told me they'd head to Canada. Vancouver has a huge Asian community, and Lian would try to blend in. Remember Claire Bouchard?"

"RCMP," said Bo.

"Yes. She sealed the Washington border like war had been declared."

I could see Abbie's confusion, so I asked Bo to catch her up, keeping Mueller's input minimal. I hoped Mueller would note that Bo never mentioned the wire or the DA, and he was smart enough to take the cue. Once she was up to speed, Mueller continued.

"We picked up their van in Seattle. Let them keep going to save resources—make our stand at the border. They pulled off near Mt. Vernon, spent almost four hours in a barn, then came out in a four-door Camry heading for the checkpoint. We were waiting. Lian and Alisandro didn't expect trouble. They even left the Glock behind. We found it before they reached the checkpoint. We had it tested—by the way. Ballistics matched it to the weapon that killed Tadeo. The greenbacks were crammed in the doors of the Camry."

"No Bonnie-and-Clyde shootout?" I asked.

"No weapons fired, but words were flying. If f-bombs could kill, it was a bloodbath."

"Have you questioned them?" Bo asked.

"Not formally. Transported them separately back to Portland. Alisandro is a talker, so I rode with him."

He stopped abruptly. "You know I can't give out details."

"Jesus, George!" exclaimed Bo. "Pull the stick out of your ass already. Marty nearly died, my brother-in-law did die. Our families have been through hell. Give us a break."

Mueller nodded in private acknowledgment. "Alisandro Falco—born Alisandro Morales in Cupertino—changed his name the second he left for Hollywood. This guy is something else. A motor-mouth with a room-temperature IQ. I mirandized him, but I don't think he cared."

"Falco?" I asked.

"Formerly Morales," he answered.

"Very Hollywood," I acknowledged.

"Why'd he kill Tadeo?"

"He didn't, Bo. She did. According to him, Ed Cruz was always flirting with Lian—'working her.'" Mueller added the air quotes and a scowl.

"More likely she was working him," Bo said.

"Probably. Lian needed a confederate to get them into your warehouse when her shipment arrived. She offered Cruz fifty grand in supernotes. He was nervous—worried Radford would be pissed, and that Zor and Ming might find out. He also didn't believe the notes were as good as she claimed.

"Then Lian screwed up. She gave Cruz a counterfeit bill along with a genuine one and challenged him to tell them apart. She told him to study them, not to use them. Cruz showed the bills to Radford, and the two of them were comparing them in his office when Tadeo walked in unannounced and invited everyone to an impromptu birthday party in the cafeteria—typical office nonsense. Cruz tucked the bills inside the folded delivery schedule on his desk, assuming he'd be back in seconds. When he returned, they were gone. He panicked and told Lian, and she went ballistic. Cruz blamed Tadeo—and he was right. Tadeo had lifted them while Radford and Cruz were singing 'Happy Birthday.' I'm not even sure he knew what he'd grabbed. He just took whatever looked suspicious. A piece of paper with numbers on it and a couple of hundred-dollar bills fit the bill, so to speak."

"Tadeo got shot over a couple of hundred bucks," Bo muttered. "Shit. I barely remembered I had them."

"Cruz tried to get them back," Mueller continued. "He couldn't confront Tadeo directly; he'd just deny it. So, he set up a meeting at Shangri-La to win him over. But when he told Lian, she told him not to go. Instead, she and Falco waited in the lot until Tadeo came out and shot him. Falco jumped out and rifled through his wallet.

"But why kill him? Why not just confront him?"

"Lian worried Tadeo was close to figuring things out. He'd been asking many questions. She couldn't risk exposure. This shipment was her exit, and she didn't want it to go up in smoke before her ship came in, literally and figuratively."

"That's why the date on the schedule was underlined. It wasn't a regular delivery. It was the counterfeit money, not cigarettes," said Bo.

I frowned. "If they searched him, why not grab the recorder?"

"I asked him that," said Mueller, pointing at me. "Falco said that when Lian shot him, Tadeo fell face down. The recorder was in his front pants pocket. He was lying on it. Cars kept arriving in the lot, and Falco was scared the headlights would ID him, so he cut the search short after the wallet."

"That's why they ransacked his house," I said.

"And his office," added Bo.

"Why not Noble's house?" I asked.

"Who says they didn't?" Mueller replied. "Falco hated Noble. Lian told him to search his house. Falco didn't tear it up, but Jeff caught him anyway. He said Jeff berated him, called him every name in the book." Mueller paused. "Ever hear of suicide by cop?"

"Of course," Bo said.

"I think this was suicide by Falco. Noble kept screaming at him, goading him, calling him a has-been grade-D actor. That snapped him. Noble never had a chance. Falco tied a cord around his neck, ran up the stairs while Jeff struggled, and pulled him up. Then he let him hang there until he stopped breathing. Said he weighed less than a swag bag. Want to know what else he said?" No one answered. Abbie winced.

"He said it shouldn't count against him because he killed a dead man." Mueller exhaled. "What a character."

"Can I ask something?" Abbie said. "Is Lian smart?"

"Yes. And cunning," Mueller replied.

"Then why take up with someone like Falco?"

Mueller shrugged. "I'm not a couples counselor, Mrs. Schott."

"Call me Abbie," she said.

"Abbie," he nodded. "She liked guys. Many guys. Before Falco, she had a Taiwanese boyfriend—serving six years now for smuggling two million fake tax stamps into the US."

Bo and I exchanged a glance, having heard the story from Heller at the warehouse meeting.

Mueller pressed on. "Wilton used Lian's contacts to supply the supernotes. The money went through Banco Delta Asia in Macau via a BVI front, then into Hong Kong, disguised by rugs and cloth—dense enough to hide it from X-rays. It was loaded onto a Panamanian vessel and arrived here a few days ago. We cleared it and put it on a truck the night you were shot. Lian diverted it from our warehouse to yours. We knew Radford and Cruz were aware of the shipment because they'd underlined it on the schedule you gave us. We didn't know how they knew, and didn't attach a possible heist to it."

He paused. "Want to hear something funny?"

Again, no one answered.

"The reason Cruz and Radford weren't available to open the warehouse? We had them under custodial watch."

"Custodial what?"

"We're allowed to hold suspects for up to forty-eight hours without charges. As the op wound down, we knew they knew something—just not what—so we kept them on a short leash. We brought them in, confiscated their phones, and rotated them from room to room in an interrogation merry-go-round. While Lian was calling them from Emerson, they were cooling their heels at the bureau."

"So that's why my husband nearly died," Abbie said.

Mueller's expression faltered. Not funny after all. He looked sheepish.

A nurse entered to check my catheter bag. Silence fell. Everyone understood my embarrassment. Once she left, Bo closed the door.

"What about that Mongolian man and his Chinese teammate?" Abbie asked. "I want Andrew and Ali to come home safely."

"Both in custody," Mueller said. "Picked up in the larger sweep."

"Sweep?" I asked, wincing.

"I can't get into details. You'll read about it."

"You answered only half my question," Abbie said. "Is it safe to bring the kids home?"

"Safe is subjective," Mueller said. "For our investigation, you and your children are no longer in danger. The operation has shut down. Nate Radford, Ed Cruz, Altan Ganzorig, Zhao Ming, Wilton Kao-Su, Lian Hua Chen, and Alisandro Falco have all been arrested. Additional arrests will follow, including your controller and several lower-level employees."

Even as he spoke, I couldn't shake the thought that the most dangerous person left in my life was DDA Autumn Flener. I lay there, tubes snaking out of my body, my face mummified in gauze, and a woman I barely knew—met only three times—held my life in her hands.

CHAPTER FORTY-THREE

The Deal

I SCHEDULED A MEETING WITH MAREK SOKOL for the next day, when no one was there except the nurses hustling back and forth. I was hoping for the best, but preparing for the worst. I knew I'd have to pay for my sins—I just wanted to survive the invoice.

Marek stepped into the room like he was looking for directions. His expression was that of someone not comfortable with injury. As tough as he was, I thought I'd found his weakness—pain.

"How are you?" I asked as he gently approached the bed.

"Better than you," he said, squinting, as if that might improve the view. "I heard you'll live."

"To the disappointment of many, I'm sure."

I gave him the blow-by-blow of the shooting. He took notes and asked pointed questions, building a case to impress the deputy DA. At one point, he pulled a small Samsung digital camera from his briefcase and snapped a few photos.

"Mind if I send these to Natalya and Dmitry? She's constantly asking about you."

"Where is she hiding out?" I asked, knowing she'd left the country while the authorities circled.

"Cyprus."

"Yes," I said, "Dmitry has a compound there. Very nice. Lots of beach."

"You've been there?" he asked matter-of-factly.

"No. I've heard about it."

"I've been there. Lovely place. Like a royal getaway."

I was suddenly annoyed. Not from envy, but from the subtle reminder of how little I mattered in that world—Dmitry's world—even though I'd taken his money and shared his woman for over a year.

We finally got around to what really mattered: Marek's efforts to keep me out of prison.

"It's good news and bad," Marek said, pulling the larger, more comfortable chair over to the side of the bed. "Good news is you're not under arrest. Not today anyway. Flener is looking for a resolution. I can see the disdain for this case in her eyes."

"Then why doesn't she just drop it?" I asked, irritated. "I nearly died because of this sting, and she still wants to come after me?"

"The FBI case has nothing to do with why she's after you. It's collateral to the charges. The sting may have triggered the investigation, but it's not relevant anymore—other than what I can use to help you at sentencing."

"Sentencing!" My head throbbed. "I am so screwed."

"No," he said. "You have leverage—listen to me. The wire transcript is your burden, but it's also your bridge."

"Bridge to what?"

"A deferred prosecution, or, if she prefers, a limited admission to obstruction. Something that stops further investigation and gives her a scalp to wave, albeit a small one. That protects … other things." He gave me a sidelong look. "You know what I mean." He was referring to the affair.

"I do," I said flatly. "I need to bury that. Nothing else matters."

"Good. Then here's the plan." He straightened his notes. "You admit to specific acts of obstruction during the Baron Von Baltruschat investigation—facts you failed to disclose, ways you misled the detectives. I'll negotiate the questions she can ask and help you craft your responses. Nothing about Vasili. Nothing about anyone else's death. This gives Flener a clean, provable offense to present to the court, and you can keep any ancillary secrets private. The outcome *could* be probation, but more likely, a brief stint in a low-security facility. It's a survival plan, not a public execution."

"What about Bo? He lied as well."

"I'll negotiate that with Flener. She has no basis to ask about him. You answer only for what you personally did. You're not obligated to volunteer anything about anyone else."

The pain I'd felt yesterday was just a dull ache today. Or maybe it was still sharp, but my brain had turned down the volume so I could focus on my bigger woes.

Marek exhaled. "Marty, you bragged about putting a bullet in a man's head and then sleeping with the woman who helped you dump the body." He flicked a glance at my monitor to check my numbers. "This isn't the sort of thing people overhear while taste-testing a new chardonnay at a garden party. The DA can't pretend it didn't happen. You have to give them something to keep them from looking for something else."

He tilted his head. "Courtrooms are for people who fail to settle."

"So, I plead to obstruction," I said slowly, "sign paperwork, skip court appearances, and that's it?"

"I can't promise that," he said. "Flener and I are close to agreement. She'll file obstruction charges with the court. On your behalf, I'll waive arraignment, keeping you out of court for that step. I can get that done while you're still in the hospital. Once you're out of here, though, you'll need to turn yourself in, be booked, and processed. You'll be released on OR until the official plea date."

I cocked my head.

"Your own recognizance," he said. "You'll get a court date to enter the plea. I'll be with you, holding your hand. The judge will order a PSI—pre-sentence investigation—that'll take about three weeks. You'll remain free on OR until sentencing. Then you return to court, the judge will pronounce sentence, and you'll be taken into custody immediately."

"Christ."

He leaned back. "You could fight this, Marty, and odds are you'd win. The case is weak. Flener knows she can't prove much. That's why she's digging for anything else credible. The problem for you is that Bo, Natalya, Alex, Dante, Charley—even Abbie—could be dragged into depositions. Some won't take the Fifth. Your secrets become evidence. Your relationship with Natalya will come out. This plea keeps it from going that far. You sacrifice a *little* to protect a *lot*."

"A little!" I sputtered. "Holy shit, Marek, going to prison isn't a little."

"Compare it to what you're protecting."

Point taken.

"Will the record be sealed?"

"No. But access to evidence in your case requires court authorization and standing. I don't see anyone doing that, so your secrets should stay secret."

"What does 'sentencing' look like?"

"Can't be certain. The judge decides after the PSI. The educated guess is you'll be committed to the Columbia River minimum-security facility, most likely for twenty-four months, plus possibly a year of unsupervised probation. Flener has already agreed she'll recommend no more than that. You'll do routine duties, take classes, count fence posts, catch up on your reading. It's not hell—it's limbo."

He closed his notebook. "It sucks, Marty. You're getting a raw deal. Maybe there's pressure from above. Maybe Flener wants to drop 'deputy' from her title. Not sure. Think about it and let me know."

"Who would apply pressure? Why? Could it be Adams? That detective definitely hates me."

"No. Too low in the food chain to nudge a DDA."

He gathered his papers and tucked them into his briefcase.

"Or Dmitry," I said as he started for the door.

He paused. "What?"

"Someone with enough pull to squeeze the county DA. Maybe Dmitry's pissed … he has the money."

"I don't think a Russian oligarch has much juice in the Multnomah District Attorney's Office."

"I'm not saying directly. Maybe indirectly. I've seen his money buy a mafia war in Italy—buying a favor in our little backwater would be chump change."

Marek's mouth curled. Not quite a smile—more a private acknowledgment of a potential truth.

"Justice is blind, Marty. But money gives it a pretty good sense of direction."

And then he was gone.

CHAPTER FORTY-FOUR

Smoking Dragon and Royal Charm

THERE'S A PARTICULAR KIND OF HELL IN HEALING. Hospitals have mastered it. I'd lost weight eating what seemed like the entire color spectrum of Jell-O. My back ached more than the bullet wound. Everything carried that sterile, chemical tang, even my own skin. By the seventh day, I was mapping escape routes and calculating which nurses, orderlies, and night-shift interns might get caught in the crossfire as I bolted for the parking lot—gown flapping behind me, exposing more than anyone should have to see.

"Don't sit up. You'll rip something, and the doc will blame me," said Bob Heller, sauntering into the room. He'd shed the lumberjack façade, wearing standard khakis and a light sweater. He looked different, though I couldn't put my finger on it. Maybe a haircut? Either way, he seemed lighter, less gnarly, more agile.

"Look at what the cat dragged in," I said, smiling.

"Look at what the cat nearly killed," he said, coming up to the bed and shaking my IV-puffy hand. Bo bounced out of his chair, and so did Abbie.

We'd all settled into the same routine: They spent the day in chairs, chatting, dozing, and solving the world's ills, while I complained about one ache or another. Both Bo and Abbie pointed out that I had taken whining to a whole new level.

Heller had called me the day before to let me know he was in town finishing things with Mueller and that if he had time, he'd drop by.

Abbie was introduced, and she launched into the story of the shooting—having heard it so many times that she could recite it from memory. Knowing her, she preferred to tell it herself, quick and succinct, rather than sit through me wandering off on tangents and turning a five-minute story into a fifteen-minute ordeal, peppered with heroic embellishments.

Heller then said he could finally reveal everything he had been unable to before, and that the entire operation would appear in most national papers over the next couple of days.

"The sweep went down the morning after you got shot," he reported. "So, while you were getting sewn up, the bureau closed the net on one of the biggest stings ever conducted."

"Rose Smoke was that big?" asked Bo.

"Hell no," Heller scoffed. "Rose Smoke was a side show. Think of it as the porch to a mansion. The real operation was national. Coast to coast. And two-headed." He held up two fingers. "Royal Charm on the East Coast. Smoking Dragon on the West. Smoking Dragon was my baby, my ulcer, my slow death—depends who you ask."

He smiled casually. "Royal Charm was our sister op—we kept each other in the loop, but only through controlled channels because one whisper in the wrong ear … everything would evaporate."

"Where on the East Coast?" asked Abbie.

"New Jersey, Atlantic City area, Port Newark. On the West, it was Long Beach and Portland. Long Beach is probably eight to ten times the size of Portland. Wilton liked Portland only because it's more controllable. Fewer eyes, fewer moving parts. Easier to track containers. It's why the money was shipped here rather than to LA."

"How long has this sting been active?" Bo asked.

"Over three years for me, almost six for the East Coast guys. We planted roots. It started as a modest counterfeit tobacco job and then ballooned—from Marlboros to supernotes to surface-to-air missiles and a carnival of other delights. Things only started to get dicey right around the time you two wandered into the frame."

"Yeah, that tends to happen when we show up," Bo said, flashing a grin that bordered on proud.

Heller motioned toward the edge of the bed. I nodded, and he eased down, settling in like an instructor before his pupils.

"Wilton and his counterparts in Jersey—a husband-and-wife team—were already concerned about the whole state of play. So were we. We were juggling close to a hundred suspects, trying to keep everyone calm and clueless. So, we made the call: end it, simultaneously on both coasts, the moment the six million in supernotes arrived."

"You arrested everyone at once?" Abbie asked.

"That was the trick," Heller said. "How do you corral all those felons? The second you knock down a door, phones light up, and half of them disappear. So, we needed something smart. The Jersey team came up with a wedding."

"Wait—what?" Abbie said. Heller already had her hovering; now he had her hooked.

"We needed a single event big enough to reel them all in. Put them in one place without tipping our hand. These guys love to chase parties. Weddings, divorces—doesn't matter. So, the Newark UCs staged a fake wedding. One UC marrying another who'd been posing as his girlfriend."

"UC?" Abbie asked.

"Undercover agent," Bo and I said together like we were showing off.

"And I went the other way," Heller said. "Told Wilton and his crew my wife finally dumped me, and I was celebrating my freedom with a party at the Playboy Mansion."

Abbie blinked. "You got Playboy to let you use the mansion for an FBI sting?"

"Easier than you'd think," Heller said. "If you know the right event promoter. We had a guy in LA—a legit one—who handled

VIP parties. He'd booked Hefner's house a dozen times before. We just slid our 'divorce party' onto his roster."

We weren't surprised. Bo and I had attended a charity function at the mansion a year ago. We even presented Hefner with a Vatican sculpture. Katherine had been so annoyed by how excited Bo was to meet Hefner that, in the dead of summer, she packed a wool winter suit for him to wear. He thought he'd drown in his own sweat that day.

"We had agents everywhere," said Heller. "Gardeners, pool guys, limo drivers. Mansion security, caterers, even a butler whose real job was long-range acoustic surveillance. Same on the East Coast. Feds everywhere."

"And they came," said Abbie.

"They did—dressed for decadence. We staggered arrivals so we didn't spook them. Some came through the front gate, some through a side entrance set up for VIPs. A few even made it to the pool patio—drinks in hand—looking around like kids at Disneyland.

"They never saw it coming. We swept up more than thirty from Wilton's crew in the first pass. The rest were taken in satellite sweeps—cars, hotels, airports. By happy hour, the operation was bagged and sealed."

"How'd the wedding work out?" asked Abbie.

"Ah, the wedding." He rubbed his jaw, amused. "They held a rehearsal party. Champagne fountains, ice sculptures. A couple of guys even brought Rolexes for the bride and groom."

"Nice," I said.

"Couldn't keep them," he added with a frown. "The place had more recording equipment than a TV studio. Even the band was FBI. The operation netted more than fifty suspects. Combined, both operations swallowed up eighty-seven felons. One of the biggest hauls in bureau history—not including the dozen in Portland, which pushed the total past a hundred."

We spent another half hour talking about undercover life—or

what he was willing to share—how identities are built and buried, how invention turns into instinct.

"Stay as close to reality as possible. When lies are truth-adjacent, it's easier not to get burned."

I thought about how Bo and I had learned that lesson long ago, and how we'd applied it in ways that never ended well. Eventually, he glanced at his watch, the small, reflexive movement of a man whose time never quite belongs to him.

"What now, Agent Heller?" Abbie was clearly smitten.

"A couple of weeks off, I guess. Long enough to see my family, remember what's normal. Undercover life… it eats at you in little bites. You don't notice it until you catch yourself staring in the mirror, wondering who that is staring back."

That doesn't just happen to FBI agents.

CHAPTER FORTY-FIVE

Confession

FOR A LONG TIME, I HADN'T BEEN CHOOSING between right and wrong. I'd been choosing which wrong I could live with.

This choice was no different. Whichever way I turned, I would forfeit something I loved—my freedom or my family. Sleep became an exercise in accounting, measuring one loss against another.

One path demanded I tell Abbie the truth about Vasili—but only about Vasili. I might save my marriage, but go to prison.

The other path offered a chance to keep my freedom, but only if I confessed to my affair. Neither offered safety. Neither promised peace.

The hospital had become less a place of recovery and more a holding pen. The IVs were gone, the catheter finally removed, the wound stiff but healing. In certain light, I could almost recognize my face again. Every breath of that recycled, disinfectant-laced air reminded me that the decision ahead would shape every day that followed.

Abbie would arrive soon. I could see her in my mind: alert, impatient to hear what she didn't yet know, ready to judge, forgive, or crumble. And I would have to tell her everything—not just that I was going to prison, but why, and what I had done.

If I lost her over killing a man—if divorce was inevitable—then saving the marriage would be pointless. I'd tell Marek to fight the charges with everything we had. I might avoid prison, maybe even walk away clean. The affair would surface, but the cause had already been lost, the harm irreversible.

But if Abbie accepted what I'd done—if she could forgive the lies and live with the fact I'd killed Vasili—then I'd take the plea, keep the affair secret, and pay for it with two years of my life.

Some choices aren't really choices. They're reckonings.

//

Abbie arrived at noon to pick me up. She'd prepared the house for my slow march back to normal—pillows piled, favorite foods, and a lit path from the bathroom to the bed.

She looked incredible—fresh cut hair, manicured hands, clothes that clung in all the right places. The stress had stripped a few pounds off her, and I definitely noticed. She was greeting home a husband who'd cheated death, and after all the stories she'd heard, saw me as a little bit gallant.

I'd spent the last two days hinting that there was something important I needed to tell her. Something I wanted to say in private. The kids were still in Michigan, packing to come home. Boomer was thrilled to see me and promised to listen without passing judgment. She'd asked if it was about my legal troubles, which I still hadn't fully explained, and I told her it was.

I asked her to make us both some hot tea and brace herself for a story that would shock and anger her. She agreed, giving me a stern look that chilled me. Between us, Abbie was always the tougher one—and the less flexible. Her conscience was as clean as an operating room; mine was as dirty as a gas station toilet. This was going to hurt more than the bullet that tore into my gut.

And then I told her everything—the parts she didn't remember and the parts I tried to forget.

I started at the end. "I killed a man."

She answered exactly as I knew she would. "I don't believe you."

"Remember, a few years ago, when the business was dying, and we were desperate for money?"

She nodded.

"Remember when Nico Scava disappeared?"

Another nod, more wary.

"Well, Nico, Bo, and I were kidnapped by a Russian psychopath named Vasili Bobrov, who shot Nico in front of us."

I took her through the entire episode. I left out the part where I pissed myself. Some details weren't necessary.

As I talked, I could see acceptance slide across her eyes like dawn. Understanding settled into her face.

"So, Nico has been dead all this time, and you knew? Why didn't you go to the police? If they threatened us, the kids, Bo's kids, wouldn't we have been safer if you'd gone to the police? What were you thinking?"

All fair questions. I answered them all, clumsily. I was out of practice. They'd stopped haunting me a long time ago because the worst had come and gone, and we'd made it through.

Next came the horror of Baron Albert Von Baltruschat and his wife, Crystal. Again, I chose my words carefully. She didn't need the particulars.

She listened with her head bowed, hands covering her face. She was curiously uninterested in the painting. What had mattered then, years ago, had shrunk in the light of what mattered now—her safety, the kids, and the truth I'd kept from her.

I told her about Vasili—his menace, his impulsive cruelty, the malice in his eyes.

How he'd kidnapped Boomer, spied on her, and threatened to kill her before anyone else.

How I'd shot him.

Abbie stayed silent. I'd been confessing for almost an hour, and I think the part of her mind that kept her tethered to reality began to fray, leaving her without words—caught between comprehension and shock.

I stayed clear of Italy. The death toll there was too high for her to accept, too much for her to understand. I wanted her to see the Vatican in a pure light—a place we might visit someday. I ended by telling her the truth about Natalya and Dmitry's investment in Paladin Holdings: how it changed everything, and how we'd built the company with Dmitry's money.

She began to emerge from her stupor. I was finally on familiar ground. She was already comfortable with our Russian partners and had long maintained a cordial relationship with Natalya. What she didn't know was the link between Natalya and the man who had threatened her life—the man I had killed.

"Natalya sent this maniac into our lives?"

"Yes, but not to destroy them. He did that on his own."

"Natalya helped get rid of her own nephew's body?"

"They weren't very close."

"And knowing this, you still worked with her?"

"That ended over two weeks ago."

"Was it just for the money?'

"For the most part."

She looked at me with disgust. I think the money motive was worse than the killing motive.

"I never want to see that woman again, do you understand?"

"Yes."

"Marty? I mean it."

"I understand."

She wanted to know why, after three years of letting this mess lie quietly under the floorboards, it had decided to crawl back into the light.

I told her. The rant. The wire. I left out the "sleeping with Natalya" part.

"Jesus, Marty," she exhaled. "And Marek can't get you out of this? I'm no lawyer, but admitting you killed a guy on a recorder isn't much of a case."

I felt sweat gather under my arms. We were now close to the fire, and I could feel its heat. I repeated what the DA had laid out to Marek and me at our meeting, matching the same accusatory tone. I made it sound devastating—legally lethal.

"It's why I'll take a plea for lying to the cops about the Baron killing rather than exposing my own. If I take the plea, the investigation stops. If I don't, it keeps going. It's a choice between a guaranteed two years or risking twenty-five to life at trial."

We sat in silence for a while.

Boomer had kept his promise, lying at the foot of the bed and minding his own business.

Abbie's eyes started to water. She sniffed, bent to stroke the soft fur on his head, and kissed it. He barely opened his eyes—probably as dispirited as she was.

"I need to take a walk," she said, and I nodded self-consciously.

"I need to stop talking … my jaw still hurts."

She returned two hours later, transformed. She'd left slumped with fatigue and defeat; she came back with shoulders squared and eyes sharp. Abbie never wore surrender well. It simply didn't fit her. Round one had been punishing, but round two would be different. She looked ready for the fight—wanted it.

"I want you to make me a promise," she said.

"Anything."

"You're done with Paladin Holdings. When we get through this, if we get through this, you won't go back as if nothing ever happened."

"I already told Bo I was done."

Her eyebrows arched. I caught her by surprise. "Good," she said. "You can't change your mind on that."

"I promise."

She paced, as if her fortifying walk had continued into our bedroom.

"Our finances will be fine. I'll go back to work. The firm I left a year ago will welcome me back. Have you talked to Bo about your equity in Paladin? It should be worth a lot."

"I haven't talked to Bo about it," I said. "I'm still pretty pissed at him. Yes, my equity's worth a lot, but Paladin's a private company. When we split from Dmitry and Natalya, we took on a ton of debt. There's no public market for the stock, so selling it won't be easy."

"It doesn't matter, Marty, we'll pull through this. My two biggest worries are the kids and you in prison. How dangerous is that for you?"

"I'll be okay. It's minimum security. I did two months of boot camp in the service—it's probably like that, only longer. I also survived a year in Vietnam. That wasn't a vacation either. I'll manage it."

"I'm worried about how the kids will handle it. This is going to be traumatic for them. They'll be without a father for two years. Will they visit you in prison? Do we want them to?"

"It's a lot to think about. I don't have all the answers," I said.

She took my hand and held it firmly.

"We'll get through this together."

And just like that, my path was clear. I'd take the plea, keep some secrets sealed, and above all, protect our marriage.

CHAPTER FORTY-SIX

Charged

THE NEXT DAY, MAREK DROVE US TO THE STATION. He'd called ahead, arranged the appointment, and made sure the desk knew we were coming. When we arrived, the clerk gave a polite nod, and a uniformed officer led me to a small processing room. I remembered the layout from three years earlier. Nothing had changed except for the posters on the walls. No loud voices, no shoving—just quiet efficiency. Everyone called me Mr. Schott.

I signed forms, gave fingerprints, and posed for the mugshot while Marek double-checked the paperwork with the clerk. The room smelled faintly of sanitizer and paper. The coffee was unusually good. A camera clicked. A scanner beeped. Every movement felt ritualistic. In and out in less than two hours, released on my own recognizance until the court date.

Sitting in the car afterward, with Marek driving, the weight lingered. There was no turning back. The law now had its claim on me. The ride home was silent. I stared out the window. I felt outside my life, watching it from high above—unbroken, fragile, but still mine.

For the next few days, everything felt better. My body, my face, my mind … my marriage. The house was quiet. Not empty—just smaller, cozier, as if it had gently contracted around Abbie and me. The air between us felt lighter, free of its usual clutter.

There's a quiet choreography between confession and intimacy: one leads, the other follows, a fragile current running between them.

She felt it, too, and we took careful advantage of it before our teenagers arrived home and everything would change again.

At one point, I called Bo. He'd been living at the office, captaining the ship. I told him what I'd confessed to Abbie. "I told her everything. The only truth I kept secret was my relationship with Natalya."

"What about the DA? What happens there?"

I told him I had turned myself in. It was now out of my hands. I explained the plea. I assured him the DA would not pursue him.

"I don't care about that," he said.

I dealt with the reality of prison by making it a pivot point. I would leave one life and start another. There was a perverse excitement in that. It gave me both courage and purpose. Two years away from my family could not just be an interlude. It had to be more. Abbie and I spent the time in our brief, intimate cocoon, talking about the life we'd rebuild when this part was over.

I would break my bond with Bo and with Natalya. I loved them both, but they occupied the world I needed to step out of. They were my past, not my future. I would never speak to Natalya again. I would reshape my friendship with Bo, shift it from confederate to comrade. I'd cash out of my equity, leave the company, and do something entirely different—I'd promised Abbie.

Maybe learn to write—become a novelist.

Marek called and said my plea hearing was the following week. I put the call on speaker so Abbie could hear.

"It's just to enter the plea, Marty. A single obstruction count. There's no testimony, no witnesses, nothing dramatic. We'll be in and out in under an hour unless the docket's backed up. Abbie can come. She'll sit in the gallery. You and I will be at the counsel's table. The judge will ask you a few routine questions. If you understand the charge, if it's your decision, if anyone's forced you, if you're satisfied with my representation."

"What if I'm not?" I asked.

"I'll double my fee."

"Shouldn't I get a discount?"

"Not by being a dick." I could sense the smile through the phone. "Then the court will accept the plea and set a sentencing date. You'll walk out the front door with Abbie and me. No cuffs that day."

"I looked up Columbia River Correctional Institute," I said. "It doesn't look too bad."

"Minimum security," Marek replied. "Dorm-style housing. Shared rooms. Routine work. Yard time. Meals on schedule. Guards aren't in your grill all day. You'll have structure, some privacy, and predictability. Not pleasant, but manageable. You'll be in with low-risk guys—fraud, embezzlement, tax issues, counterfeit cases."

"Counterfeit?" Abbie asked.

"Not the ones you've been dealing with," Marek said, amusement in his voice.

"Feels like a step up for me," I said.

"A whole new class of people," said Abbie, running her hand slowly across my back. "I won't recognize you when you get out."

"I'm happy to hear you're taking this so well," said Marek.

"We don't have a choice," said Abbie. "We'll swallow this pill as best we can."

//

Crisis has a way of folding your life into a box small enough to hold; whatever doesn't fit gets left behind.

I answered only calls from family and friends. I mainly communicated by email. I let Marek explain my plea deal to Natalya—I knew she'd pass it on to Alex and Dmitry. She sent me an email that was both sad and affecting. It said, "I'm sorry. We will talk when you come back." As if I were going on vacation.

"No, we won't," I muttered to myself.

Andrew and Ali returned, and our little amatory cottage once again became the cacophonous castle it had always been. Between Boomer's swinging tail and the constant comings and goings of teenagers, the house vibrated with the energetic pulse of a reunited family.

Then it came time to sit down with them. Abbie did most of the talking. We wanted the kids to see that she wasn't just a bystander. We couldn't tell them about the shooting—and didn't want to—so she focused on the Baron murder instead. She explained that their father had withheld information from the authorities to protect the family from possible Russian mob retaliation, and that he'd finally confessed and would now face the consequences. I was a little embarrassed by how much better she made me look.

It didn't go well.

Andrew went very still, the way he had as a child when he was scared. He didn't ask anything at first. He watched me steadily, as if recalibrating who I was. When he finally spoke, his voice sounded older than he was.

"So … you're going to prison." Not a question. A verdict. "For two years."

I nodded.

"What happens to us?" he asked, and I could tell he meant all of it—college, friends, reputation, where we lived, what the neighbors would whisper. He accepted our answers without emotion, the way he'd accept weather. It didn't make me feel better.

Ali cried first and fast. Her questions came in bursts. Would I be safe? Could she visit? Would Mom stay married to me? Her fear and curiosity tangled together, and she pressed herself into Abbie's shoulder.

We told them what we could—and I realized, not without shame, that Abbie had grown comfortable with the same trimmed truths I'd used on her for years. There is no graceful way to tell your children you're leaving on a schedule measured in birthdays. My punishment was prison; theirs was its aftermath. I deserved mine. They didn't deserve theirs. And perhaps that was my greatest punishment.

When it ended, nothing was resolved. We weren't healed. But they knew. And knowing, however hard, was a kind of relief.

CHAPTER FORTY-SEVEN

The Plea

THE MORNING OF MY PLEA HEARING carried that early September edge—the heat was softer, the sunlight was thinner, and everything tilted toward change.

Andrew drove the car. Ali and Abbie rode in the back seat, our little caravan of solidarity. I wore my best suit, the one for weddings and funerals, and carried an empty briefcase. Abbie had bought me a cane—black, topped with an absurdly ornate silver crown. I didn't need it, but she wanted the judge to see what I'd been through. The kids walked us as far as the corner, then peeled off to wait at a Starbucks. We argued about it, and Abbie won; she didn't want them inside the courtroom. It's the kind of memory once built that can never be razed.

Abbie and I joined the cluster of suits outside the courtroom doors. Marek stood there with a folder tucked under one arm, radiating practiced calm.

"They won't make you wait long," he said. "Single obstruction count. You answer a few questions, they set a sentencing date, and you're done."

The DDA arrived moments later—brisk, composed, not unfriendly. "Mr. Schott, ready to proceed?" she asked.

"As ready as I'll ever be," I said.

Abbie refused to look at her. She kept her eyes focused forward. The clerk opened the doors. We filed in.

The courtroom was bigger than I expected and colder than it needed to be. The judge sat high on the bench, robed, formal, expression unreadable. When our case was called, Marek and I stepped forward. I felt Abbie behind me, close enough to touch, and it steadied me.

"Mr. Schott," the judge said, voice carrying easily across the room, "I'm going to ask you a series of questions to ensure your plea is knowing and voluntary. Please answer out loud."

I was sworn in.

He walked me through it methodically: my name, my age, whether I was under the influence of anything, whether I was satisfied with my lawyer, and whether anyone had threatened me or promised me something not contained in the agreement. Then the heart of it:

"Do you understand the charge of obstruction of justice and the rights you are giving up by pleading guilty?"

"Yes, Your Honor."

"And did you, in fact, commit the conduct described in the plea agreement?"

"Yes, Your Honor."

The DDA summarized the facts. Marek confirmed there were no objections. The judge asked whether I had read and signed the agreement. I had. I had also memorized the parts that scared me.

He nodded once, decision formal and impersonal. "The court accepts your guilty plea as knowing and voluntary. Sentencing is set for September 26, 2005, at 11 a.m. You will return at that time for final disposition. Until then, you are ordered to comply with all conditions of release. Do you understand?"

"I do, Your Honor."

The gavel didn't fall. It didn't need to.

And it was done.

I walked out on the cane Abbie had bought, but didn't need, past people whose lives had nothing to do with mine. Marek stayed behind to cover sentencing issues with Flener. We met the kids at Starbucks.

They were sitting with Bo and Katherine. Ali had told Natalie, and she had told them. The look on Bo's face was devastating.

We hugged and cried, and then coughed and wiped our eyes. The women did the same, but without the cough.

CHAPTER FORTY-EIGHT

Parting Company

THE WEEK BEFORE MY SENTENCING DATE, I drove to the office.

After the handshakes and obligatory smiles, I made my way to the glass cage. It felt like crossing an invisible border—a place I'd practically lived in for years and would probably never enter again.

Bo and I had a couple of conversations about my exiting the company. They were more collisions than conversations. He insisted I stay, I insisted I go. I came to sign whatever documents our corporate counsel had prepared.

"I don't care how pissed you are at me—I still think this all sucks," he said, pouring me a cup of coffee as I stared out at the lake for what I knew was the last time.

"Yeah," I said. "Sucks for me too."

"I haven't told you this because you already had enough on your plate, but now that everything's settled, I need to tell you something."

"What?"

"Dmitry bought our debt out of the Refco bankruptcy."

My mouth dropped. My body dropped. The coffee dropped—straight onto my shirt.

"Shit ...," I said.

"Shit," repeated Bo.

"I meant the coffee."

"I didn't."

Silence.

I soaked up the coffee with a paper towel.

"Our dead exit wasn't so *dead* after all," I said, shaking my head.

"It wasn't even an *exit*—more like a transfer."

"What happened?"

"Refco Inc. filed bankruptcy. Our loan went up for auction."

"I know …" I said. "But how'd Dmitry get it?"

"One of his companies. He's got more than I have shirts. They bid on it, bought the entire loan for a twenty percent discount."

"So, they paid eighty million for a hundred-million-dollar loan."

"Which carries a five percent interest rate."

"Well, he doesn't really own the company," I said. "He owns our debt."

"Which is the same thing," said Bo. "If he decides to call the loan, I'd have to hand him the company. He actually has more power now than before."

"Will he do that?"

"Hope not. When I talked to him …"

I cocked my head.

"He called to rub it in. It's how I know he owns the company. He assured me nothing would change. It's business as usual. He gave me some Russian saying: 'If you've shared bread and salt with someone, don't fight them hand-to-hand.'"

"Russians have a lot of sayings," I sighed. "Doesn't he have enough money already?"

"He doesn't give a damn about the money; it's dust on his ledger. He wanted the kick to our groin."

"But why?"

"You know why. You said it yourself."

I looked at him, puzzled.

"You fucked his girlfriend."

"And I'm going to prison for it."

"You think that's enough for him?"

We sat for the last time on our couch, staring out at the lake. We traded memories. Some funny, some not.

Finally, he pulled out the bottle of Glenlivet from the lower drawer of the desk, for emergencies and celebrations.

We toasted ourselves.

I would miss the scotch.

CHAPTER FORTY-NINE

The Package

MAREK SOKOL CALLED JUST AS BO POURED US A SECOND DRINK. I walked
to the other side of the office. Bo's eyes followed, curious.

"Marty?"

"Yes, Marek."

"Minor hiccup. Nothing to panic about. Glad I caught you."

"O-k-a-y …"

"I'm working out of this temp office, as you know. Temporary
secretary, part of the package."

"Yes …"

"The court filed your plea on the docket. The DA got its copy.
For our records, I asked for the complete set of materials tied to
the plea—just the Baltruschat exhibits. Someone in the DA's office
pulled the wrong binder and dumped the entire underlying investigation into the packet. The Vasili material. The wire transcript.
All of it."

"But that's all been closed."

"Closed but not sealed. The DA still has its internal files, and
somebody reached for the whole stack without thinking."

"Okay … so what?"

"I told my temp to copy the plea agreement for your personal
file. I'm traveling, so I called her. But she copied everything. The
whole file, FBI wire included. I'm not there to review it, so the

entire bundle went out by courier and was signed for by someone—Christine—at your office."

"Great, I'm here right now."

"You need to grab it and burn it. Don't sift through it. I'll assemble a clean package and send it myself."

"Will do. By the way, I've officially resigned from the company, so in the future, don't send anything here again."

"I'm sorry to hear about that," he said. "How do you feel?"

I hesitated. Bo was watching me, reading the pauses between my words.

"Relieved," I said.

Bo gave a sad grin.

I hung up and called Christine into the office.

"Can you give me that package that came in today from Marek Sokol?"

"Sorry, Marty, but I didn't know you were coming in, and you're not getting mail here anymore, so I had my assistant drive it to your house."

"What? When?"

She checked her watch. "Before you arrived. About two hours ago."

The word barely landed before I was out the door. Bo ran after me.

"What's wrong?" he yelled as I fired up the Z8 and shot out of the parking lot. I took the back roads—shorter, tighter, and blind in places. I laid on the horn more than once. I swung into the driveway too hard, left the car door open, and ran.

Abbie was at the kitchen table.

The package was open. The papers were spread—a pale scatter across the wood. She sat very still, as if movement might separate what had already broken. Tears traced her face. She didn't look up at first. When she finally did, there was nothing in her eyes I could negotiate with. No sentence in the world could fix this moment.

My mouth went dry, words evaporating before they formed. The damage had already spoken for me.

CHAPTER FIFTY

The Evening Thins

WE SAT ON THE DECK AS THE SUN SLIPPED BELOW THE HORIZON, pulling dusk in around us. His eyes were soft and patient, fixed just beyond mine. I rested on the sun-warmed planks instead of taking a chair. I wanted to be level with him.

Abbie and the kids had left days ago. They wouldn't return until I was gone. They gave me Boomer and the house because I would not see either of them again. It was my last night of freedom. I didn't eat. I wasn't hungry. Abbie and I had planned a big family dinner for tonight—the Bishops and the Schotts, a farewell party. She'd whispered, warm and conspiratorial, *"And afterward I'll give you a reason not to forget me."*

But that was then—and this was now.

I drank scotch instead.

I rested my hand on his head, felt his warmth. He had never judged me. Not for the choices I'd made. Not for the lies I'd told. Not for the wreckage I'd left.

"Boomer," I said, my voice thin, unsteady. "I wonder if this world will still exist when I get back. This world with you in it. This world I once belonged in."

I rubbed the hollow behind his ear and felt its velvet heat. "I don't deserve you. I don't deserve them. I don't deserve this." I gestured at the empty deck, the quiet yard, the life already fading at the edges.

Boomer lifted his gentle brown eyes—soft as fall leaves after rain—and he understood. Not the wrong I'd done, not the morality of it, not the tangle of my failures. What he caught was the heartbreak, the apology, the love I couldn't put into words.

"I don't know how long you'll have, old friend," I said, voice cracking. "Probably not long enough for me to come back. But if you can … just … stay. Stay with them. Keep them safe. And remember me … not for what I lost, or what I destroyed, but for how much I love them. And you. And maybe even for the things I couldn't outrun."

He eased his head against my knee. I felt the quiet certainty that this, at least, was real—that this love, unbroken and straightforward, would survive the ruin. And for the first time in days, I let myself grieve without fear or anger or loss—with only the faint hope that he might remain when nothing else had.

We stayed like that as the evening thinned from gray to black.

And I allowed myself to mourn, to let go—

and to leave.

Author's Note

If you enjoyed *Dead Exit*, I would be grateful if you could leave a review. It truly makes a difference. Marty and Bo's story will continue—please visit **mbalter.com** for updates.

This novel was inspired by real events.

In August 2005, the FBI announced two coordinated bi-coastal sting operations—Smoking Dragon and Royal Charm—targeting an international smuggling ring dealing in counterfeit cigarettes, currency, drugs, weapons, and other contraband. Eighty-seven defendants were arrested across eleven US cities. I remember reading about it at the time, unaware it would one day find its way into a novel.

Years later, while researching cigarette smuggling for this third Marty and Bo crime thriller, that memory resurfaced. A close friend of mine—the real-life inspiration for Bo—had once been swept into a major FBI investigation involving a company in which he had invested. He described being summoned into a room filled with agencies and acronyms, the atmosphere controlled and intimidating—the kind of room where no one needs to raise their voice to make the threat understood.

His experience became the spark for this story.

As I developed the plot, I revisited the 2005 sting through multiple news articles and Te-Ping Chen's reporting for the Center for Public Integrity. I also contacted former undercover FBI agent Bob Hamer, who was involved in the original operation and later wrote *The Last Undercover*. While he understandably couldn't share specific details, he generously pointed me toward interviews and resources that helped me better understand how such complex investigations unfold. I am grateful for his guidance and service.

Dead Exit is fiction. There was no Smoking Dragon or Royal Charm operation in Portland, Oregon. I used the real investigation as a framework and built my own story upon it.

In researching, I also discovered another dramatic real-world event that occurred in that time frame, the collapse of Refco Inc., whose 2005 bankruptcy involved approximately $33 billion in assets. I adjusted the actual event timeline slightly to better serve the novel's plot.

At a few points in the story, I quote writers whose words felt particularly appropriate: Jiddu Krishnamurti's observation that "Intuition is the whisper of the soul," Raymond Chandler's line from *The Big Sleep*, and a variation on the title of Judith Viorst's *Alexander and the Terrible, Horrible, No Good, Very Bad Day*.

My sincere thanks to my beta readers—Ted Wozniak Sr., Larry "the Dentist" Freedman, Warren Anderson, Andy Allen, Emery Scheibert, and Tom Barnes—whose suggestions strengthened this book considerably. Special thanks to Valerie Snyder, my sister-in-law and a probate court judge, for her guidance on legal matters, and to Dr. Jonathan Alterie for reviewing the medical details. Any remaining errors are mine alone.

Thank you to my children, Andrew and Ali, for allowing me to borrow their names and bits of their personalities. I am grateful to Amber Parsons for her kind indulgence in letting me sit in Harwood Gold—the best coffee shop in all of northern Michigan—day after day, while I write. Thanks as well to my regular tablemates for their friendship and humor.

My appreciation goes to Doug Weaver for his mentoring, editing, and sage advice. I am very fortunate to have been introduced to him by Anne Stanton, and even more fortunate to call him a friend. I also want to thank everyone at Mission Point Press—their expertise and professionalism make these books award-winning, and I am deeply grateful for all they do.

This book is dedicated to Roy Rose—my best friend and the inspiration behind Bo.

And finally, I want to thank my lovely wife, Suzanne Balter. She is my agent, my muse, my boss, my editor, my marketing director, the mother of our children, and the love of my life. To say I couldn't do this without her would be an understatement.

She said to me once, "I'll help you with this writing idea, but you have to make the bed every morning."

… That's a deal I can live with.

MICHAEL BALTER is an award-winning author known for his sharp wit and high-stakes crime fiction. His debut novel, *Chasing Money*, received multiple honors, including the Best Indie Book Award for Crime Thrillers, gold medals from the Feathered Quill and the Military Writers' Society of America, the Reader's Favorite Gold Medal for Crime Fiction, and the 2024 Crime Thriller of the Year Award from BestThrillers.com.

His second novel, *The Vatican Deal*, won the CIPA EVVY Gold Medal for Thrillers & Suspense and became an Amazon #1 Hot New Release.

Born in Berlin, Michael grew up in a bombed-out building. When the Berlin Wall went up, his family fled to America. During the Vietnam War, he served as an air traffic controller at Udorn Air Force Base in Thailand. Michael earned a degree in aerospace engineering before joining Intel Corporation in the early days of Silicon Valley. He later became an entrepreneur, launching ventures ranging from a voice-recognition startup to an art company and a private equity firm. The kidnapping of a business partner by a Russian mobster inspired elements of *Chasing Money*.

Michael lives in Charlevoix, Michigan, and is working on his next novel. Learn more at mbalter.com.

www.ingramcontent.com/pod-product-compliance
Lightning Source LLC
Chambersburg PA
CBHW020141170726
47995CB00003BA/657